D1251623

ZERO
MOMENT

Also by M. G. Harris

The Joshua Files
Invisible City
Ice Shock

THE JOSHUA FILES

ZERO MOMENT

M. G. HARRIS

Walker & Company   New York

Originally published in Great Britain in 2010
by Scholastic Children's Books, an imprint of Scholastic Ltd.
First published in the United States of America in July 2012
by Walker Publishing Company, Inc., a division of Bloomsbury Publishing, Inc.
www.bloomsburyteens.com

For information about permission to reproduce selections from this book, write to
Permissions, Walker BFYR, 175 Fifth Avenue, New York, New York 10010

Library of Congress Cataloging-in-Publication Data
Harris, M. G. (Maria G.)
The Joshua files : zero moment / by M. G. Harris.
p.   cm.
Sequel to: The Joshua files : ice shock.
Summary: When Josh learns that a special artifact, the Bracelet of Itzamna, is the key to both
his father's death and the mystery of the codex, he returns to the hidden city of Ek Naab—
alone this time, because as the stakes rise he can no longer trust even his closest allies.
ISBN 978-0-8027-2835-7 (hardcover)
[1. Fate and fatalism—Fiction. 2. Mayas—Fiction. 3. Fathers and sons—Fiction.
4. Science fiction.] I. Title. II. Title: Zero moment.
PZ7.H242245Jow 2012   [Fic]—dc23   2011038058

Printed in the U.S.A. by Quad/Graphics, Fairfield, Pennsylvania
2 4 6 8 10 9 7 5 3 1

For Ana-Elena, Kizzie, Deborah, and Alison,
in memory of wonderful days in Brazil

I would like to swim against the stream of time.

Italo Calvino

The Oxford Repor

DNA scientist found dead in Middle East yacht mystery

DOHA, QATAR The body of Cambridge professor and biotech entrepreneur Melissa DiCanio was discovered earlier today by fishermen in a yacht off the coast of Doha, Qatar. The boat was abandoned and had floated into the Persian Gulf.

DiCanio had been missing since the middle of January. The cause of death has not been released.

CCTV footage from Doha Harbor has helped police to make an arrest. Three men were photographed at the site, and one has been arrested—Simon Madison, who is also wanted by the FBI and CIA as a suspected terrorist.

Authorities intend to bring Madison to the United States of America. It is believed he will be charged with a number of offenses.

Doha police were unable to comment as to the possible motive for the murder.

A spokesman for the FBI said, "We've been after Madison for a long time. This is an important and very satisfying arrest."

DiCanio was born in Houston, Texas. She began her career at Baylor College of Medicine before moving to Oxford University in 1997 as a visiting professor at Aquinas College.

In 1999 she cofounded the pharmaceutical company Chaldexx BioPharmaceuticals, a privately held company based in Interlaken, Switzerland, that developed and markets the drug Tripoxan, with annual sales of US$50 million.

In 2005, DiCanio was awarded the Chaldexx Chair of Molecular Genetic Neuroscience at Cambridge University. DiCanio divided her time between her university research group and her post as chief scientific officer at Chaldexx BioPharmaceuticals.

Dr. Marcus Anthony, Master of Aquinas College, Oxford, said, "Melissa was a brilliant scientist, a true innovator. It was an honor to know her during her time at Aquinas College. She will be sorely missed."

From: Ixchel<ixchel1996@aol.com>
To: Josh Garcia<mariposajosh@gmail.com>
Subject: Hey there, Mister Promise-I'll-Write . . .

Josh!

You said you'd write, but you haven't. What's going on with you? Benicio tells me a few things about his life there in Oxford with you.

But it's not the same as hearing it from YOU.

How is Oxford? Your friend Tyler? Your mother?

I visit your father's grave every week, just the way I promised. The sun shines on him for many hours here. I enjoy my visits. I don't forget anything that happened. I'm there with him, for you.

Come on, write me a little message. And what happened to your blog?

You've gone pretty quiet, Josh. Should I be worried?

I have some important news for you. It's about the strange inscription on the Adapter, in case you're still interested . . .

Your friend always,

Ixchel

3

Hey Ixchel,

Yeah . . . it's been a while. I just haven't been on the computer much. Benicio keeps me busy . . . I'm not sure how, but we seem to hang out quite a bit. Which is cool, you know? All the girls at school want to know about this college-student cousin of mine. Tyler and I, we've been training hard for a capoeira thing in Brazil. We're leaving in a couple of weeks.

It's like . . . finally I'm starting to have a life again. A normal life, I mean. I try not to think about what happened, but when things are quiet, when I'm alone, I can't stop thinking about . . . Well, you know. I try to be out all the time doing stuff. I try not to think. Kind of hard to talk about it, really. I'd rather not, if it's all the same to you.

So I'm not sure I want to know about any "strange inscription."

It was nice to hear from you. I mean that.

Josh

Josh,

But you're talking to someone about this, yes? It's no good to keep such strong, hard feelings inside. You have Benicio and Tyler and your mother. Do you talk to them?

About the inscription on the Adapter—we found something that I think you WILL want to know. I don't want to write details in an e-mail; you never can be sure where it will end up.

I think YOU should know because . . . well, because of the You Know What. (I'm guessing we have to call it something like this?)

We need a more secure way to communicate than e-mail. Do you know anything about that?

A hug,

Ixchel

Hey Ixchel,

Wow . . . I wasn't expecting this. I don't know what to say. Of course I'm interested in anything new about the You Know What. But on the other hand, maybe I should let sleeping dogs lie, right?

Things have settled down for me since then. I'm in a good routine here: I get up at six thirty and go to the gym with Ty. We spot for each other—he's bigger and stronger than me, so he does more reps and uses heavier weights than I do, but I'm gaining on him. This is every day. It wasn't my idea to be a maniac, but Ty is obsessed—OBSESSED—with winning a medal at the World Capoeira Championships next month, and he wants to be TOTALLY buff. But after about a month I started to notice that I was beginning to get pretty ripped too. I've got these biceps and shoulder muscles now, and even a six-pack! Not like Ty, obviously, but he had one to start with. So I'm not going to stop now—I'll turn back into a flabby shrimp.

Then we train for a while. Not fighting, just the moves. Handstands, backflips, cartwheels without hands—so we can start our capoeira routine with something really

6

awesome. I can hold a handstand for ninety seconds. That's freestanding. Then we go to school, then home, and after a snack and some Xbox, we're back to the training.

We meet every single day. We only call each other by our *apelidos*—capoeira nicknames. We're getting so good now; we're faster and faster. People stand around and watch us. Benicio usually turns up too—doing his job, keeping an eye on me.

I'll tell you the truth: I don't like remembering what happened on that mountain. Don't even want to think about it. Because every time I do, I feel sick, sick in my gut. I can feel that rope tightening around me again, all my internal organs being squeezed like it's going to slice me in two. I think about the moment when my dad cut the rope. Over and over again. The rope going slack. Him falling without making a sound. His last words—"This isn't over."

And why did it happen; why did I go up that mountain? Who is—or was—Arcadio? How did he know so much about me? Why did I listen to him—why did I let him lead me to Mount Orizaba?

I used to have this dream, last year, about my dad. Maybe I told you; I can't remember if I did or not. In the dream, Dad wasn't really dead. He and Mom, they'd been pretending, keeping things from me. Pretty crazy, right? It made me sad, but at least it was like seeing Dad, like being with him again. Then I *did* see Dad—for real.

7

That's when it all went to pieces.

I mean, was it all meant to happen? I don't know anything anymore.

I don't like these questions. It's enough to drive you crazy.

So . . . let me think about it some more, before I decide whether I want to start this stuff again. Okay?

Hugs,

Josh

From: Ixchel<ixchel1996@aol.com>
To: Josh Garcia<mariposajosh@gmail.com>
Subject: reps? ripped? buff??

Josh,

It's good that you've found something to take your mind off the painful memories. You seem very focused on the capoeira, but I don't really know what you are talking about when you write "reps" and "buff" and "six-pack" and "ripped." Something to do with getting muscles, yes? That's good too—you told me that you were going to get stronger so you could protect yourself and your mother.

But the world keeps turning, doesn't it? We're still here in Ek Naab, and everything is going to happen in 2012 exactly the way it is written. The galactic superwave—all the computers in the world are going to be wiped, the end of civilization. Unless we can stop it, using all the information in the codex you found, the Book of Ix. No wonder no one in Ek Naab really thinks about anything but our job now—solving the 2012 problem.

What I've learned about the inscription—it isn't just about the You Know What. There is also a link with the 2012 problem.

This is a big deal in Ek Naab. I can sense it in the air. It's the usual thing, Josh—people talking in hushed voices. *Don't-tell-that-I-said-this-but* . . . is how every sentence starts. The only person who has all the information is . . . we both know who I'm talking about.

Please let me tell you what I've discovered. You are the only person I can tell.

A hug,

Ixchel

De: Josh Garcia<mariposajosh@gmail.com>
Para: Ixchel<ixchel1996@aol.com>
Asunto: Re: reps? ripped? buff??

Ixchel,

Okay, you got me. Now I'm really curious . . .

There is a way we can communicate secretly.

I've set up a room for us at this online 3-D place. We can talk with avatars and put up pictures and videos and stuff. The room is locked—I'll send you the password and all the details. Delete the e-mail after reading, then meet me in the chat room. I'll be online all evening, waiting.

Josh

<J-MARIPOSA has joined>
<MENINHA has joined>

MENINHA: Hello . . . J-MARIPOSA! Josh—you're named after a butterfly?

J-MARIPOSA: It's my *apelido*—my capoeira nickname. After my favorite move.

MENINHA: And I'm just "girl" . . . *meninha* is Portuguese for "girl," am I right?

J-MARIPOSA: *grin* Sorry. Couldn't figure out what you'd like. Ooh, how do you make your avatar scowl like that . . . ?

MENINHA: I've never seen you dressed in white pajama bottoms and no shirt . . .

J-MARIPOSA: They're *abada* pants. For capoeira.

MENINHA: Oh. Please give your avatar a shirt next time.

J-MARIPOSA: *sigh* There's so much I have to teach you . . .

MENINHA: So—you have a favorite move?

J-MARIPOSA: Yep. *Mariposa*—the butterfly twist. It's awesome.

MENINHA: We can talk freely here?

J-MARIPOSA: Talk away. What's this big news?

MENINHA: Okay. You remember the Adapter? That weird
object that Simon Madison stole, then we found it in the
hands of the Sect of Huracan, in that strange
chamber under the pyramid in Becan?

J-MARIPOSA: Of course I remember. I was carrying the
Adapter around in my back pocket trying not to let it
blow poison gas in your face most of the time . . . how
could I forget it???

MENINHA: Sorry, Josh, it's just that you said you've been
trying not to think about what happened the last time
you were here.

J-MARIPOSA: Trying not to think about it . . . don't see
how I could ever forget . . .

MENINHA: Well, then you'll remember that the Adapter
has an inscription . . .

J-MARIPOSA: The same inscription that appears at
the beginning of the Ix Codex, the fifteen symbols. I
remember. And . . . ?

MENINHA: Well, they deciphered the Adapter inscription.

J-MARIPOSA: Whoa!

MENINHA: The entire project is locked down. All of a
sudden—top secret! One of the codebreaking team
members is my teacher at the Tech. You know I'm
learning ancient Sumerian, yes?

J-MARIPOSA: You said you might.

MENINHA: Now my teacher can't say ANYTHING about the project. No one is allowed to know what's written in that inscription. Apart from the members of the ruling Executive.

J-MARIPOSA: I might have guessed Carlos Montoyo wouldn't want to be left out.

MENINHA: You're right. But this time, he isn't in charge.

J-MARIPOSA: Then who is?

MENINHA: Lorena. The *atanzahab*, the matchmaker, you remember her? Our chief scientist.

J-MARIPOSA: They put a scientist in charge of this project? Why?

MENINHA: I have no clue.

J-MARIPOSA: Why are you so eager to tell me about this?

MENINHA: Because you want to fix the You Know What, don't you?

J-MARIPOSA: You can call it the Bracelet of Itzamna. No one here but us chickens.

MENINHA: What . . . ?

J-MARIPOSA: It's just a saying.

MENINHA: Here's the thing. The Bracelet needs a replacement Crystal Key . . .

J-MARIPOSA: We don't know that for sure.

MENINHA: Yes, but we know that some ancient technology uses the Key.

J-MARIPOSA: Yeah, yeah, how could I forget? The piece of the Ix Codex I gave away, with all those secret instructions about how to activate the Revival Chamber using the Adapter and the Key. The Key can be a liquid, but works best in crystal form.

MENINHA: Nice of you to finally talk about the Ix Codex. All that secrecy about what you were allowed to say was getting kind of annoying.

J-MARIPOSA: Hmm. It's only because I think you know more about what's in the Ix Codex than I do by now.

MENINHA: You may be right.

J-MARIPOSA: If only I'd always been as careful about the Ix Codex as I was with you. Thanks to me, the Sect of Huracan knows how to make the Key. . .

MENINHA: You couldn't have known that your friend Ollie was spying on you. She and Simon Madison working together . . . she used your friendship against you. That's why it's called a betrayal. Not your fault, Josh.

J-MARIPOSA: Believe me, I still feel like an idiot. At least the Key they made didn't work.

MENINHA: True. That was pretty funny, actually, when they tried to activate the Revival Chamber and it failed. Remember how those people from the Sect of Huracan, the "Professor" woman and Marius Martineau, started screaming at each other? And at Simon too?

J-MARIPOSA: Didn't seem all that funny to me. I

remember we were pretty scared they'd find us hiding in the tunnels.

MENINHA: I guess we were.

J-MARIPOSA: So . . . any news about what the Revival Chamber actually does?

MENINHA: No clue, it's all secret. Lorena had her team take over the chamber right away. They sealed the Sect's secret entrance and created another, direct from Ek Naab.

J-MARIPOSA: When we were climbing Mount Orizaba, you told me you thought it might be a time-travel device.

MENINHA: Yeah. But now I'm not so sure. Your father—he seemed to use the Bracelet of Itzamna to transport from wherever he was to the volcano, didn't he? So maybe the Revival Chamber does something completely different. Like, maybe it revives the dead?

J-MARIPOSA: Jeez. That would be cool! Do you think Lorena's team has managed to activate it?

MENINHA: I don't know! Like I say, TOP SECRET! They don't tell someone like me.

J-MARIPOSA: Okay, what about this inscription on the Adapter? You need the Adapter to activate the Revival Chamber, right? The Key goes into the Adapter and makes it work in the Container, and that makes the Revival Chamber work . . . isn't that how it goes?

MENINHA: I haven't been able to find out what the
inscription on the Adapter says, but what I do
know is that Lorena's scientists are talking about the
Key. That's the whisper, the rumor. The inscription tells
them how to make the Key.

J-MARIPOSA: Those fifteen symbols on the Adapter—
they tell you how to make the Key?

MENINHA: Correct. They're trying to make the crystal
version—the Crystal Key. The ancient instructions in
the Ix Codex say that the Crystal Key is the most stable
form.

J-MARIPOSA: Make a crystal . . . like with a chemistry
set?

MENINHA: I guess. Lorena *is* a scientist.

J-MARIPOSA: So those fifteen symbols are, like . . . a
chemical formula for the crystal?

MENINHA: That's what I think. But I haven't been able to
see the deciphered text.

J-MARIPOSA: If it's chemistry, we're out of luck. I wouldn't
know where to start with making a crystal.

MENINHA: Yes, the same with me. But here in Ek Naab,
they are confident. They're going to have the Crystal
Key here in a few weeks. A month at most.

J-MARIPOSA: Are you sure?

MENINHA: I read some e-mails of Lorena's. Over her
shoulder, actually—she didn't realize. It was just a short

message to Montoyo. He asked, *When will it be ready for a test?* And her reply was, *Maybe a month*.

J-MARIPOSA: But when we were in the caves, I heard that Professor woman from the Sect say that you had to make the Crystal Key in zero gravity.

MENINHA: Yes, I remember that. But maybe zero gravity is not a problem for Ek Naab. They could take a Muwan up into space.

J-MARIPOSA: Hmm. If I could get my hands on that crystal . . . even for a bit. Just to try it in the Bracelet.

MENINHA: YES! Just what I was thinking.

J-MARIPOSA: I need to find an excuse to go back to Ek Naab.

MENINHA: EXACTLY.

J-MARIPOSA: But what?

MENINHA: It could be me.

J-MARIPOSA: You?

MENINHA: Yes, your excuse for coming back to Ek Naab. Say you want to see me again.

J-MARIPOSA: *blush*

MENINHA: Say that you miss me. Montoyo and Lorena— they're so eager for us to like each other, since they tried so hard to arrange our marriage. They'll fall for it.

J-MARIPOSA: Okayyyy . . .

MENINHA: You and I, we'll know the truth.

J-MARIPOSA: Well, if you're sure. I'll tell Benicio. And he'll tell Montoyo.

MENINHA: Mmm . . . maybe you should ask Montoyo directly. Don't involve Benicio.

J-MARIPOSA: Why not? He seems to like talking about you.

MENINHA: I'd prefer you and Benicio don't have that conversation. Later he might find out we weren't telling the truth. Then he won't trust us.

J-MARIPOSA: I guess.

MENINHA: Good. Okay. Well, I'll drop by this room again in a few days.

J-MARIPOSA: We can leave messages for each other on the wall. THIS wall!

MENINHA: Good-bye, then.

J-MARIPOSA: Later.

MENINHA: What later?

J-MARIPOSA: I mean SEE YOU later.

MENINHA: Oh! Okay . . . later!

Long minutes after Ixchel's avatar disappears in a puff of animated smoke, I still can't tear my eyes away from the screen. I can't seem to move from my chair.

Why did I choose the screen names "J-MARIPOSA" and "MENINHA"? Why do I try to be funny around Ixchel? I could kick myself—I don't seem to make her laugh. It's a good thing the 3-D chat room doesn't keep a log of our conversation, because if I could, I'd read it over and over. Just to see how much of an idiot I made of myself.

I'm so distracted that it doesn't even occur to me—for well over an hour—to think seriously about what Ixchel is suggesting.

It's everything I've tried so hard to avoid. The mysteries of Ek Naab and 2012. The Bracelet of Itzamna.

Three months of struggling with the urge to bury that bracelet in the garbage can. Or to chuck it into the River Cherwell on a rainy day.

Three months of trying to forget about traveling back in time, to forget about fixing what happened to my dad.

Persuading myself to let things fall—wherever.

Then Ixchel sends me some messages about an inscription, and something creeps back, something I thought I'd banished.

Hope.

Since I got back from Mexico, Mom's treating me completely differently. It's as though she's heaved a big sigh of relief that her kid has finally grown up and she doesn't need to take care of him anymore. He can take care of her.

You'd think a guy would be happy about it, and at first I was. Not anymore. I don't mind putting up shelves and making furniture from IKEA, but I don't want to listen to Mom talk about how lonely she feels, how she misses my dad.

I feel pretty awful about it too. After all, I was there when he died. He died saving me—not something I'll ever, ever be able to put out of my mind.

Mom asks me to buy her cigarettes at the store. I can't believe it—she's actually forgotten my age.

"You're almost sixteen," she says.

"I'm not even fifteen until summer!"

She frowns as if she'd forgotten where she put her keys. "Really?"

"Anyway, you have to be eighteen," I tell her, annoyed.

I go to the store all the same and buy her a paper, a bottle of Perrier, and a snack. When I return, Mom takes one look at the headline and remarks, "Melissa DiCanio—your father knew her."

It takes me a few seconds to focus on what Mom is saying. There's a story in the Oxford newspaper about a scientist who's been found dead in Qatar, a country in the Middle East. While Mom talks, trying to remember how Dad had known the woman, whether Mom had met DiCanio at this college dinner or that one, I read the story.

Right away, something leaps out at me: "one has been arrested—Simon Madison, who is also wanted by the FBI and CIA as a suspected terrorist."

Simon Madison. Somehow he survived the avalanche that he started on Mount Orizaba, the avalanche that led to my father's death. Just as I'm feeling a surge of disappointment that Madison didn't get what was coming to him, I read the next part.

"Authorities intend to bring Madison to the United States of America. It is believed he will be charged with a number of offenses."

So that's it, then. Madison has been caught. Too bad for DiCanio, that scientist he seems to have murdered. For her, it's too late.

Madison is not often out of my thoughts. How could I forget him? He's bound up in my single most painful memory—the memory of my dad's death.

That day, the *whole* day, is the last thing I think about at night and the first thing I think about in the morning. It's in the back of my mind most of the time too, but night and morning are when it comes right to the surface. As soon as the thoughts start, I work at pushing them away. I visualize capoeira moves. I plug in some headphones and listen to music or a funny podcast. I get to sleep and everything goes blank. No more dreams.

Ground zero—blank.

For the first time in many weeks, I open the drawer with the Bracelet of Itzamna and gaze at it. Then I touch it, lightly. That ancient Erinsi technology. There's a really distinctive feel to those surfaces. I remember the same from the Adapter and the cover on the Ix Codex. Like stroking a sheet of magnetized iron filings.

I put the Bracelet on my wrist and feel the familiar buzz of energy, so tiny that you could miss it if you weren't prepared. The hairs on my arms prickle and a shiver runs up my spine. But it's not me reacting to the Bracelet—it's the Bracelet reacting to me.

Those first few weeks after the avalanche that killed my dad . . . if I could have fixed the Bracelet, I would have. No question. I'd have gone back in time and done whatever it took to make sure he didn't end up on that volcano.

But then . . . then I thought about it.

Everything I've done so far has been rushed. I get an idea

21

in my head, and I just go and do it. Find out what happened to my dad, go to Mexico, find the Ix Codex, break into J. Eric Thompson's house, take on Simon Madison, follow some mysterious message in a bunch of coded postcards . . . climb a volcano and risk my life . . .

All in the name of some bizarre, prophetic letter from Arcadio Garcia—a weirdo who claims to know my future.

No planning. Just reacting.

Where has it gotten me?

My dad is dead. That's all I can see.

Any way you look at it, I've messed up. The only good thing I did was find the Ix Codex. Everything else . . . ?

You can talk about "destiny," the way Arcadio did in that letter. Yep, you can do that, and accept things, the way Montoyo said.

I don't buy it.

There has to have been a better way.

I have the Bracelet of Itzamna. A chance to travel in time. To put the clock back, to change the past: a way to fix everything. There's no way I can afford to screw this up.

But the Bracelet is broken. It can't travel in time, because the crystal burned out. The Crystal Key might fix the Bracelet. It isn't just another lost relic waiting to be found.

The Crystal Key can be made.

I've been waiting for some news like this, some ray of hope. I didn't even dare to think it would happen so soon.

Problem is, it's too soon. This is make-or-break.
And I'm not ready.

Message Posted on the Wall of *J-MARIPOSA's* Place:

GET READY . . .

. . . for a BIG surprise, Josh. Montoyo has a plan. I'm sworn
to secrecy. Just to annoy you, I'm gonna join in his little game.

So, do nothing till you hear from me.

"Meninha"

J-Mariposa says . . .

Woo, mysterious . . .

"Do Nothin' Till You Hear from Me" . . . that's a song, did
you know? By Duke Ellington. Another of my dad's favorites.
I guess I'll never forget stuff like that.

Meninha says . . .

Why would you want to forget things your father showed
you? Like it or not, he's part of who you are.

I don't hear from Ixchel over the next few days . . . which stretch to a week, then eat into the following week. Maybe I'm taking it too literally—"do nothing till you hear from me."

Well, whatever. I can't have the girl thinking I've got a thing for her, which she might if I e-mailed for no reason . . .

The time arrives to pack for Brazil. Me, Tyler, my mom, Benicio; we're all flying to the beach resort of Natal for the World Capoeira Championships. Sun, sand, sea, and the land where capoeira was invented. Mom's been totally getting into it; she's been showing me YouTube videos and everything.

"Children practice capoeira right there on the beach!" Mom tells me in a tone of discovery.

I just sigh. *Mom, I know* . . . Haven't I been talking nonstop about capoeira for two years now? Nice that she finally takes an interest.

The afternoon before we leave, Mom drives us all up to Shotover Country Park. For some reason, we haven't taken

Benicio there yet. I'm pretty sure Benicio must be fed up with my mom insisting he spend every weekend learning something new about life in Oxford. I told her he'd be happier hanging out with some Oxford University students. But does she listen . . . ?

The parking lot is almost full when we arrive—it's a typical family-weekend type of outing. Most people disappear straight into the woods, following one of the walking trails. Tyler and I walk along in silence a little ahead of Benicio, who, as usual, is talking to my mom. The bluebells are out, dotted around the woodland undergrowth. That means a trip to the bluebell woods at the arboretum is next on Mom's list. Dad or no Dad, every year is just like the last.

Now that I think about it, that's okay by me.

Every trail leads to the sandpit clearing, and that's where we end up. We stop for a while and sit on a log, looking out over the woods.

"Strange to think that there was sea here once . . . so far inland," Benicio says to no one in particular.

"And dinosaurs," I add. "The first one was found not far from here."

"Nothing lasts . . . ," my mom says softly. "Not even the 'terrible lizards.'"

"Overgrown chickens," Tyler says, sniffing. "Nothing to miss . . ."

"No one to miss them, Tyler," she murmurs. "It's different with people."

I look away, instinctively hiding my eyes from the others. It must show, what I'm thinking. How could it not? I feel it so strongly, as though it were seeping from my pores.

If I could fix the Bracelet of Itzamna, I wouldn't have to miss anything or anybody.

The past, the present, the future; they'd all open up before me.

When is Ixchel going to get back to me? I don't like having my hopes built up, and then . . . silence.

"So . . . how is it you like to be called," Benicio says with a wicked grin, "'Mariposa' and 'Eddy G'?"

"It's serious, man," Tyler says with a straight face. "The *apelidos* help us get into the zone. When I'm fighting, I'm not Tyler—I'm Eddy Gordo, capoeira titan."

Benicio smirks. "And what's Josh? A butterfly?"

Tyler winks. "He's a guy who *still* can't do the *mariposa* move."

For that, I shove Tyler hard enough that he lands on the ground, cracking up with laughter.

As evening draws in, we end with a final practice of our capoeira routine, up there on the sandy hill. Walkers and their children stop to watch as Tyler and I fling ourselves around, flying through the air, spinning kicks that miss each other by closely timed fractions of a second. Until my leg links with Tyler's and wraps around his knee; he stops in midcrouch, flashes me a quick grin, and then pulls away.

26

My problem is, *I don't really want to miss*. Next time someone goes for me, I have to be ready.

Night falls. Before locking my laptop away in the cupboard, I log in to the 3-D chat room. Still no word from Ixchel.

I'm quiet all the way to Brazil. I think about Benicio getting into his Muwan, throwing a backpack into the belly of the craft, putting his headset on over his scruffy hair, starting up the antigravity engines, and docking his iPod to listen to his favorite new rock tunes from England. Heading out alone, all the way to Brazil.

Yet it occurs to me how different everything would have been for us both if Benicio's grandmother had been a man.

He'd have been the son of a Bakab's son. Then *Benicio* would be the Bakab Ix. They'd never have needed me. My grandfather wouldn't have been the one to search for the Ix Codex. My dad would still be alive, and I would be living a quiet, ordinary life in Oxford. Never even dreaming that a place like Ek Naab could exist.

Whichever way you look at it, Fate dealt us all a pretty random hand.

I've always been kind of envious of Benicio. It's hard not to be—he's obviously a genius, he gets to fly a futuristic spacecraft, and he's the hand-picked secret lieutenant of Carlos Montoyo. And for some reason girls really like him.

But *I'm the Bakab*. One of the four sons of the god Itzamna, according to Mayan mythology. Only it turns out that Itzamna was real—he was the founder of Ek Naab. I don't know if the original Bakabs really were his sons, but they were definitely special. All male descendants of Bakabs inherit a genetic immunity against a certain poison—the ancient bio-defense toxin that protects each of the four Books of Itzamna. Those four books contain the inscriptions that Itzamna found in a superancient ruin near the Mayan city of Izapa. The inscriptions aren't Mayan—they're much older. The Books of Itzamna are the writings of the Erinsi, a civilization that's been lost from the record. Something destroyed the Erinsi civilization—the galactic superwave, a massive burst of energy from the center of the galaxy. And it's coming our way again . . . at the end of 2012.

For hundreds of years, one of the Books of Itzamna had been missing—the Ix Codex. Only a Bakab Ix could find it. It should have been my grandfather, but he died in the search. Then my own dad disappeared after using the Bracelet of Itzamna to zap himself to another time and place. So it came down to me, the only Bakab Ix left. At least, as far as the people in Ek Naab knew.

The Bakabs are pretty important to Ek Naab—in fact, four of them sit on a ruling Executive of just six people.

As the Bakab Ix, I'll join the ruling Executive of Ek Naab once I turn sixteen.

From the window of our airplane, my eyes search the endless horizon of clouds, hunting for even the tiniest sign of Benicio's Muwan. I wonder; could it be that Benicio envies *me*?

It's evening when we land at Natal's airport. The sun is just going down. As we step out of the airport, a blast of warm air hits us. Within minutes, the thick weave of my T-shirt sticks to my back. Tyler grins in delight. "Real heat! Hey, *Mariposa*—this is the life."

The guest house—Pousada Florianopolis—is right next to the promenade of Natal's wide beach. After dumping our luggage and changing into flashy board shorts, Tyler and I hit the beach.

It's flooded with yellow light from tall lamps all along the promenade. The sea disappears into dark shadows. Whitecaps on the surf lines glisten in the artificial light. We race into the sea, frothy warm water spreading around our legs. Wading along in the line of the first wave, we follow my mother. She's showered and changed into her evening beachwear, and now strolls along the sidewalk above the sand, peering out toward us.

Mom was right about the capoeira on the beach. About fifty yards up the beach, two tanned, lean boys around twelve years old practice slow handstands followed by measured sweeping and turning kicks—*queixada* and *armada*. Tyler and I pause briefly to watch them. From the moves they're doing, I'd guess they're beginners, but still . . . their technique has a fluidity that mine has only just begun to capture.

We slosh along in the surf, keeping one eye out for Mom, who's taking her pick of the beachside bars. Finally she stops and waves us over. We cross the beach as white sand-crabs shimmy around our feet across the powder. In this light the sand looks like snow.

Tyler bounces along, then gives me an experimental shove. With a low chuckle, he tries harder to unbalance me. In a second we're both cartwheeling across the beach, going into the final part of our routine. Our feet are a blur in the air.

Warm currents brush my skin as I whip through the air. The sand is cool to the touch under my hands and feet. I push back all memories of Tyler and me in the pool at Hotel Delfin, showing off in front of Ollie, seconds before Camila arrived . . .

Ollie, the gorgeous girl who betrayed me. I thought she was a little out of my league—beautiful and a couple years older than me. I never suspected that she was actually a spy, and even worse, an agent of the Sect of Huracan and Simon Madison's girlfriend!

And my sister, Camila—another painful memory. She was a fantastic girl—well, a woman, really. She had a husband who was crazy about her, and most of her life was ahead of her. The memory of Camila drowning in that swamp is one of the most horrible things I have in my head . . . I try pretty hard to keep from remembering that.

At the beach bar, Mom orders drinks. Goblet-shaped glasses appear, filled with foam-topped fresh juices, bright purple and orange; grape for me, passion fruit for Tyler.

We sip our drinks in contented silence. Mom drinks from a frosty glass of cold beer. Her eyes are still on the beach, continually sweeping back and forth. She seems distracted, but I'm too wrapped up in my own thoughts to notice right away.

Two tables down from us, a couple of slender girls are sitting eating ice cream from sundae glasses. They both wear green-and-yellow-trimmed white *abada* pants and short, sleeveless green tops. Capoeiristas. Here, they're everywhere.

So I don't notice my mom staring in the opposite direction until Tyler pokes me, hard.

"Look."

When I do, I see something that, for just an instant, makes my heart leap straight into my mouth.

Carlos Montoyo. But not just him—Ixchel, strolling toward us along the promenade, grins all over both their faces. Yep, Carlos's too. For once, even he looks happy.

I shuffle to my feet. Tyler follows.

"So this is your girlfriend," he murmurs under his breath.

I hiss back, "She is not!"

I told Tyler everything when I got back from Mexico. I was fed up with keeping Ek Naab a secret from my mom and friends, with them thinking I was a person who invented stories about alien abduction. Looking back on it, obviously *Ollie* never thought I was making anything up. No; she knew everything, right from the beginning, right from when she set out to spy on me.

I didn't know that, though, and that's what counts. I'm the one who felt like a secretive freak.

So I wasn't having that with Tyler, not any longer. Now he knows it all: Ek Naab, who Benicio is, Ixchel, the codex, almost everything. Of course, he can hardly believe it—and he's not happy about the fact that Benicio refuses to let him see his Muwan. Then again, Tyler has to believe it, doesn't he? By

32

now my life doesn't make much sense unless you know the crazier parts.

Except—Tyler doesn't know about the Bracelet of Itzamna. No one but Ixchel and me knows about that.

That's how it has to stay.

I might have guessed Ty would tease me about Ixchel.

"She's just a friend," I mutter as I step forward, pushing one hand through my hair before I realize that I'm nervous.

I don't know which of them is making me feel this way—Montoyo or Ixchel. But that's what's going on as I wait for them to reach our table.

Ixchel looks nice—better than nice, actually; really cute. She has a new haircut, she's using a little bit of makeup, and she's dressed in white beach shorts and a cropped, sleeveless top. She's not dressed up and elegant the way she was at my dad's funeral. The sassy-waitress look has vanished too. But it's her smile that gets me.

Jeez. I don't remember her being this pretty.

I have to drag my eyes away from Ixchel to Montoyo. Probably already too late; I make a mental note to keep my eyes off Ixchel as much as possible for the rest of the evening.

Tyler whispers in my ear, "Dude, be cool . . ."

I manage a nod. Montoyo hugs me first, clapping my back twice and looking deeply into my eyes, like he's searching for a sign of how upset I might still be about my dad. "Josh, look at you! You're really turning into a man now!"

I redden; I can't help it. I guess he's talking about the bodybuilding. But, of course, I'm glad he noticed. This took work—and more than a little pain!

Then it's Ixchel's turn. Cool as silk, she gives me the once-over with her eyes. "Good work!" she says, like she's congratulating someone who just carried heavy suitcases to the door. We kiss hello, a bit awkwardly. Then she moves on to Tyler.

"This is Tyler," I say with a shrug. "He likes to be called Eddy G . . ."

"How's it going, Ixchel," he says calmly, as though they've known each other for years. He pecks her cheek, even throws in a little shoulder hug. "I've heard a lot about you . . ."

So of course, everyone looks straight at me. I blush so hard that I have to stare at the ground. I just about force a laugh. "Right! Yeah . . ."

Montoyo hugs my mom for what seems like a tiny bit too long. He says something to her quietly, staring for just a second right into her eyes. I don't catch what he says, but I sense it right away.

Things have changed.

In the past three months, while I've had my mind on other things, something has changed with my mother. Sitting at the table with her and Montoyo, I can't escape the sensation; they know something that I don't.

As we sit down, I try to hide the fact that I'm concentrating hard, trying to figure out what the heck is going on. Ixchel and Montoyo order snacks and drinks. It's obvious right away that Montoyo knows exactly what he's doing. Is there any place this guy doesn't look and act completely in his element? I watch for a few seconds as he stretches an arm around Ixchel while also patting my shoulder, eyes roving contentedly around our little group.

He walks in, he takes charge.

Montoyo looks almost exactly the same as the first time I saw him, right down to the black silk shirt and short gray-flecked ponytail. He carries a small leather satchel over his left shoulder.

Montoyo orders something called *pastel* for both him and Ixchel, and a drink called *guarana*. He starts chatting easily about this part of Brazil: what there is to see, places we should take in after the capoeira championship, excursions we should book. It's the same sort of thing I've heard my mom talk about, but instead of saying, "Yes, I know all about that," like you might expect, she just listens, like she's fascinated to be hearing this for the first time.

What the heck is going on with those two?

Ixchel starts asking Tyler and me about our capoeira routine, our workout regime, all the stuff I told her about the gym, and everything. She shows no sign whatsoever that she and I have been discussing this by e-mail and in the chat room. I sit there saying almost nothing, letting Tyler do the talking.

So Ixchel and I, we're pretending that we haven't been

talking about anything; I get it. I'm not sure why, but Ixchel seems to have it planned out. So I play along. I catch her eye every so often. No sign at all that this isn't the first time she's said this, either.

Ixchel and my mom are good at this play-acting thing.

Tyler enjoys talking. He gestures with his hands, demonstrating the theory of capoeira, explaining the rules of the competition.

"Josh and I are competing in the student tournament. I'm a higher belt than him, so we'll never fight each other in a match. We do have this routine, though, just for show, for our capoeira school in Oxford."

Meanwhile, Montoyo and my mom talk quietly between themselves. I try to look as though I'm involved in the Tyler–Ixchel conversation, which is louder and punctuated by short laughs; but actually I'm trying to hear what Montoyo is saying to my mom.

What could they have to talk about?

Listening to them, it slowly dawns on me that this isn't a conversation that began here and now, this evening on a Brazilian beach.

This is a conversation they've been having for some time.

Montoyo and my mom—they've been in touch with each other. By phone or who-knows-what. Since they met in Ek Naab around Christmas, they've gotten to know each other. They've become friends.

As I realize this, a wave of fury rises in my throat, tightening my chest.

He's got some nerve . . .

Montoyo glances at me. In that moment I see that he knows. He can tell I'm angry—I don't know how, because I'm using all my energy to control my face. He purses his lips and narrows his eyes for a brief second.

"Tyler, Ixchel, I need to borrow your friend. We need to speak alone, Josh, if that's okay with you. There's Bakab business that you should know about."

With that, Montoyo whisks me off onto the sand, where the rhythmic slapping of waves on the shore will drown our words.

I'm guessing he expects me to lose my cool.

He's right.

Montoyo and I head for the beach a few yards from the ocean. We walk in stony silence for a minute, putting fifty yards between us and the beachside café where Ixchel, Tyler, and my mom sit. Something about the way Montoyo gets me out of there—the very second he realizes I'm angry—makes me feel even angrier.

Almost as though it's okay for me to react that way, like Montoyo thinks I'm justified.

"You don't seem happy to see me, Josh," he begins. He speaks slowly, every word considered. "Or Ixchel. Not a very warm welcome for a girl who's been . . ."

"I'm not marrying her," I break in, speaking so mildly that it surprises even me.

Montoyo stops walking. His eyes widen. ". . . for a girl who's been through some very tough experiences with you, is what I was going to say. Josh! What's wrong with you? We've already explained—the arranged marriage only happens if you *both* agree."

38

You always get me to do what you want, is what I'm about to say. But I bite my lip. At least I'm still keeping the Bracelet a secret from Montoyo.

He looks at me in silence. I stare back, pushing out my chest.

"You're angry," he says. He sounds disappointed. "About my friendship with your mother."

In fact, I'm so angry that I can't speak. I want to yell at him, but I'm suddenly scared that it might come out as a sob. So instead I gulp hard and keep it in.

"We're just friends, Josh," Montoyo says, very simply. "I like her. Eleanor . . . she's a very interesting woman; very intelligent and cultured. We have had some nice conversations—principally about you. She's been telling me about her life with you, about how Benicio is getting on in Oxford."

There's another long silence.

"You're a credit to her, and you should know—if you don't already—that your mother is tremendously proud of you."

As calmly and quietly as I can make myself speak, I say, "My dad's been dead for three months. That's all."

"Maybe so, but Eleanor has already been mourning him for almost a year," Montoyo says.

That does it. I yell, right in his face, "So she can forget him, is that it? So she can move on . . . to you?"

Montoyo doesn't flinch, I'll give him that; he takes it on the chin.

"Maybe one day, if she decides. I would be the lucky one. But that's not your decision."

It's all I can do not to punch him.

"She's your mother, Josh, and I understand that you feel protective—even possessive—toward her. But women aren't possessions. I should know," he says, suddenly regretful. "I've made that mistake myself."

"Why couldn't you let her be?" I shout. I've barely heard a word he's said. "She's my mother! It's my life! It's like you have to be *everywhere*: Ek Naab, Oxford, here."

"Let this go, Josh," Montoyo says, very serious. "Or it's going to become a problem between you and Eleanor. Between you and me. Your mother's already worried enough about you."

"You could have fooled me," I say bitterly. "She's not even that interested."

Now that Montoyo's here in Brazil, it's suddenly obvious to me why Mom was so eager to come. Not to watch me do capoeira, after all.

He continues, "You're wrong. Just because she doesn't crowd you and coddle you as though you were a little boy. She respects you! She thinks of you as a young man—one who's ready to take his place in the world. But that doesn't mean that she doesn't worry about you."

I start to walk away from Montoyo along the shore. Tears of fury are prickling in my eyes. I can't afford to let him see.

Montoyo walks along beside me. He pulls something out of his bag and puts a hand on my arm.

"Before we get back to the others, I brought something for you." He places a book into my hands. I recognize it immediately. What I see completely takes my mind away from any worries about Montoyo and my mom.

Incidents of Travel in Central America, Chiapas, and Yucatan, Volume I, by John Lloyd Stephens.

It's part of the same book that was taken from my house— same book, different volume. A copy of my dad's first-ever gift to my mom. The same edition that I tried to replace, the book I found in a bookshop in Oxford that was stolen right out from under me. All thanks to Simon Madison and the mysterious global network he works for—the Sect of Huracan.

"The book . . . ," I say in wonder, turning it over. I look up at Montoyo and notice that now, he's hardly more than an inch taller than me. "Is this supposed to be for my mom? 'Cause the one that was stolen was Volume II . . ."

He taps his bag with a hint of impatience. "Yes, yes, I have the second volume also. It's the first volume that interests me. I remembered what you told me about the dedication in that book you found in the shop. From John Lloyd Stephens to Arcadio."

I stare at him in disbelief. As if in a dream, I open the book to the flyleaf. In the top left-hand corner there's a scribbled name.

J. Arcadio Garcia, 1843.

"No way! This book belonged to Arcadio Garcia too . . . you think it's the same Arcadio?" I mutter, amazed.

Montoyo nods. "Maybe."

"Where did you get it?"

"Ever since you told me about the letter that Arcadio Garcia left for you with Susannah St. John, I've thought it an interesting coincidence," he replies. "It never occurred to you? A book dedicated to 'Arcadio,' and then this strange letter from 'Arcadio Garcia'?"

"A coincidence? It's just the same first name."

Montoyo taps the flyleaf. "But this book was owned by Arcadio Garcia. The same name as your mysterious correspondent Susannah St. John's friend."

Well, okay . . . except that . . . it couldn't be the same guy. Could it?

"But the date . . . ," I stammer. "1843? He couldn't still be alive in the 1960s, when he met Susannah."

Montoyo grins, showing his teeth. I get a little shiver, watching him smile like that. This must be how a mouse feels, being toyed with by a cat.

"Not unless he has a time machine."

Okay, Montoyo . . . you got me.

I don't want him to see my excitement, so I pretend to stare closely at the book. But I can feel his eyes on me, watching me like a hawk.

Montoyo continues, "It struck me as an interesting

42

coincidence, so I began looking for that book in rare-book shops. Do you know what I found? There's a collector in the USA who's been collecting that same book . . ." He pauses for a minute, staring directly into my eyes. "All copies inscribed by J. Arcadio Garcia."

"Weird," I agree, slowly. I don't really follow . . . yet.

"But the *dates*, Josh. That's the strange thing. The dates are all over the place. Nineteenth century, twentieth century. Always the same book. The collector has eight. He *had* nine; I persuaded him to sell one set of volumes to me."

"I bet that cost you," I say, flipping through the pages.

Montoyo agrees drily. "He very nearly refused to sell. Now why do you suppose, Josh, that Arcadio Garcia had a collection of these books, all inscribed with different dates?"

I stare blankly. "No idea."

Montoyo gives me a long, searching look. Eventually he nods at the book. "Look at the back."

I turn to the back flap. There's more of the same handwriting—is it Arcadio's?

Curtly, Montoyo says, "Read it."

I read aloud: "I would like to swim against the stream of time . . . so the more I seek to return to the zero moment from which I set out, the further I move away from it . . ."

I stop reading and face Montoyo with what I hope is a vague expression.

He asks me, "You understand . . . what this is saying?"

43

Maybe I do. I can't help but think these words have some kind of meaning for me.

But I don't want to let Montoyo know that. Then he might guess that these days, all I think about is how I can do exactly that: *swim against the stream of time*.

To go back in time and change the past.

So I shake my head. "Not really, no."

"I looked this up. He's quoting from a writer named Calvino. The character in the story makes a terrible mistake and longs for a way to turn back the clock, to alter what went wrong in the past."

I force myself to shrug, to act as uninterested as possible.

Montoyo taps the book. "Why do you suppose Arcadio is writing this?"

Mumbling, I reply, "I don't know."

"The inscription of Arcadio's name in the book says 1843 . . ."

"So . . . ?"

Montoyo gives me a quizzical smile. "And yet the quotation comes from a Calvino story . . . a story published in 1979. Over a hundred years later."

"Arcadio's a practical joker?" I suggest.

The smile doesn't leave Montoyo's lips. "You think so? What if I told you that I saw all the books in this collector's possession? *And every one of them has the same quotation in the back.* What do you say to that?"

I scowl. "Why ask me? I don't even know who this Arcadio is!"

"Who is Arcadio . . . ?" Montoyo wonders. "Now *that* . . . that is really the question, isn't it?"

We climb the stairs to the paved promenade and stroll back to the café. Montoyo stops to buy some T-shirts from a stall. They look a little tight for his beefy shoulders. I don't comment. Then he surprises me by handing me one—it's yellow and green, and shows the flag of Brazil.

"We're going to a restaurant, Josh," he says, tight-lipped. "So put on a shirt."

We pick up Mom, Tyler, and Ixchel from the beachside café, and Montoyo leads us down to the main street on the seafront of Natal. The narrow palm-lined boulevard is packed with artists hawking their canvases and boys pushing wooden carts loaded with pirated CDs. Their loud sound systems blast out samba rhythms. The sidewalk crawls with fortune tellers, mystics, crippled beggars, and guys offering buggy rides on the sand dunes. Opposite the sea there's a solid line of restaurants and bars, half-filled with lazy-eyed tourists.

The whole place pulses with a warm, steady rhythm, a beat that lies somewhere between relaxing and energizing.

As I pass one mystic's tent, he breaks off his conversation and stares at me from under a silky purple turban, white bangs, and thick black eyebrows. His expression is so piercing that I glance around to see if he's looking at something behind me. When I turn back, he gives me a knowing smile.

Tyler notices him looking at me. "Check out the weirdo in the turban and cloak."

My eyes lock with the guy in the turban for one second before I look away. Something about the mystic makes me feel uneasy. He reminds me vaguely of the bus driver I met in Catemaco, the one who offered to interpret my dream for cash.

The dream, I remember with a shudder, that led me right to the Ix Codex.

Tonight, though, I don't want to think about the past. It's a warm, sultry night, and Ixchel's here. So I ignore the weird vibe I get from the mystic and walk faster, catching up to Tyler and Ixchel.

Montoyo seems to know what he's doing. He picks a café, shakes hands with the owner, and guides us upstairs. We take a table next to the concrete dance floor, by the stage. Talking directly to the owner, Montoyo orders plates of seafood, rice, steak, and fries, all without asking any of us what we want.

I glance slyly at my mom. Montoyo has decided that she's sharing a mixed seafood platter with him and drinking a *caipirinha*—the local lime-based, sugar-cane spirit cocktail. Mom doesn't seem to mind having her food and drink chosen for her.

I sit quietly and seethe, then lean across to the waiter just as he's leaving and change my drink order from *guarana* to grape soda.

Tyler and Ixchel have stopped talking. In fact, I notice they keep giving me these little glances—who knows what they mean. If they're bored with chatting to each other already, that's fine by me.

I'm wondering whether or not to tell Ixchel about the book I'm holding. I can see she's curious about why I'm carrying a famous old travel book about the Mayan ruins. She's smart enough to figure out that Montoyo gave it to me on our walk just now. Aside from that, it won't mean much to her.

Then Tyler speaks up. "Hey, isn't that the same book we were looking for in Jericho that time?"

I glance at him, taken aback. "Actually . . ."

The stage comes to life then; musicians start pounding on the conga drums. Two capoeiristas emerge from the edges and burst across the smooth concrete floor, flying head over heels in a series of spectacular crisscrossing somersaults.

The words freeze in my mouth as I watch. Tyler's the same—eyes riveted to the stage.

More capoeiristas follow, bouncing onto the stage in pairs. They fly at each other with cartwheels and backflips and then perform a couple of swift, basic moves before moving aside to let others join them on stage.

When the entire group has assembled, they pair off and begin to spar, whirling in a blur of yellow and green *abada* pants. The musicians on stage sing the same capoeira songs that Tyler and I have learned. I notice that, like me, Tyler sings along quietly, under his breath.

The players perform within yards of us. Their moves become faster and more violent with every turn they take. Within moments, all the men gleam with a shiny film of sweat, while the two girls still look daisy fresh. By the end of the show, I know for a fact that I'm watching the best capoeira players I've seen in my life. The students at the championship aren't going to hold a candle to these guys. When they're really going for it, their kicks have the power and speed to kill . . . and yet every move is intricately timed. They miss each other by the breadth of a hair, laughing with delight, clapping as they land another daredevil handstand and backflip.

Tyler and I are speechless. We're clapping along with everyone else in the audience. I notice Montoyo watching me.

You like this, don't you, Josh? he seems to be saying. *I finally found a way to put a smile on your face.*

Well, okay, Montoyo. Maybe this time . . .

49

On stage, the *berimbau* player hands his instrument to another guy and then bounces lightly, landing barefoot on the dance floor. They start playing "Happy Birthday" to a capoeira rhythm. Everyone grins happily as the capoeiristas take turns sparring with Birthday Guy.

At the table next to us, two women in their twenties remove their flip-flops and line up to dance with the birthday guy. The capoeira moves are now the slow, lighthearted, easy moves that two beginners might play. If anybody accidentally lands a kick, it's blocked and laughed away like an old joke between friends.

Tyler stands up.

"I'm gonna give it a shot," he says.

Ixchel smiles. "Go on, Eddy G! That would be so great!"

Just like that, he does. Tyler steps in, touches hands with Birthday Guy, and without a word, they begin. Birthday Guy can handle more than the easy moves he's been playing so far. When Tyler moves the pace up a notch, so does he. Their movements speed up rapidly. I can see that Tyler is being pushed right to the edge of his abilities.

Tyler looks incredible. I've never seen him do capoeira with anyone this good. Now I realize just how talented Tyler is. Soon everyone in the restaurant is cheering him along. They give him a round of applause and a cheer when he finishes.

When Tyler returns to our table, breathing hard, he wipes a sheen of sweat from his forehead and neck.

"Wow, Ty, that was amazing." I'm filled with pride in my pal.

"Yeah . . . ," Tyler says with a quick grin at everyone at the table. "Thanks. It wasn't bad, was it?"

It's only then that I notice another presence at our table. Benicio. Without any fuss, he's joined us. He's already sipping a drink and clapping for Tyler, who's the first one to greet him.

"Hey, man, you made it!"

There's something like a squeal of joy from Ixchel. She turns around, delight in her eyes, and throws herself against Benicio. I sit by, uncomfortable once again. I watch as Benicio and Ixchel hug tightly. Her hand lingers on his shoulder. For some reason, I can't tear my eyes away from that hand. When I finally glance away, I catch Montoyo gazing at me again, with a sort of knowing look.

Montoyo is really starting to get on my nerves.

On the dance floor, the capoeira players have given way to three couples dressed in casual black. They dance together to tropical music with an accordion backbeat. It looks a bit like ballroom dancing, only funkier, less formal. The lead singer calls it *forro*. After the demonstration, the dancers invite people to join them on the dance floor.

Benicio winks at Ixchel. He offers his hand. "Do you dare?" She grins back, putting her hand in his.

So then I have to watch them dance. It gets worse. Montoyo leads my mom onto the stage, where it's obvious immediately that he knows what he's doing on the dance floor too. My eyes flicker from them to Benicio and Ixchel, who aren't nearly as proficient. But at least they can dance in time. When they make a mistake, they just giggle helplessly, pressing their foreheads together.

I feel something then that is completely new. Nausea throbbing somewhere underneath my diaphragm. The feeling gets more intense when I finally put a name to it.

I'm actually *jealous*, more than I can remember being in my entire life.

It's so overpowering that for a few seconds the sheer novelty is almost funny. It's like unlocking a whole new part of my brain.

Who knew it could feel this bad?!

Looking from Benicio and Ixchel to Montoyo and my mom, it's hard to tell which of them is causing the feeling. In fact, they both are. But it's worse with Ixchel. After a while, I literally can't bear to watch her dance with Benicio—I have to look away, suddenly acting very interested in the lobster tank in the middle of the restaurant.

I'm conscious of my heart pounding like a metronome. I concentrate on the lobsters crawling around in their tank. It suddenly strikes me as pitiful, watching them experience their last few minutes of life. I sense the tropical rhythms of the dance band; they enter through the soles of my feet, through my fingers, deep into my bones, which feel like they're trembling inside my skin. Try as I might, I can't stop exhaling sharply—more like a tiny gasp of pain.

I like Ixchel; I like her a *lot*. When did this happen? Why didn't I see it coming?

Later, Tyler lies snoring in the bed next to mine. I'm hypnotized by the ceiling fan, watching it slowly rotate among the shadows. In my head, I can still hear the music from the beach restaurant pulsing away in the background.

I've been awake for almost twenty-four hours since waking up in Oxford. Although I'm exhausted, I can't sleep.

My mind can't stop speeding along, not for a second. My thoughts flit to the last minutes of my dad's life, replaying the whole incident on the volcano in detail. Then I think about Ixchel. She's falling asleep against me on the bus to Tlacotalpan. She's holding my hand as we whisper to each other, the night before we climbed the volcano. She's standing beside me at the funeral. I remember how aware I was of her, our shoulders almost touching all the way through that ordeal. The way she took my hand and murmured, "You'll get through this, Josh". . .

Then I'm on to thoughts of the Bracelet. That quotation in the John Lloyd Stephens book that Montoyo brought me: "I would like to swim against the stream of time."

A perfect way of putting it. That poet Arcadio quoted from, Borges, in the letter he left me all those years ago . . . Borges wrote that "time is a river."

Well, if that's the way things are, then yes, I want to swim upstream.

Why is Arcadio writing something like that in so many copies of the John Lloyd Stephens book? Is that the reason why Madison stole a copy of the book from our house? And as Montoyo says—who is Arcadio Garcia?

From there I think about Montoyo. The way he looked at my mom. The way she smiled at him. Jeez . . . she's *my* mother! I'm not thinking of her as a possession—what a jerk that Montoyo can be. I've never thought of a *girl* as a possession either. But what my mom is to me, she can't be to anyone else. I'm her firstborn and only child, her son. I have rights, whatever Montoyo thinks. I don't have to just stand by and watch him try to steal her away from my dad.

Dad is not just a memory. For us, things can be different.

I have the Bracelet of Itzamna. *I can change everything.*

I roll out of bed, fed up with hearing Tyler snoozing so happily. I step out onto the balcony, listening to the breeze whispering over the sound of the waves. In the garden below, the palms are lit up with blue and red lights. Suddenly I notice a movement in the shadows, beyond the pool. I stare hard into the depths of that darkness. The more I stare, the more I grow certain that someone is sitting there quietly, concealed by the dark, on a deck chair.

As I lean on the rail of the balcony, I have an eerie sensation of being watched. My gaze falls into the blackness, with nowhere to focus. Whoever sits down there can probably see me clearly, outlined by the dim orange glow of a citronella candle.

I suddenly hear my mother's voice. She's speaking very quietly, but there's no doubt about it—it's her.

Is she down there in the darkened garden with Montoyo? Immediately, I lose interest in the mysterious presence in the garden below.

I'm rigid with tension when I realize that I hear *both* their voices—Montoyo's and my mother's. The sounds are coming not from the garden but from the path that leads to the beach.

Montoyo and my mother have been together at the beach. They've only just returned to the hotel.

I pull back from the rail and lean against the hammock that's stretched across the balcony. I fall into the hammock, carefully wrapping it around me so they can't see that anyone is on this balcony. I lie still inside the hammock, one arm against the balcony door, holding the hammock motionless.

I listen for their footsteps on the stairs. There's the sound of one door shutting, and then another.

They've each gone to their own rooms, which is a relief. Yet clearly Montoyo and Mom wanted to keep their conversation going. They took a midnight walk together, along a tropical beach. Well, that's enough to keep me from sleeping for the rest of the night.

It's a disaster. Tomorrow is the first day of the capoeira contest. I'm going to be wrecked.

Outside, it begins to rain. Within minutes, the downpour has built to a torrent, drumming loudly on the roof and balcony.

Back in the room, I turn on my bedside lamp. I pick up the two volumes of the John Lloyd Stephens book and flip through them. I'm looking for the story my dad always told me about, where Stephens relates hearing rumors of a living city of the Maya—in 1840, hundreds of years after the Maya collapse, and after the Spanish invasion too.

There shouldn't have been Mayans still living in the ancient cities—not by 1840. Only in Ek Naab—the secret city beneath the ruins.

Ever since I discovered their invisible city, I've always wondered whether that story could have been a clue. Was it John Lloyd Stephens' way of hinting about Ek Naab?

Montoyo once told me that Stephens had secretly been to Ek Naab. That Stephens taught the people of Ek Naab

English. And that's how they finally figured out that the Ix Codex is written in Mayan hieroglyphs that spell out words in English.

On page 195 of Volume II, I find what I'm looking for. "A Living City."

I read the page once quickly, then more carefully. That's when I notice that two of the letters on the page are very faintly circled in pencil. I glance through the rest of the book to see if there are any similar marks anywhere else.

There aren't.

I pick up Volume I and make the same check. Nothing in those pages. But now that I'm examining this volume closely, I find something bizarre in the back flap, tucked right under an old Stanford University library sticker.

A series of numbers, beginning with 195.

195: 1, 1, 6; 2, 7, 4; 5, 3, 2; 6, 1, 4; 6, 4, 4; 6, 6, 1; 8, 5, 3; 8, 5, 5; 9, 1, 2; 9, 2, 2; 10, 4, 3; 10, 5, 4; 15, 2, 3; 16, 2, 1; 16, 2, 5

I'm so still I can almost hear my own pulse. I stare at the numbers—tiny, meticulous handwriting. Like something a librarian might write, or a bookstore owner, to help them catalog the book. But I'm fairly certain this is no coincidence. A set of numbers starting with 195 in Volume I of a book I . . .

and then traces of pencilled circles on *page* 195 of Volume II . . . ?

The whole situation seems to remind me of something. It feels like there's a telephone ringing in the distance, muffled, and I'm hunting down the phone in room after room.

This should make sense to me. This should be easy.

I'm just so tired, though. I can't force my brain to calm down and think it through in a nice, calm, logical way. It's like a TV image when the satellite signal breaks down. Doesn't make sense.

Yet it should. Volume I and Volume II. Numbers in one volume of a book, circled letters in the other.

Like a jolt of electricity, it hits me. An idea so incredible and yet so simple that I can't believe it could be true . . .

The numbers in Volume I refer to the page in Volume II.

My hands shake slightly as I open the two books again and locate the first circled letter on page 195. It's a *Y*. I mumble slightly, counting how many lines down, how many words across, and how many letters into the word the *Y* appears.

Five lines down, three words across, two letters in. *Y*.

Now, my breath catching with excitement, I scan the long list of numbers in Volume I for that same triplet: 5, 3, 2.

The triplet is there. Amazing . . .

I struggle to calm myself as I test the theory a second time, now with the second circled letter, a *K*.

Fifteen lines down, two words across, three letters in. *K*.

Now I'm looking for the triplet 15, 2, 3. And there it is.

I gasp, then stuff a fist into my mouth to stop myself from yelling with triumph.

Each triplet of numbers corresponds to one letter. Two of them have been circled—a *Y* and a *K*.

The string of numbers written in Volume I is a cipher—a coded message.

Someone started to decode this message. Who?

I work my way through the entire cipher text, translating the triplet code into the single letters. But after the first three letters, my spirits begin to plummet.

This doesn't spell any word in English; in fact, it doesn't look like any kind of word.

I plow on right to the end. But by then I'm totally disillusioned.

AGYLIHRPPREIKGR

It's meaningless to me. It might as well be another code.

I still can't sleep, and I don't see why Ixchel should. So I slink into the corridor and knock softly on her door, then a little louder. She comes to the door instantly. Although she's in her pajamas—shorts and a T-shirt—it doesn't seem like she was asleep either.

"Hey," she says with a surprisingly shy grin. "Couldn't sleep?"

"I found something."

60

"Your mom's in the shower. She just got back from the beach with Montoyo."

Impatiently I reply, "I know. Let's go to my room. We can sit on the balcony."

The instant I say the words, I realize that's a bad idea. It takes me a few seconds to figure out why. Thinking about the balcony gives me a creepy feeling—a sense of being silently observed by whoever was just sitting out in the darkened garden.

It's okay, though, because Ixchel kicks the idea out. "Too dark. Let's go downstairs, to the lobby."

Behind the high reception counter of the lobby, a tall, gangly guy with a shaved head and trendy black glasses sits reading a paperback folded almost double. He glances up for just a moment when we approach. We help ourselves to a fistful of candies from a goldfish bowl crammed with fruit drops. It's late and everyone else in the hotel is in bed, but after we sit on the sofas he doesn't give us a second look.

I unwrap a grape-flavored drop and pop it into my mouth. Ixchel chooses lime.

"Okay, Josh—what have you found?"

I show her the volume of the John Lloyd Stephens book I've been carrying, as well as the separate piece of paper on which I've scrawled the deciphered code. I explain how I figured it out, and then my voice trails off as I watch for her reaction.

Ixchel is quiet for a couple of minutes.

"You worked this out, just now?" She looks at me intently, and I find myself stammering slightly.

"Well, yeah . . ."

"You really have a talent for codes, Josh. This is brilliant, you know."

She really seems to mean it.

"Thanks," I mumble, feeling myself redden. "But it doesn't get us any further."

"Yes," Ixchel says, "it does. It tells us a lot. I just don't understand how or why . . ."

"Huh?" I say. "Explain."

"Well," Ixchel says, pointing at the string of letters. "Have you noticed that there are fifteen of these letters?"

I actually hadn't bothered to count them. If I'd noticed that there were fifteen, I probably wouldn't have thought too much about it. But now that Ixchel mentions it . . .

"You're right," I mutter. "That *is* weird." And a crackle of excitement zips along my spine.

"Fifteen symbols on the Adapter," Ixchel whispers. "Fifteen glyphs in the front of the Ix Codex fragment. And now *fifteen letters* in Arcadio's book."

"You think it's the same thing?"

Ixchel chuckles. "I know it is! Look—see this combination near the end? RPPR-something-something-something-something-R. I've seen it before."

"You've seen this sequence of letters before?"

"No—not as *R* and *P*. It could have been *ABBA* something-something-something-something-*A*. Or *BCCB* and the rest. I never knew what it was—I just saw the glyphs. I saw them plenty of times. This pattern is pretty memorable. The same pattern of two different glyphs: glyph *A*, glyph *B*, glyph *B*, glyph *A*, then four other glyphs, then glyph *A* again."

A slow grin spreads across my lips. "You think this is the Adapter sequence?"

"What are the chances of a sequence like that happening by accident—in a fifteen-letter sequence?"

"Hmm . . . I'm not great at math."

"This could be the formula for the Key, Josh. Don't you think?"

"I think you're right, *Meninha*," I say. I can't help smiling at her. "You're a bit of a genius yourself."

"Yes," she says, no hint of joking, ignoring that I just called her "girl" in Portuguese—or, at a stretch, "babe." "I know."

"Doesn't look like any chemical formula I've seen."

"Well, me neither, but I don't know chemistry. We could find one—a chemistry expert."

"You want to find a chemist here in Brazil?"

"Well, sure," Ixchel replies with a smile. "We'll use the Internet."

She's been strangely calm all the way through this. Me, I'm

63

sizzling with wonder at our discovery. But then Ixchel puts her finger on the one thing that makes me a little uneasy.

"The thing is, Josh—why? Why is Arcadio writing the Key sequence in code? And why in these books?"

I don't know the answer to that yet. But for some reason, the question sets off a tiny little alarm bell. It feels like the source of something dangerous.

Maybe even life and death.

7

The next morning, Tyler has to shake me awake. I can hardly move. He's shouting at me to get dressed, but it's all I can do to prize my eyelids apart.

"Hnuhhh?"

"Breakfast in an hour!" Tyler says. "Just enough time for a swim first . . ." He chucks a pair of shorts at my head.

Maybe the ocean will wake me.

When we get down there, it's barely 8 a.m., yet I can already feel my shoulders roasting under the sun's rays. The beach is nice and empty; just a few guys are selling sunglasses, bags of fresh-roasted cashews, and ice pops. I'm a little surprised to see that Montoyo and Mom are already lounging under a beach parasol. The ocean is blue gray, speckled with foam. Waves are dotted with surfboards, their riders bobbing around the breakers. Once in a while someone catches a long wave and rides it all the way to shore.

Ixchel is in the water, riding a boogie board among the

surfer dudes. She's not very good at it. I guess she's hardly ever been to the beach. I watch her for a minute. She looks happy, laughing every time a wave knocks her off the board.

Mental note—teach Ixchel how to bodysurf.

Tyler and I take a quick dip in the ocean and then hit the beach for another capoeira warm-up session. We go through the routine twice and then do some freestyle. A handful of local people watch us, smiling in appreciation.

With capoeira, when everything is going well, there's an energy that flows through my entire body. The air, my hands, the ground; it all merges into one. I am a free particle, energized, bursting with *axé*—an Afro-Brazilian word we use in capoeira. It means something like "life force," but also "cool."

But today there's no *axé*. Today I'm slow, clumsy, rough.

When we finish, Tyler eyes me curiously for a few seconds.

"Something wrong, Josh?"

"Yeah," I tell him tightly. I want to talk, but I don't. I hate this feeling. Can't take a step forward for fear of going back. I glance out toward the surf again. Tyler follows my eyes to Ixchel and then looks back to me. He raises an eyebrow.

"You *like* her."

I snort. It's probably not very convincing.

"But she likes *him*, doesn't she?" Tyler continues thoughtfully. "She likes Benicio."

So simple and everyday when Tyler says it. Ice cream is cold; the girl you like wants someone else.

"Hmmm. Change the subject."

Tyler stares at me curiously. He throws me a towel. "All right, Josh. Try to keep your mind on the capoeira. What was up with those *queixadas*? Even your *ginga* looks off."

Annoyed, I say, "You think I don't know?"

He's right, though; I can't even pull off the basics today. I'm doing the moves, but my mind is somewhere else completely.

Even worse—I hardly care. I just want to be alone with Ixchel so that we can sort out this mystery. Instead, I have to go and compete in the capoeira tournament.

Tyler is going to kill me, because he's right; my heart isn't in it. Not today.

The championships are being held in a fancy hotel farther along the beach to the north. After the morning swim and a quick breakfast of ripe yellow mangoes, pineapple juice, and fried eggs, we head out as a group, walking along the sand. Montoyo is even more brazen than he was last night; he offers my mother his arm as they walk. Benicio strolls along with one arm dangling around Ixchel's shoulders.

I couldn't feel more gutted if she actually kicked me in the stomach.

It's almost like they're doing it to irritate me. I'm itching to hit someone. That or find some isolated place and vent my rage. Tyler and I walk on ahead. He keeps flashing me these anxious looks.

"Chill, Josh."

"Shut up."

"I know what it's like, man."

"No," I scowl. "You don't."

"Yeah," he says calmly. "My mom and her new boyfriend. That's terrible. And how do you think I felt about you and Ollie?"

I turn to Tyler in amazement. "Me and Ollie? There is no 'me and Ollie'; there never was."

"Yeah, I know that now, but she played me too. All part of her plan to spy on you. She used me. Winding me up, going on and on about you."

I stop walking and gape at Tyler. "You're joking. You liked Ollie? You never said."

Tyler presses his lips together. "I liked her. And course I didn't say anything."

My eyes focus lazily on the sand, the horizon, anywhere but Tyler's flat, bitter gaze.

"So I know what it's like, man."

With a throat so dry it almost chokes me to speak, I say, "With Ixchel, I think I might be. . . You know."

"Blatantly," he agrees. "She's *nice.*"

I sigh with relief that I don't have to spell it out for Tyler.

"But, Ty . . . I mean, how? I thought . . . me and her . . . we're just friends, right? Then I see her again, and it's . . . like . . . *bam*. It just hits me."

Tyler just nods. "It was probably there all along. That stuff is weird."

I stare at him. "You were supposed to tell me I'm imagining things . . ."

He grins, shaking his head. "Nope. I believe you've got it bad."

"What am I going to do?"

Tyler laughs, shrugging. "No idea."

The others have almost caught up with us, so I start walking again. Tyler follows.

"Let it out in the capoeira, Josh."

That sounds like a great idea. If only I knew how.

The hotel is one of those big fancy ones with lots of marble and a bunch of ritzy swimming pools surrounded by palm trees. As we approach the conference room, we hear the pulse of the *pandeiro* drum and a raw, stringy twang, the buzz notes of the *berimbau*, the chorus chanting in response to the singer: the music of capoeira.

Tyler perks up the moment he hears the sounds and turns to me with a huge grin. "Dude, we're here, we're really here!"

The conference room has been laid out with tiered seating around a wooden roll-out dance floor. By the time we arrive, the early stages of the tournament are almost over. Just five more matches for students with the same belt as me.

I've drawn a fifteen-year-old boy from Austria. One look at him stretching is enough to make me worry. He's about the same height as me, but looks skinnier, less muscular. But he's got that long, raggedy, sun-bleached ski-bum hair. I just know he's one of those mountain kids who spend six months of the year on a snowboard.

I don't like snowboarders. Ever since Madison got my dad and a bunch of other climbers killed by starting an avalanche while riding a snowboard.

Snowboarders are reckless.

I shake my head in silence, going into my breathing exercises. I can see Tyler talking with the British team coach, Mestre Joandy. I'm expecting a big pep talk before I get into the *roda* with the snowboarder.

But all Mestre Joandy says is, "Have fun, Josh. Relax. Enjoy—that's capoeira."

I look up, mystified. I guess they've really given up on me.

From the second we touch hands, Snowboarder really is wild, totally fearless; he throws himself into the match with a quick series of flips ending with a *mortal*—a somersault. From then on, he keeps upping the ante: I do an overhead kick, and he'll do *aú sem mão*—an aerial cartwheel with no hands. If I miss him by ten inches, he'll skirt my face by five. I go for the *mariposa*. It's not the best one I've ever done, but as I fly past Snowboarder, I catch his delighted grin. This guy is not just good—he *lives* capoeira. Winning doesn't matter to him. He just wants to play. His own *mariposa* follows—faster and sleeker than mine. Then a barrage of rapid variations on *meia lua*—circular kicks.

The judges don't even need to discuss it. They pick

Snowboarder to go through to the next round. Snowboarder can't stop beaming. I should be happy for him. A guy like that *should* win. But none of that helps. I wasn't as good as I can be, and I know it. I never once got into the zone. With all these people watching too . . .

"There's still plenty more team display stuff to look forward to," Tyler says. He pulls on his UK team shirt, getting ready for the next round—the yellow and blue belts.

I glance up into the audience, where Mom is giving me a "never mind" sort of look.

"I guess," I mutter.

Ixchel joins me at the side of the dance floor, watching as Tyler and the other yellow and blue belts warm up. I can hardly look at her, so I just give a quick nod.

"You're not in the mood, are you?" she says, in what for Ixchel is a very kind voice.

Slowly, I say, "Nope . . . apparently not."

She seems to consider her next words. "This whole Bracelet thing . . . it's taken you over. Hasn't it?"

I can hardly believe what I'm hearing. Has she only just figured that out?

Ixchel continues, "Because maybe . . . maybe you should be thinking more carefully about what you'll do . . . if you fix it."

I've never really talked about that in detail, not with anyone.

"You're going to use it to go back and save your father—right?"

"Yes."

"What if that changes things?"

I gaze at Ixchel in disbelief. "I want it to change things!"

"If your father isn't there on the volcano when we climb it—how do you know that you won't die? Or me?"

Exasperated, I say, "No one will die! I'll bring Dad back *in the past*. None of that mountain stuff will have happened. Dad can find the Ix Codex. Then everything will go on like before. Except that *Dad* will be the Bakab, and I'll be back to my normal life."

Looking right into my eyes with what I'm sure is a hint of a blush, Ixchel says, "So if this works . . . you and me . . . we might never meet?"

I mumble, "I'm sure Dad will introduce us one day . . . he's the one who agreed to us being fixed up, after all."

Softly she says, "And you're so sure that your father will find the Ix Codex?"

"Yeah . . . of course . . . he had the same dream as I did, the one with the *brujo* who says 'Summon the Bakab Ix' . . ."

Ixchel shakes her head. "You're taking a big risk. Your father had that same dream since he was a child. But even so, it never occurred to him to search for a Mayan codex in Catemaco."

"Me neither."

"No, Josh—*you* were led there."

I laugh. "It was a coincidence. I took a bus. Never planned it. I just wound up in Catemaco."

Incredulous, Ixchel says, "After everything that's happened to you—after the ghosts of Chan and Albita saved us in the caves—you still believe that it's all been a coincidence?"

"Yes," I say firmly. "A coincidence! They happen all the time. My dad could have found the Ix Codex in Catemaco, just like me!"

I stop talking. Why is she trying to talk me out of this? It's not so complicated. This isn't a Chosen One–type situation. Anyone with the Bakab Ix gene could do what I did.

Even Madison—and all those other guys in the Sect of Huracan who happen to have the Bakab genes.

I move away from Ixchel, letting her see the anger that's rising within me. "I just want things back the way they're supposed to be."

Then I turn and walk away. From behind I hear Ixchel's firm, quiet voice following me.

"But Josh . . . how can you know *what that is*?"

I ignore her. To my surprise, the ache I feel when I look at Ixchel is replaced by something colder, something easier to take: resentment.

This is good. This will cure me. Get mad at her! I should have thought of it before.

As I leave the dance floor, a spectator who's been sitting

73

in the front row stands up. I catch his eye for a second and he gives me a quick nod. Now that I think about it, he was watching my game very closely. He's fair-haired too. Maybe someone else from the Austrian team?

I don't give him another thought. But I should.

We're outside enjoying drinks and general festivity beside the moonlit waves. The capoeira tournament is over, and Tyler has won not one, but two medals—best in his belt class and best all-around under-sixteen. I'm happy for him— really happy. It's everything Tyler has wanted for months and months. Watching his incredible performance in the finals this afternoon, it struck me that I couldn't be prouder of my best friend. Which, I realized today, Tyler has become.

The tournament closed with celebratory team displays, followed by another beach party.

Boy, do the Brazilians know how to party!

With music pumping through my senses, feeling dizzy from drinking lime juice laced with sugar-cane brandy, it's hard to have a care in the world. Of course Mom doesn't let me have enough *cachaça* to really forget my troubles. So it's not long before I'm back to brooding, watching Benicio and Ixchel laughing, chatting, and dancing together on the sand.

Okay, she asked me to dance before asking Benicio. It was only because she knew I was going to say no. I can't dance, Ixchel knows it, and I'm not going to look like an idiot in front of everyone.

Get mad at her.

It's working. Anger is something I can deal with. If Ixchel's not going to support me, if she's going to be all weird about me using the Bracelet, then she's going to find herself off my friend list. I stare out at the bluish-black beyond the horizon, where a half moon is rising.

In a beach paradise like this, surrounded by friends and family, I should be happy. I'm not.

Montoyo notices that I've broken away from the group. He joins me, our feet submerged in warm surf every time the waves break.

"So, Josh," he begins. "Having a good time?"

"Yeah." I attempt a smile. "Tyler was amazing. He made up for me being so terrible."

"You weren't terrible. You were . . . distracted."

I nod, resigned. "True."

Montoyo eyes me watchfully. "The question is . . . by what?"

The real answer to that would bring me scarily close to mentioning the Bracelet. So I try to be vague. "By wondering why . . . why everything has to be so complicated."

76

Montoyo seems perplexed. "What is complicated? Your life?"

"Yeah. Being a Bakab and everything. When all I want is . . ."

"What, Josh?" Montoyo's eyes take on a stern glint. "What do you want?"

I shrug. "I just want to be happy."

I don't know if I'm expecting sympathy or what, but I don't expect Montoyo to actually laugh.

"Happy?! But what *is* that?"

It seems pretty obvious to me—so obvious that I start to think he's making fun of me. "Happiness . . . ," I blurt. "Like, having fun and friends and things to look forward to and not be dreading stuff all the time."

Not feeling jealous either. Or sick when certain memories flash into your mind . . .

"Is that actually happiness? The pursuit of pleasure, the avoidance of pain? That's not what Aristotle believed. You know Aristotle, the philosopher? He thought that happiness was about seeking personal excellence."

I shake my head slightly. "Personal excellence" sounds like a recipe for hard work.

Montoyo continues, "For men like us, Josh; for men of will, men of action, happiness is something else. It's about always having someone needing you, depending on you.

Always having someone to protect. Always having difficult problems to solve. Always having so much work to do that . . . sometimes you don't have time even to drink a glass of water."

I stare at Montoyo in silence. He's actually smiling. He *does* look happy.

"Maybe it's time you were really honest with yourself, Josh. What's really important to you in life?"

Before I've even realized, my gaze has wandered over to Benicio and Ixchel. Like Tyler earlier today, Montoyo's eyes follow mine: he watches me watch Ixchel. Then he breathes a light sigh of discovery.

"Ah . . . !"

I force my stare to become glazed; I move my eyes in a controlled fashion so that they appear to sweep the dancing couples, the bar, the restaurant, all with the same feigned lack of interest. A last-ditch attempt to make Montoyo doubt what he thinks he saw.

Montoyo shifts his position in the water-furrowed sand. This time, he sighs deeply. "Well, you'll be happy tomorrow, I guarantee it."

"Why?"

"We're going to take a nice long ride on the dune buggies. Ride down giant sand dunes. Eat barbecued shrimp by a river in the cashew-tree forest. Zip-line into a freshwater lagoon. And drive right along the sand until we find a beautiful beach that's just for us."

"Really . . . ?" I can hardly believe my ears.

Montoyo nods. He claps a heavy hand on my shoulder and squeezes once. "That sound okay for you, Josh?"

"Yeah," I manage. "That sounds *amazing*."

The party winds down. We walk back along the beach to the hotel. Ixchel catches up to Tyler and me.

"Josh, is something wrong?"

Tyler throws me a knowing look and then hangs back, leaving me to walk alone with Ixchel.

I make myself look at her, as vaguely as possible. "Nothing's wrong," I answer shortly.

We walk along in silence for a few seconds. Beside me, I can sense Ixchel tensing.

"You're mad because of what I said," she begins. "About not changing the past."

Yes, Ixchel, and so much more . . .

But all I say is, "You're entitled to your opinion."

Ixchel reaches out and takes my arm. "Stop it, Josh."

"Stop what?"

"This. I've never seen you like this before. Cold. Angry. Just because I warned you not to do something that could be incredibly dangerous?"

I stop moving and turn to face her. "What did you think I was going to use the Bracelet for?"

A confused expression comes over Ixchel's face. "I don't know . . . maybe I didn't fully think it through either."

Challenging her, I say, "You didn't think I'd ever fix it."

"Well, sure! It's still a long shot."

"I know the formula for the Key. And I know they probably have the Crystal in Ek Naab. One way or another, I'm going to fix the Bracelet, Ixchel." I pause, enjoying the look of unease on her face. "With or without you."

She looks hurt and withdraws her hand from my arm.

Get mad at her.

"So this is how you get when people don't agree with you, is it?"

"That's right." I nod, staring directly at her. "This is how I get."

In the artificial glow of the beach lights, I notice tears glistening in her eyes. I don't allow the shock of what I've done to register on my face. A cool wave of relief seems to pass through me. When it's gone, I feel numb.

Controlling her voice with difficulty, Ixchel says, "Well, I'm glad I found out."

I can only nod. "Uh-huh."

She turns and slowly walks back to where Benicio, Montoyo, and my mother are ambling along in a leisurely fashion. Tyler picks up speed, jogging slightly until he's alongside me again. I'm already walking even faster than before.

He asks, "What happened?"

"Oh, she's just throwing a tantrum."

"What about?!"

"That's between me and Ixchel."

Tyler pauses. "At least Benicio's got the guts to own up to liking her."

Now Tyler's annoying me too. "This has nothing to do with any of that."

"No?"

"No, this is about . . ."

"What?"

But my voice trails off. Suddenly it hits me that by pushing Ixchel away, I've lost the one person I trusted to help me figure out how to use the Bracelet.

I've left myself totally alone in my quest—again.

Well . . . Okay. Good.

Trust no one.

I sleep fitfully that night. At least twice I'm stirred awake, certain that I've felt my cell phone buzzing underneath my pillow. I don't answer it, of course. It costs a fortune to take a call from someone in the UK. And there's really no one there I want to talk to right now. The second time it happens I turn the phone off. And then I think I even dream that the phone is buzzing.

I don't let myself think too much about Ixchel, or Benicio, or Montoyo.

Instead I focus on the next steps in fixing the Bracelet. First I need to understand that fifteen-letter chemical formula. Then I need to figure out who Arcadio is—and if there's any way of contacting him.

Unless I decide to patch things up with Ixchel, I'll be doing it alone. Which suits me fine.

What worries me slightly is this: What if Ixchel decides to tell Montoyo about my plans for the Bracelet? Montoyo has been after the Bracelet of Itzamna since the day I met him. If he finds out that I've got it, he'll take it from me. It's as simple as that.

The next morning we all meet for a quick breakfast in the reception area. Tyler, Ixchel, and I are all wearing the matching yellow-and-green Brazilian-flag T-shirts that Montoyo bought at the beachside stall. Tyler and I think it's funny, but Ixchel seems a bit miffed to be dressed in matching outfits. She's about to go change, but Montoyo tells her it's too late: the dune buggies are here.

Stepping onto the beach outside, we meet our buggy drivers—the *bugeiros*—tanned guys in their twenties who wear uniform white T-shirts made of football-jersey fabric. They stand beside two stocky, squat-looking buggies with chunky wheels. A scent of sweet, alcohol-blended gasoline hangs over the vehicles. They look a little like beefed-up Mini cars with the roofs cut off. An overhead bar sits across the middle of each car, from which a plastic tarp hangs, protecting the front seat passenger and driver from the sun. For passengers in the back, though, there are no seat belts and zero shade, just the cool of a racing breeze to keep them from frying.

Mom chooses to sit in the shade in the front of the red buggy. She straps herself into a front seat with the only safety belt. Tyler and I sit up on the back of the roofless, brightly painted car. We grip the overhead bar in front, our sandaled feet on the plastic-covered cushioned bench in the back.

Benicio and Ixchel do the same in the back of a second, silver-colored car, while Montoyo takes the front seat.

We take off, racing over the cobbled streets of Natal behind the hotels, up to the highway and then along the main beach road. It's only nine a.m., but once again the sun pelts down from a deep blue sky. A wind whips through the buggy, refreshing, exhilarating.

After about twenty minutes of careering through the city, our drivers leave the main road. We head for narrow chaos in the backstreets of hillside fishing villages. We cross a red-tinged river on wooden rafts paddled by muscular villagers. They laugh and joke with each other, talking in laid-back, slangy-sounding Portuguese.

The buggies storm through another couple of villages, splashing through mud and cloudy puddles of last night's rain. Then the *bugeiros* veer off-road. We cut across damp, brick-red sand and shallow mangrove swamps toward a golden mountain—the beginning of the giant sand dunes.

Up there, it's like being in a ski resort—except instead of the gleam of powdery white snow, it's just pinkish-yellow sand as far as the eye can see. Behind the dunes in the distance is a line of deep blue—the sea.

We climb out of the vehicles, stretch our legs, and take some photos. A young girl approaches, holding a plump green lizard along her arm. Ixchel, Tyler, and Benicio are immediately drawn to the lizard girl, cooing over her exotic pet.

A third buggy pulls up beside ours. The driver is short and squat, his mouth a straight line under wraparound sunglasses and a baseball cap. His green uniform shirt looks too tight for him, stretched thin across thick shoulder muscles. Four male passengers climb out, snap a couple of photos, and swig from water bottles. Three of them are probably Brazilian; strong-looking guys accompanying one fair-haired European—or maybe Canadian? He looks kind of familiar, although behind his dark glasses I can't be sure. Seconds later the passengers climb back in. Their buggy pulls away sharply and disappears down the nearest slope.

I stroll away some distance, gazing out over the sands. I notice then that Mom has followed me.

"Josh . . . you've got to stop sulking. It isn't fair to your friends, or me."

I'm stunned. *Sulking?*

She continues. "Ixchel was crying last night. She was very quiet, but I heard. What did you say to her? It's really not okay to be mean to your friends, just because you're upset about your performance."

I draw myself up to my full height. Something feels ready to explode inside me. I wish Mom would just shut up.

"And Carlos mentioned that you were a bit moody with him too . . ."

"What, suddenly I'm surrounded by all these tattletales?" I say coldly. "But you, Mom; you don't understand anything. You don't know anything about me at all!"

85

"If I don't, it's because you don't tell me anything! Josh, be careful. Or you're going to grow into one of those cold, distant men. It won't make your life easy, I promise you."

The explosion feels very close now. In disbelief I say, "Easy . . . ?"

"Yes. You should be more open. None of us can read your mind, you know."

"Easy," I repeat, even more amazed. "You think my life is easy *now*? Well, it's not!"

"You're still upset about your father, aren't you?"

I stagger. "Upset . . . ? Mom—are you kidding? Upset?"

"I should have insisted you see a grief counselor. I'm sorry, that was my mistake."

That does it.

"A counselor? You think you can just hand me over to some counselor and it all goes away? Like back when I was the only one who refused to believe that Dad's death was an accident? You *never* listen to me!"

Mom tries to touch me, but I push her hand away. "You don't listen to me," I repeat. "And you know what, Mom? What I've learned is this: I can't count on anyone but myself. When I needed you, you couldn't help me. You couldn't think about anyone but yourself. Maybe if you'd listened to me, things would have been different. Maybe I would never have ended up on that mountain."

There's a long, agonizing silence.

In a voice that trembles slightly, Mom says, "I don't pretend to understand everything in your life, no, but I do try my best to be supportive. As for everything that's happened, Josh . . . you must learn to accept things. To let things go."

Now I'm trembling too. Maybe a part of me—a tiny part—can see the sense in what Mom says. But that part is swamped by raw anger.

I hate that Mom is so wrong about me. I hate that she is so right about me. I hate that I can't control anything—outside of me or inside. That I just want Mom to hug me and make it better, but she can't, ever, and I can't rely on anyone but myself.

"I can't . . . *let things go*. I won't. Because everything in our life is wrong—can't you see that?"

But I can fix it . . .

Mom's tone becomes disappointed. "I'm sorry that you feel I'm such a failure as a mother . . ."

I give a bitter laugh. "That's right; try to guilt-trip me."

With that I storm off, right past the red buggy and into the silver one, where I sit fuming in the back.

Ixchel approaches. "I think you've really upset your mother, Josh."

I squint up at her in the dazzling sunlight. "What's it to you?"

Ixchel shakes her head. "Wow. You have a real mean streak, don't you?"

To that, I don't reply, just glare back at Ixchel. After a second or two, she picks her bag out of the silver-colored buggy. "I'm gonna ride with Eleanor. This isn't a nice way to treat her. You're lucky to still have a mother."

With that, Ixchel walks over to the red buggy, where Mom is standing, dabbing at her eyes.

I almost give it up right there and then, go over and apologize. But what would I say? I wouldn't know where to begin. This has all somehow spiraled out of control. All because of this . . . *thing* . . . I have for Ixchel. What kind of an idiot does that make me?

This is too complicated. I'm not going to have everyone feeling sorry for me just because I've gone soft—over a girl who likes someone else.

Better that they think I'm moody, angry, whatever.

So I stay put, blinking in the intense light because, stupidly, I've left my baseball cap in the other buggy. The way things are now, it would just be too undignified to get it. Then I notice that Ixchel has put my cap on. She turns around and glares back at me, shadowed under the peak of the cap. Daring me to come and get it. But I won't.

Eventually Montoyo, Tyler, and Benicio gather around the silver buggy.

Tyler gives me a steady look. "You want me to ride with you, man?"

I shake my head. "Stay with them, Ty."

He looks thoughtful. "Okay."

Montoyo's expression doesn't alter. He doesn't even glance at me, just sits in the front seat and straps himself in. Benicio resumes his seat in the back, next to me. We both avoid each other's eyes, saying nothing.

I can almost hear Benicio's mind whirring away. If Tyler guessed, then so will Benicio. I exhale very slowly and fix a blank gaze on the nearby slope of the dune.

If this is what love feels like, then . . . you can keep it.

Ahead, a valley of shimmering sand stretches across our entire field of view—a view that might easily belong to the Sahara. The dunes are dotted with a few other buggies. Their riders screech with pleasure as the buggies tumble down the slopes like giant sleds. But even that thrill is going to leave me untouched. The weather may be sizzling hot, but inside there's a cold front sweeping through me.

Oblivious doesn't even come close.

The *bugeiros* are probably wondering why their fun party of dune-surfers has suddenly turned so cold. As they rev up the buggies to tackle the first slippery slope, we're all a little solemn. But once we start hurtling down the monstrous sand hills, even I perk up.

It does feel amazing.

The drivers seem to have the curves of the dunes etched into their minds. From the top, the craters at the bottom of the dunes seem terrifyingly distant. The expanse of sand is so bright that staring at it, I lose all sense of perspective. The next patch might be wildly steep or loose, require a hard turn to the left—or to the right: who knows? As a passenger you can hardly predict where you'll be going next, which gives a crazy exhilaration to the ride.

Soon enough, we're all whooping as we zigzag across the landscape. It's as much as Benicio and I can do to hang on to the overhead bar. A couple of times we're actually lifted off our seats. It only adds to the thrill.

Holding on takes concentration. We're aware of the other buggies on the dunes, but we don't pay much attention to their positions.

So what happens next really takes us by surprise.

Seemingly from nowhere, a metallic-blue car leaps through the air in front of us. It lands between our silver buggy and the red one that carries Mom, Ixchel, and Tyler. Our driver curses loudly to himself but doesn't alter his course. For some reason, the blue car's driver was desperate to pass us in the craziest way, scrambling across a patch of trees and scrub to cut in.

Now we're one of three buggies in a row. The red one carrying Mom, Tyler, and Ixchel; then the weirdo blue buggy; then us in the silver.

Between catching my breath as we swoop down and up those sandy hills, I begin to catch glimpses of something odd happening ahead. I don't speak Portuguese, but from his tone, I can tell that our driver is getting irritated with the driver of the blue vehicle in front. He keeps muttering under his breath until Montoyo asks him something—I'm guessing it's "What's going on?"

Our *bugeiro* gestures wildly toward the blue car.

Benicio shouts into the wind, "What's up?"

Montoyo turns unsteadily in the front seat. The buggy jumps slightly. Montoyo's head bounces against the soft tarp sun shade.

Still wincing, Montoyo tells us, "That driver—he's being very aggressive . . . trying to force them off the hills."

I look around, puzzled. There's sand for at least three hundred yards in either direction.

"Force them off . . . into where?"

Montoyo shrugs blankly. He turns away and faces forward again, rubbing his head. I glance at Benicio. Both he and Montoyo get very quiet. I sense there's something they're not saying. I stare at the red buggy. The blue one is right behind it.

No doubt about it—red is in trouble.

The crest of the last slope looms ahead, fleshy pink against the white-flecked, navy blue of the sea. A three-hundred-yard sheer drop, straight into the Atlantic Ocean.

For safety, our *bugeiro* pulls back as we near the edge. There's no hiding his astonishment when the blue buggy driver does the opposite, sticking dangerously close to the red buggy as it tumbles down the slope.

Benicio gasps. "That guy is nuts! Someone's going to get hurt."

Finally, the driver of the red buggy seems to realize that he has a crazy guy on his tail. He uses the drop to speed up, pulling away at the bottom of the hill. The red buggy is already a hundred yards ahead, almost at the shoreline as we go into the final drop. The blue buggy speeds up too.

Benicio speaks again, this time ominously. "I don't think that buggy is trying to pass Ixchel's." I turn to him. He pauses. I definitely don't want to hear Benicio complete this thought. "I think they're chasing them."

The driver of the red buggy seems to have reached the same conclusion. He's really turned on the speed now, trying to get away from the nutjob behind him. Ixchel and Tyler are yellow and green blurs in the distance as their buggy zips across the flat wet sands. The blue buggy speeds up too, its four burly passengers sitting impassively in their seats.

"Josh, Benicio, time to sit properly. Hold tight!" Montoyo yells. Then he tells our *bugeiro* to speed up.

As I drop from the back onto the rear car seat, a sense of foreboding flashes across my mind. Something bad is happening—in probably the last place I expected. In the very next second our buggy takes its turn at the sickening, almost-vertical drop. We zip down the sand, sometimes sliding, sometimes bumping. Tangy sea air and sand sting our faces. We practically fly down the dune. I hardly breathe.

Then we're onto the beach, rushing to catch the blue car in front. The low tide whips at the wheels of our vehicle; a spray of salty water lashes our skin. Blue buggy chases red buggy. Silver chases blue. Could it all be a stupid game? If this was happening to anyone but me, I'd be tempted to say it was just some local *bugeiros*, rivals possibly, playing a joke.

But this *is* me. In my life, incidents like this have a habit of turning nasty.

A few minutes into the situation, I'm more than nervous.

I'm downright scared.

In the red buggy, Ixchel, Mom, and Tyler are still around a hundred yards ahead when their buggy actually jumps across a stream of water slicing into the sand. They make a hard left and disappear into a tangle of cashew trees behind the low dunes.

A second or so later, the blue buggy follows suit. Another second after that, so do we.

The path cut through the cashew trees is just wide enough for one buggy. All three *bugeiros* are driving like lunatics—I'm not surprised to spot tourists spread-eagled against the side of the path, desperately trying to stay out of our way.

The forest path twists and turns—I can only glimpse the blue buggy ahead. The obstacles have slowed it down. Now I can see the passengers more clearly. It's the three muscular fellows with their fair-haired guy. They don't even glance behind them. They're obsessed with chasing the buggy in front.

Why?

In a few minutes, we clear the cashew forest. We crash through broken fencing and onto the red sandy dirt track of a village. The makeshift road is lined with single-story shacks; simple houses from which locals stare at us as we zoom by.

I'm starting to wonder where this will end. Are we just

going to hurtle madly through all the fishing villages until we get to Natal? What then?

The road is riddled with deep puddles of milky reddish-brown rainwater. The *bugeiros* swerve to avoid the deepest puddles, but it's not always possible. The blue and red buggies ahead keep being lost from view, hidden behind a cloud of brick-colored spray.

As the town gets more built-up, the road narrows. We hit a paved section. Even though we're in the thick of the village now, the drivers hardly slow down at all. Why doesn't the red buggy driver just stop, call off the chase? I crane my neck to get a better look at the passengers in the blue buggy. But every time I move, my head or knees get a wallop from some part of the buggy.

"Why don't they just stop?" I yell at Montoyo.

He replies curtly, not bothering to turn around, "Because they have a gun. In the front seat. He's pointing a gun at them."

"What?!"

Montoyo doesn't answer. I steal a glance at Benicio.

"What the heck . . . ?"

Benicio frowns. "It looks bad, Josh."

Ignoring the fact that my head crashes against the overhead bar, I raise myself up to a place where I can see over the three guys in the back of the blue buggy.

Montoyo's right. Calm as can be, the guy in the front has a large pistol aimed at the red buggy.

Yet he's not firing. Why?

Villagers are literally leaping out of our way now. Some of them hurl garbage at us, furious at the ruckus. But nothing seems to stop us.

The road slopes along a steep hill. Buildings here are a mixture of ramshackle concrete huts that might be half-built or half-destroyed—it's hard to tell which. Our wheels slip and slide as the driver forces the buggy to climb way too fast. At the top of the hill, the red buggy halts.

It's not just the hill. There's something in the way—two more buggies packed with passengers. They've come up against something. I peer up the hill. There seems to be a white van across the road, blocking it.

The blue buggy stops a few yards behind the red one carrying Mom, Ixchel, and Tyler. The guy in front, the fair-haired white guy, steps out. The gun is raised now, held sideways at eye level.

He shouts toward the red buggy in heavily accented English, "Get out, all of you!"

Montoyo grabs our driver's arm. "Stop!"

The three dark guys in the back of the blue buggy are climbing out. Two of them turn toward us.

Urgently Montoyo hisses, "Back up!"

Our *bugeiro* slams the buggy into reverse. We screech down the hill backward.

The two guys from the blue buggy are reaching into their

shirts. One pulls out a gun. Our *bugeiro* forces a handbrake turn. We spiral for a second, then jolt forward. The buggy leaps across someone's front yard, bursting through a line of hanging laundry. We head for the shed at the side. We keep going, breaking down the makeshift straw wall at the rear and heading into a construction site. Laborers in hard hats leap out of our way, yelling out in fury. The buggy skids unsteadily over patches of wet concrete and clambers over a pile of broken cement that blocks the only exit.

That takes us into another alleyway, for the moment deserted. The buggy driver mutters again. But like us, he can see there's no choice but to keep moving.

Those guys have guns.

"That was a roadblock!" Benicio shouts, breathless as we navigate the narrow, dusty lane. "Those guys were organized!"

I'm stunned. "Are you saying it was a trap?"

Before anyone can answer, there's an engine roar from behind us. It's the blue buggy, revving loudly, screaming down the tight street to catch up with us.

Our driver turns into an even narrower alley. The sides of the vehicle scrape against crumbling concrete walls. Instinctively, I suck in my breath. We squeeze through the narrow gap and into a dusty clearing overlooking the edge of a ravine. The *bugeiro* curses loudly. He spins the buggy around and around, throwing up clouds of sandy red powder.

He's looking for options. There's only one.

The blue buggy has followed us again. This time it's carrying only one passenger—and he's armed. It blocks the narrow lane as, carefully, its driver forces through. In two seconds they'll be in the clearing with us.

We're pointing straight at the edge of the flat clearing. The ravine is beyond, about four yards wide. On the other bank is a line of banana trees. Behind them, more scrub-covered sand dunes.

Our driver changes gears and slams the pedal; the buggy leaps forward until we reach the edge of the ravine. We're airborne. It only lasts a fraction of a second. I can hardly believe we're going to make it. We drop dangerously low, almost slamming into a wall of banana palms. But amazingly, the driver manages to land between two of them. We're through and onto the sand dunes. I turn around just in time to see the blue buggy stalled at the edge of the patio.

They've stopped.

Benicio gasps with relief. "I guess we weren't worth the extra risk . . ."

Montoyo replies grimly, "Or they need to leave someone to pay the ransom."

Ransom?

"The others have been kidnapped, Josh," he says gravely. "Benicio is right. This was a trap."

For several long minutes I struggle to grasp what Montoyo has just said.

Kidnapped?

Ominous tales of South American kidnapping gangs spring to mind. I didn't know this kind of thing happened in Brazil— at least, not in a nice place like Natal. Mexico, Colombia, Peru, sure; everyone's heard of kidnapping in those countries. It's a big business in Mexico City these days, so I've heard my mom say. A bloody one too.

People get kidnapped, yanked right out of their cars on the street. Young people, old people; it doesn't matter. What matters is that they matter to someone—someone who will pay.

Simple economics. Give us cash, or your son, daughter, cousin gets it.

On the way, victims can lose a finger or two, maybe an ear. Sliced off by ruthless kidnappers, delivered to the terrified relatives. When the kidnappers get impatient, people die.

My mind reels. Mom. Tyler. Ixchel.

The things they're going to go through. I'm sick with fear.

Benicio and Montoyo are silent with their own thoughts. A sense of deep shock settles over us. The *bugeiro* drives along, not muttering or cursing anymore, chewing nervously on his shirtsleeve.

I summon up the courage to speak, my voice cracking. "What happens now?"

"Let's get back to the hotel first, Josh," Montoyo says. "Try to relax, if you can." He twists backward in the seat, facing me. "And breathe. The next few days are going to be difficult. You need to be strong."

He's right, I realize. I'm so tense that it's hard to breathe.

This can't be happening. Not now, not after everything we've been through.

The driver takes us onto the main highway. Soon we're crossing a huge bridge into Natal. I stare up at the parallel lines of the bridge's suspension cables, slicing the sky into deep-blue segments.

I'd forgotten about the real world, the outside world. So wrapped up in my own problems: Ek Naab and its massive destiny, the mystery of Arcadio, the Bracelet of Itzamna, and a fate I believed I could alter . . .

I forgot about the everyday brutality of the real world. Why should I be immune to ordinary crime? Obviously, I'm not. But it doesn't seem fair.

This is just too much.

The second we arrive at the hotel, Benicio leaps out of the buggy. Without a word or a glance, he storms into the room he's sharing with Montoyo. I watch him climb the stairs two at a time.

Benicio is angry with me.

I don't understand why, but there's no mistaking the rage pouring off him. It must have brewed up during the buggy ride. I look at Montoyo, puzzled.

"Why's he angry with me?"

"Don't worry about Benicio now," Montoyo advises. He sits me down in the lobby. It's deserted apart from one maid laying the dining table for lunch.

The receptionist strolls over and murmurs quietly to Montoyo in Portuguese. When she's gone, Montoyo stares at me, his eyes deadly serious, his mouth set.

"The kidnappers have been in touch."

Hesitantly, I nod.

His voice becomes soft, deliberately calm. "Let me explain what has happened. It looks as though your mother and friends have been abducted by a new gang that's operating in the area. They also took seven other tourists, the ones in the two buggies in front of your mother's. They blocked the road with that white van, rounded them up, and took everyone into their van at gunpoint. Minutes later, they were gone."

"A new gang?"

"Kidnapping is rather unusual in this part of Brazil. But the gang members seem to be from a place where kidnapping is big business—Rio de Janeiro. Definitely professionals."

"I get it . . . ," I mutter.

But I don't.

Montoyo says carefully, "This is all about money. The kidnappers judge how much they can ask for each hostage. They will come back to us with what's known as 'proof of life'—photo evidence that the hostages are alive and well. Then they'll name a sum of money. That's when we start to negotiate. Somewhere in the middle ground, we find a figure we can all agree on."

"So Mom, Tyler, Ixchel—they won't be hurt?" I'm starting to glimpse some hope.

Montoyo shakes his head. "Try not to worry. We have access to plenty of cash. Obviously we'll negotiate, just so it looks like we're being pushed to our limit. The fact that we're staying in such a simple hotel should make the kidnappers believe we aren't rich."

I can't keep the admiration out of my voice. "You can fix this?"

With a little smile, Montoyo says, "Don't worry. I've dealt with many, many difficult people in my life. I will handle this. Stay calm, stay in your room as much as possible. Don't be alone, even in the pool. In a few days hopefully this will be over. Like a bad dream."

"What about the police?"

"If we go to the police, we force them to act for us."

"So?"

A shadow seems to cross Montoyo's face. "It makes things harder to resolve quietly. Pride comes into it. The police want to win, to catch the criminals. The safety of the hostages may not be their main objective. For now, we deal directly with the gang."

With that he stands up, pulling me to my feet. I'm sent upstairs to my room while Montoyo waits for the phone call.

Somehow I'm not surprised that Montoyo has completely taken charge. He didn't ask me once about how I felt or what I thought we should do. Montoyo seems pretty confident about the situation. Me—I'm out of ideas.

I close the door behind me, feeling shivery and numb. I lie on the bed, staring up at the motionless ceiling fan. Minutes tick by, time stretching in the growing afternoon heat. After a while I break into a sweat. It trickles down my head and neck into the pillowcase. I don't budge an inch. I can't stop remembering.

The things I said to Mom. The way I acted around Ixchel. It seems hard to believe that was me, even a couple of hours later.

What I'd really wanted this morning was simply to sit next to Ixchel, maybe put my arm around her. To be all relaxed and smiling, sharing a joke. Why was that so hard? In my imagination it was easy—no problem. In my imagination I was just like Benicio with Ixchel. Relaxed, cool, confident—the kind of guy every girl likes.

But searching my memories, I don't think I've ever let her see that side of me. Not once. I know I'm not usually a jerk around girls. Why can't I just be normal with Ixchel?

Mom's another story. She's my mom—she'll forgive me. When we see each other again, I bet it will be like it never happened.

The events of the afternoon begin to take shape in my memory, like pieces of a jigsaw puzzle. The face of the fair-haired guy in the blue buggy. I recognized him from somewhere, but where? It'll come to me eventually, I know. I replay the entire morning in my head, slowly. As though in a dream, I watch myself walk away from my mother at the sand dunes and go to the silver buggy, watch Ixchel take her belongings and join Mom in the red buggy, watch Tyler offer to ride with me but return to the red buggy.

No wonder Benicio's angry.

If not for my outburst against my mother, I'd have been the third passenger in the red buggy. Ixchel would have been with Benicio.

Ixchel would have been safe.

I want to believe Montoyo that it's all going to be okay. But a deep current of fear runs through me. How all this happened . . . how it's all going to turn out . . . it's like some complex mathematical equation.

I can't balance it.

It all looks so easy on the surface—a simple case of bad luck: wrong place, wrong time. With such a simple solution—cash.

I'd love to believe it. Can it really be true?

When I'm finally starting to relax, nicely cooled by the dampness of my pillow, it comes to me. Things that weren't in order. In a place where there should have been nothing odd, things that stuck in my mind.

The fair-haired guy in the blue buggy was at the capoeira contest.

He was watching as I walked away from my bout, the one I lost to Snowboarder. At the time, I thought he might be with the Austrian team; that's why I was confused. I didn't expect to see him in a dune buggy with three Brazilians.

That first night in Natal, when I sensed that someone was watching me from the shade of the darkened garden . . . Is there some connection? I sit up rapidly and grab my shoes. Montoyo needs to know about this. The blue buggy being on the dunes at the same time as us—what if it's no coincidence? What if something started the day we arrived in Brazil?

What if this is no ordinary kidnapping?

I lock the room behind me, then leap down the short flight of marble stairs to the lobby. Montoyo's there, holding a phone to his ear. He looks up at me, his expression open, hopeful. He gestures at me to be silent as he nods twice. He speaks briefly in Portuguese before ending the call.

"There's news, Josh. We have proof of life."

MESSAGE FROM IXCHEL

Hi Carlos, Benicio, Josh. First thing: try not to worry. We haven't been harmed. We're staying with some guys named Tiago, Nando, Mario, and Gaspar. Gaspar and Nando were in the buggy behind us at the dunes. Tiago and Mario were in the white van.

Gaspar was at the capoeira match too—maybe you noticed? He'd been watching us for a while, Josh.

There are some other tourists with us too. I'm allowed to tell you that there are seven others and that they are all fine, in case you've been in touch with their families.

So far no one has gone to the police. Gaspar told me to tell you that everyone is cooperating. If everyone keeps doing that, everything will be fine and no one will get hurt. They have people watching all our families. If they get any idea that you are going to the police, then it's going to make things bad for us.

As you can see from the photos, we're all fine, no injuries. Eleanor was very shocked and needed some medicine, but they let her take one of her antianxiety pills. She's feeling better now.

We have to spend most of the time tied up. I'm dictating this via Gaspar. I guess there's no way I can make you believe that these are my actual words. You'll just have to accept it. I can't tell you anything else about where we are.

Gaspar says that he'll let us communicate via the comments on this blog. He said not to bother to trace the IP address, that he's smart enough to know how to shield that information. If they detect any IP tracing activity, they'll assume the police are involved. So please don't!

Josh—your mother asked me to tell you that she's concerned about the bad mood you were in this morning. She says that she understands you sometimes feel things are hard and that's okay; of course she loves you anyway, so don't feel bad.

Gaspar says that if you do exactly what they want, we'll be home in a few days.

We send you lots of hugs and kisses; we are trying to be strong. Please don't do anything dangerous. Let's all stay calm, and this will soon be just a bad memory.

Montoyo pores over the photos on the computer screen. I've never seen him this anxious. I'm the same; I can hardly believe my eyes. Ixchel and Tyler, sitting on two shabby-looking plastic chairs, hands behind their backs—presumably tied. Mom sitting on another chair, her face drawn, looking ten years older than she actually is. She's holding a copy of today's newspaper. The strain shows on their faces. These aren't cheerful shots of hopeful hostages just waiting for their inevitable freedom.

These are photos of terrified people trying hard to appear relaxed.

Montoyo reads Ixchel's message over and over, muttering to himself as if it were some kind of code.

"Is this what you were expecting?" I say, breaking the tension.

"It's more high-tech than I expected," he admits slowly. "Using the Internet and blogs to give proof of life. But it makes sense. If they really do know what they are doing, it would take some serious intervention to track them down. They're probably using a mobile satellite dish to get their signal. Which means they can just keep moving from place to place. Using technology to track them down would be unreliable. Risky too."

"Track them down? I thought you were just going to pay up."

Montoyo gives me a guarded look. "Did you notice that nobody has mentioned money yet?"

I'm puzzled. "What else would they want?"

"I don't know what else, Josh. But Ixchel didn't write most of that message, however it looks. And these four names are just normal Brazilian names—they tell us nothing."

"Maybe they're still wondering how much money to ask for?"

"Money is at the top of the agenda for kidnappers."

I hesitate. "What if this is no ordinary kidnapping?"

Montoyo goes silent, clicking a fingernail against the keyboard. Then I tell him all my worries, the dark suspicions that have built up since the first night.

"You should have told me," he says eventually.

I say nothing. It's hard to explain how unimportant those tiny little details had seemed, with everything else to think about. All that anger and frustration, all those plans I made with Ixchel about fixing the Bracelet of Itzamna. Plans that are fading with every passing second. I sense the weight of the Bracelet in my pocket. Right now, it might as well be a worthless chunk of metal.

Montoyo continues, "For whatever reason, these kidnappers have identified us as a target. It's not unusual for kidnappers to stalk their prey, but . . ." His voice trails off, as though he's lost in thought.

"What?" I ask, anxiously.

Montoyo eyes me cautiously. "I don't want you to worry, Josh. Let's take this one step at a time, okay?"

I can't stop myself, though. "'Stalk their prey'? Why? Tell me!"

After a pause, Montoyo speaks again, reluctantly. "There's something called a 'tiger kidnap.' When they take someone in order to coerce someone else to do something . . ."

"Coerce someone? Like who?"

I can see from Montoyo's expression that I've pushed him as far as he'll go on this. "Let this go now, Josh. There is something strange about this kidnapping, it's true. Most likely we've wandered into some kind of territorial struggle between two gangs. The kidnappers appear to be new to Natal. That will make them many enemies here."

Benicio arrives in the lobby. His hair is all messy, his eyes blazing with unspoken anger. Montoyo calmly explains the situation to date. Benicio stays silent. Only a single resentful glance in my direction gives a hint that he blames me.

I can't return his look. Deep down, I agree with him. I'm the reason that Ixchel's in danger.

We're still staring at the computer screen in the lobby when the receptionist comes over with the phone. Yet another call for Montoyo. She rolls her eyes, grinning in mock sympathy. I bet she's got no idea what's going on. She probably imagines it's a travel agent playing phone tag with him.

Montoyo takes the phone confidently. He says "yes" a couple of times and then goes silent. His expression doesn't change one bit as he listens. Then, very slowly, almost incredulously, he hands the phone back to the receptionist.

"What?" Benicio asks. We wait impatiently. Montoyo doesn't seem to know where to start.

"We've found them!"

Benicio and I gasp. It's the last thing we expected to hear. But Montoyo's expression makes me suspicious.

"Something's weird, isn't it?"

Montoyo shrugs. "It just seems too incredible. But one of the *bugeiros* has a contact who has a contact who *saw* them. We're all forgetting that one of the buggy drivers was kidnapped too. I assumed that he was in on the plan. But maybe not." He frowns. "That was the head of the buggy tourism company. He's organizing a rescue mission. The hostages are being held about twenty minutes away, in an abandoned construction site."

I say, "But they said no police."

111

Benicio adds, "And why do you trust the guy who spoke to you? What if it's a trap—a way to lure in the rest of us?"

Nodding, Montoyo says, "You have a point. But we cannot risk that this may be genuine information. It's typical—plans go wrong. You think you have a secure plan, all the t's crossed and i's dotted. But you forget about the friend of a friend who works for another friend . . . Information finds a way to leak. We're just very lucky that it's leaked this early. We cannot delay. However," he adds thoughtfully, "the time may have arrived to call for reinforcements."

Benicio grins. "You're gonna call the Chief?"

"I think it's time some more of our guys from Ek Naab joined us at the beach," Montoyo says with a thin smile. "Don't you?"

We all go up to Montoyo and Benicio's room. Montoyo makes some lengthy calls, including one to Chief Sky Mountain, the head of Ek Naab's tiny armed force. The whole time he speaks Yucatec—the language they mostly speak in Ek Naab. I can't understand a word. Benicio paces up and down, mumbling to himself.

I feel totally left out. I get the distinct impression that I'm not going to be asked to help.

When the call is over, Montoyo sits us down. Carefully he closes the balcony door and turns up the air conditioning so that there's a loud background hum to our conversation.

"The Chief is sending six people in two Muwans. With

112

weapons. I'm afraid we have to use ordinary guns, because anything else will leave very suspicious traces."

I chime in, "What else would you use?" Do they have some kind of laser gun? It's the first time I've heard anyone from Ek Naab talking about weapons.

Montoyo ignores the question.

"We're going in tonight, as soon as it gets dark. We'll land all three Muwans—yours and the other two—on the roof of the building. It's one of those unfinished hotels. The developers ran out of money—it's the same story all over Natal. This place has been deserted for over a year. The intelligence says that the staircase is only partly completed. So we'll lower ourselves down more than ten stories, and then go into the stairwell. They'll never be expecting an attack from above." Montoyo pauses. "We could use some independent intelligence on that hotel building. But it's a risk. Chances are that any request for information may be detected. Asking the wrong person . . . could be fatal."

Benicio says, "I could take the Muwan—fly some reconnaissance."

"And if you're spotted? What then?"

Benicio bristles. "You prefer we take our information from the buggy company guy? It could be a trap."

"He's taking his group in on foot, from the ground. Naturally, he doesn't know that we're planning anything."

"So why is he telling you anything about his plan?"

113

I agree with Benicio. Why tell us anything?

"Because he wants my help."

Benicio and I sneer in disbelief. "Then it's definitely a trap!"

Now Montoyo seems annoyed. "Of course I didn't offer him any men. I offered money—if the rescue is successful. He's agreed."

"How much?"

Montoyo pauses. "It's quite a sum."

Benicio can't hide his scorn. "In that case, it's one kidnapper buying the debt from another! He's gonna kidnap the hostages and then he's gonna pass them on to his guaranteed buyer!"

"I agree, it could be." Montoyo's answer is spoken mildly. But his eyes have narrowed.

Montoyo doesn't like Benicio talking to him like this, but I can tell that he doesn't want Benicio to notice. Benicio hasn't, though—he's on a roll now. In fact, he's getting more confident by the second.

"The guy who runs the buggies might even be in on the original kidnapping . . ."

My mind reels as I try to understand the implications of what Benicio is suggesting.

"Hold on," I say. "Are you saying this is a kidnapping within a kidnapping?"

Benicio looks triumphant. "Exactly!"

Still, Montoyo doesn't seem fazed. "There are many possibilities. Who to trust, who not to trust. Maybe it's genuine. The guy is taking a big risk to deal with me openly. If he really is another kidnapper."

Benicio snorts. "No, he's legitimized the whole business! You won't be able to call him a kidnapper—he'll just claim to the police that he rescued the hostages and you paid for the rescue."

Patiently, Montoyo says, "That is precisely why I'm not telling him about our own plan."

Sitting there with Montoyo and Benicio, listening to them plan the rescue, a feeling of exhilaration grows inside me. It turns out that they are going to let me get involved—I'm going to fly in with them and help guard the Muwans in case anyone from the kidnapping gang manages to get onto the roof.

A kidnapping within a kidnapping.

Well, okay, maybe that's how these things are done.

Either way, the rescue is going to be one terrific adventure. What a way to improve my image with Ixchel, to earn Tyler's admiration, and to make it up to my mom. Just as much as Benicio, I'll be one of the heroes.

Now that we know we're being watched, we take care to lie low in the hotel all afternoon and evening. The question is, who's watching us now? The original kidnappers, or the buggy company guy?

It's hard not to marvel at the convoluted game that's being played here. Gang A watches a bunch of buggy-riding tourists, rounds them up on a day out, and then calls all the relatives. *No police, do as you're told* . . . the whole thing. But they make a mistake and kidnap a guy from Gang B. So Gang B puts together another deal with the relatives who all hired buggies. Gang B swoops the hostages away from Gang A.

It could even be like Benicio says—maybe Gang A and Gang B were working together from the start.

Montoyo's right, though—none of that really matters. Either way, we're going to get our guys back. With or without assistance.

As the sun sets, Benicio and I change into our darkest

clothes. In my case, that's an old black rock concert T-shirt and some black jeans. In Benicio's case, it's his Muwan pilot's jacket over his jeans. Benicio mutters something about getting me a bulletproof jacket later on, when we get to the Muwan. It's obvious from his tone that every word he has to speak to me is one more than he'd like.

Does that mean I'll be getting a gun too?

I'm not sure I'd be much good if it comes to shooting someone. I remember when I had a gun on Simon Madison that time we fought in the nunnery ruins. He was knocked out cold, but I couldn't even shoot him in the leg. Real-life violence is nothing like computer games.

I don't want to see anyone else die. I'll never forget how I watched those two US agents dying from the poison gas released by the Ix Codex. Their screams bubbled with the sound of blood. And Camila and Dad . . . They both died near me, but thank God I didn't actually see Camila drown or watch Dad break his neck. Although what I've imagined might be worse.

I decide that if I have to shoot, I'm aiming for their knees.

When it's dark enough outside, Montoyo receives the signal. It's go time. We leave the hotel by taxi. The taxi driver is probably part of Gang A or Gang B—but who cares? By later tonight, no one will believe a word they say about us.

Montoyo tells the taxi driver to take us to the Serhs Grand Hotel, where the capoeira championship was hosted. We talk

117

about capoeira all the way, pretending to our taxi driver that we have teammates staying there. When we arrive, Benicio and I step out, saying that we're going to pick up a friend who's waiting in the lobby.

Instead we go straight to the motorcycle parking area, where Benicio's left his Harley-Davidson. He used it the first night to drive from where he hid the Muwan down to the beach. Benicio starts the machine in a hurry, looking around nervously as the engine revs. I grip the passenger handholds as we take off. No time for helmets. We fire off onto the brightly lit beach highway. Within minutes, we've pulled off onto a side road and are climbing into the hillside neighborhoods—the poorer backwaters of Natal.

I don't know how Montoyo's going to find his way to the construction site where they're holding Mom, Tyler, and Ixchel. When I asked him, he just looked grim and told me, "You let me worry about that."

Benicio and I make such a quick getaway, it seems at first that we're not followed. But I guess we make a distinctive pair—two teenage boys without helmets on a Harley. It's not long before someone's on our tail.

Unfortunately, it's the police.

A traffic cop is the first to spot us. He flashes his lights from behind, signaling for us to pull over. Naturally, Benicio ignores him and speeds up. He makes a few rapid turns, and we're in another network of convoluted streets. Eateries, pedestrians, cars, and bikes clog the road. It's so busy, it could be the middle of the day. The police car switches on its siren. A few people look around curiously. Benicio curses. We're stuck behind a delivery van. On its open bed, stacks of plastic crates packed with bottles of Antarctica-brand *guarana* clink against each other, precariously balanced. Then we hear another siren—a second cop. This one's on a motorcycle.

"I guess they don't like these Mexican license plates . . . ," Benicio says ruefully.

We probably look like a couple of thieving kids on some rich foreigner's bike.

Benicio bumps the bike onto the sidewalk. I hold on even tighter. We zoom along, watching people dive out of our way. We outrun the traffic jam, but so does the bike cop.

We try to shake him with another series of crazy turns into alleyways, down a flight of stairs, then out onto some scrubland behind a narrow street. We lose him just as we reach the edge of the city. Our headlight beams straight ahead, lighting up scrub and occasional heaps of trash. There's just enough ambient light from the glowing cityscape to let us make out trees in the distance.

Benicio activates the Muwan via remote. Shadowed behind some trees, the aircraft's lights turn on. Not too far behind, I hear the familiar roar of the police bike, still looking for us.

Why doesn't the cop just give up?

Close to the Muwan now, we slow to a halt. Benicio scrambles into the cockpit to start the engines. I take care to stow the Harley in the hold. When I close the door, there's a brilliant light beaming straight at me. It's the other bike approaching through the trees.

"Hurry!" Benicio calls, shaking the rope ladder. I follow him into the aircraft and begin strapping myself in.

We take off right in front of the bike cop. Later tonight he'll be the person that everyone will think is UFO-crazy. I mention this to Benicio as he engages the in-flight stealth mode, turning off all the outside lights.

Benicio is not so convinced that it's going to be laughed away. "It's bad when police see us. Police have to make a report, however dumb it sounds. The National Reconnaissance Office—they're pretty high-tech guys, Josh. A joint organiza-tion of the United States Department of Defense and the Central Intelligence Agency? Not strapped for cash, the NRO. They have computer programs that can trawl all the data of all the police forces in the world. They've known about us for a long time now, believe me. They know what to look for. They're gonna know we were in Natal."

There's no time to worry about the consequences of the NRO pinning down a Muwan sighting in Natal. We're in the air for only five minutes. Benicio has set the navigation systems to lock on to a signal broadcast by the other two Muwans—both are the smaller Mark I models. They've already landed on the roof of the unfinished hotel. Benicio takes our Muwan down and lands in the remaining space with barely a whisper.

In the planning meetings, Montoyo was given information that the building is about twenty stories high, but past the twelfth floor, only the outer walls have been built. There aren't too many other buildings around, and nothing above five floors. It's a commercial district, and it seems that most people have gone home.

The strike team from Ek Naab has already assembled on the roof. The two pilots stay in their Muwans. Four guys wearing ski masks are dressed in black from head to toe. I don't recognize any of them—but then, I was never exactly given the keys to the city. One of them hands me a large bundle without a word.

It's a bulletproof jacket and a gun. I pull on the jacket and stare at the gun.

"Ever used one?" he asks. I shake my head.

"Okay. I wondered. We've been told you can handle yourself. Didn't know if that was with a gun or without."

I stare up at him, flushed with pride. I wonder—who told him that I could handle myself?

"You point, you shoot. Keep both eyes open to aim. Keep your arm really firm, and watch out for the kickback. Got that?"

I nod, biting my lip.

I'm the lookout guy. I patrol the roof and warn the pilots if anyone's coming. The gun is only for emergencies.

The strike team lower themselves down the side of the building on fast-moving quick-release nylon rope winches. They enter around the empty windows of the sixth floor. The kidnappers are holed up in a space that was planned as a conference suite, on the third floor. The plan is that they'll burst in on the kidnappers, shoot them, and grab the hostages.

They'll arrive silently, from above and not below, as the kidnappers would expect. They'll strike with deadly speed and accuracy. "These are our best marksmen," Montoyo promised me earlier today. "The kidnappers won't stand a chance."

Standing on the roof, I listen carefully, tense with anticipation. I keep expecting to hear gunshots. But there's nothing. Just the noises of a seaside city, calming down for the night.

I wander over to Benicio's Muwan, calling up to him.

"What's going on?"

Benicio is listening to a communication via his headset. There's a tense silence. He finally breaks off. Staring at me, his eyes fill with astonishment and confusion.

"They're all gone!"

Benicio and I drop down to the third floor using the rope winch. It's an adrenaline rush, but I'm too frazzled by what's happened to enjoy the moment.

Montoyo and the four members of the strike team make a painstaking search of the space, hunting for clues. I just stand there, feeling useless. I stare into the dark corners of the four bare walls that imprisoned my mother, my best friend, and Ixchel until less than an hour ago. It's chilling to think of them here in this gray, empty place, tied up, not knowing how much longer they'd be held.

"My contact has double-crossed me," Montoyo concludes. He stands still, his tone deadly calm. "He made the raid an hour sooner than we agreed. They must have disturbed the kidnappers. Now they've moved on and taken the hostages."

"How do you know it was an hour ago?"

Montoyo indicates the floor near to him. "There's blood here. It's congealed, but still wet. And over there, the floor and the wall—the concrete is still slightly warm. My guess is that's where they had their portable power generator."

I don't take in much after "blood."

"How much blood?"

"Someone's been shot, but perhaps not fatally. They probably managed to stop the bleeding before they got out. The drops fall in a trail that reaches here . . ." Montoyo takes a few steps toward the door. "And then they stop. There's a small pool. This is probably where the person stopped to be patched up."

But who?

I remember the searing pain of the bullet I took in the leg when Madison shot me last year in Tlacotalpan. It was like being stabbed with a red-hot poker. Thinking that the same may have happened to Mom or Ixchel makes me feel a powerful surge of rage. If the kidnappers have hurt either of them, I swear I'll get revenge.

There's a rustling sound from behind us, by the doorway to the elevator shafts. The four black-clad marksmen from Ek Naab turn in one fluid motion, assault rifles at the ready. One of them shines a powerful beam into the gloom.

A figure steps forward.

Standing in the doorway, his hands up, shaking, is Tyler. One side of his Brazil T-shirt is stained almost black.

I rush straight at my pal. Montoyo tells the strike team to lower their rifles. I grab Ty by the shoulders, but when he winces I pull away.

"I'm a little shot, man."

"No kidding."

I look at Tyler. That's when I notice his eyes—they're glassy, staring. His teeth are chattering. He's on the verge of passing out. He falters slightly, then falls against me.

Montoyo and Benicio surge forward. They help me to catch Tyler and lower him to the ground.

"He's going into shock."

"I've got morphine," Benicio says. He reaches for his backpack and starts fumbling around.

I pull my hand away from Tyler's side. It's sticky with his blood.

"He's been shot in the side."

There's a makeshift bandage over the wound. Montoyo's right—someone tried to patch him up. And then, what? Was it the kidnappers? Or someone from Gang B? Did they actually manage to rescue anyone? Did they just abandon Tyler?

Benicio injects Tyler with something. Then he drags a piece of dark cloth from his backpack—a fleece blanket, which he places over Tyler's shivering body. We squat in silence for a few minutes while Tyler starts to regain awareness.

"They're gone," Tyler begins, speaking quietly, with short bursts of labored breath. "They got a tip-off . . . someone was coming. One of the lookouts got suspicious. So they packed everything up. Gaspar put his gun down to untie me from the chair. I saw a chance. I got in a few good kicks . . .

then moved away. Doing handflips so that they couldn't easily shoot me. One of them caught me in the side. I didn't get much farther . . . staggered on a bit . . . fell down. They were so mad . . . they were really in a hurry. Gaspar slapped something on me to stop the bleeding. From that minute I could see that they weren't that concerned with me. It wasn't really me they wanted." He shoots me a tiny glance, eyes hooded with fear.

"They hustled everyone else downstairs. Didn't even give me a chance to say good-bye. The lookout called again. Gaspar got really mad then. He told me this. 'Tell Montoyo—you can have this one for free. And he can have the other two when he gives us the boy—Joshua Garcia.'"

I'm frozen solid. Montoyo leans in closer. "Tyler . . . how did they know Josh's name?"

Tyler shivers from head to toe, staring from me to Montoyo. "They know about all of us."

Montoyo asks, "What did they do with the other hostages?"

"I didn't see what happened after they went downstairs. A little after that, some other guys turned up, about ten of them. I hid in the elevator shaft. They didn't stay long. They took off the minute they could see everyone had gone."

Tyler's eyes cloud over again. "This is about you, Josh. It's not money. They want *you*. They were following our buggy 'cause they thought it was you, me, and your mom. We were all wearing this same Brazil T-shirt, remember? You, me, Ixchel."

In a hollow voice, Benicio says, "But Josh wanted to switch seats."

I return Benicio's cold, accusing stare. No. I'm not going to let him lay this all on me.

Tyler closes his eyes again. "I'm so tired . . ."

With effort, Montoyo stands up. "I'm finished playing games with these people. We're taking you both back to Ek Naab."

I stare at him open-mouthed. "What about Mom and Ixchel?"

Montoyo looks suddenly old, like something's sucked all the life out of him. "These aren't any ordinary kidnappers, Josh. I'm afraid your fears were justified. Unless I'm very much mistaken, what we're dealing with here . . . is the Sect of Huracan."

Montoyo wants to put me in a Muwan right away with Tyler and Benicio and send us all to Ek Naab. I don't see that I have any choice. I won't leave Tyler alone in this state.

I'm not happy to think of Montoyo back at the hotel, going through my mom's things, packing them up. The whole idea makes my blood boil. Then there's my John Lloyd Stephens books. At least I stashed the paper with the decoded message. I doubt that Montoyo will be looking too carefully at my books, not at a time like this.

I glance at Benicio. He's concentrating hard, sitting in the pilot's seat. After the way he looked at me, blaming me for the fact that Ixchel's in danger, I don't particularly want to be around him.

It's the same old story—things have been taken out of my hands. All the time we're flying to Ek Naab I keep thinking, how did I let this happen?

One minute I was making plans to travel back in time,

to change the past so that my dad doesn't die. I cracked a code that's been sitting in a book for decades—some kind of chemical formula for making the Crystal Key. A massive step on the way to repairing the Bracelet.

And now . . . this. My mother and Ixchel snatched right in front of me. I don't know where they are. I don't know where they're going. Something tells me that I may never see them again.

This is no ordinary kidnapping. This is personal—as personal as it gets. There's something about my genes—my DNA—that makes the Sect desperate to get their hands on me. This is about genetic experiments—experiments the Professor woman from the Sect muttered about in the tunnels under Becan. Marius Martineau—Madison's father—had suggested that they kill me, but the Professor told him that I was more useful alive—as a test subject. They're experiments that require someone with the Bakab gene. Most of the guys in the Sect have one of the four Bakab genes, but these experiments they didn't dare to try on their own people.

I remind Montoyo of all this, and he just nods. "We can't risk you falling into their hands, Josh. I hope you'll remember that and understand some of the choices I may be forced to make."

Montoyo can talk all he likes about negotiating with the Sect, or even about mounting another rescue attempt. Deep down I know it's pointless. The Sect wants me. They might even kill a hostage to get me. I imagine my mother tied up in some dark, dank cellar with a sack over her head, terrified that she's going to be dragged away and shot. Even the mental image leaves me gasping for breath.

Ixchel, too . . . I still can't stand to think about what I said to her. It was worse than what I said to my mom: I actually *meant* to hurt Ixchel.

How can I let that be the last thing Ixchel remembers about me?

I lose myself staring into the midnight purple of the sky. The last time I remember feeling this powerless was when, thanks to Madison, I almost drowned in the Caribbean Sea. At least I kept fighting until the end. Which probably saved me—a few minutes later and I'd have sunk too far under the waves for anyone to drag me out.

There's only one thing I can think of doing.

I could give the Sect what they want. I could hand myself over.

Benicio doesn't say more than five words to me on the way over. We're all reeling from how deeply serious this has become. It's as though the air is heavy with fear.

Tyler sleeps through most of the flight, woozy from a painkilling injection that Benicio gave him. I think about how much I'd be looking forward to showing Tyler Ek Naab, if only it were the three of us, the way it should be: me, Ixchel, and Tyler.

Until I actually watch Brazil disappearing beneath us, I don't realize how strong the link is to my mother and to

Ixchel. It's like I'm being torn away from an invisible anchor—a thread that connects me to them both. Deep inside my chest there's an actual physical pain.

I think about the first time I met Ixchel. It was in the middle of the jungle, and she was dressed in a soccer jersey and jeans. She seemed so distant. Not angry with me, exactly, but as if leading me through the jungle was a chore. I remember trying to hide that I was crying about Camila's death. I remember how Ixchel wouldn't pretend not to notice.

Now that I think about it, that's when it began: the instant that I felt Ixchel's sympathy—sympathy that I turned down. Something was planted then, a seed of curiosity. I wanted to know more about this strange girl who appeared from nowhere with all her jungle knowledge.

Right at this moment, I think I'd do anything to have Ixchel beside me again. Just to know she's safe, just to hear her say one more time, "Listen to who's talking."

Now there's no way that can happen. The kidnappers will kill Ixchel unless I hand myself in. It's literally her or me.

"You all right, man?"

Tyler's voice snaps me out of my trance. When I look at him, I'm amazed to see him giving me a weak smile. I check the level of the blood bag that's hooked up to Tyler's arm. It's almost half-empty.

"That's some hard-core medicine Benicio gave me," Tyler mutters. "I feel exactly like I'm flying."

I manage a chuckle. "They've got great doctors in Ek Naab. You'll be fine in a bit."

"So I'm finally going to see Ek Naab."

"Yep."

"I always thought you'd made it up, to be honest."

"Ty, I couldn't. Not even if I tried. You just wait."

We fall silent then, both of us thinking hard. Still looking out of the window, I say, "So, these kidnappers. What are they like?" When my gaze falls back on Tyler, I see that he's staring at me with a mixture of dread and sympathy.

"I'm sorry, Josh," he says quietly. "They're . . . bad."

It's the only thing he can say. After that his voice cracks and dries up.

I pause. "You think they'd actually . . ."

"Kill one of them?" He nods, then breathes, "Yeah."

Tyler's hand goes to his wound. His face scrunches up. I can tell that the pain is creeping back.

I touch the Bracelet in my pocket, feeling the familiar rustle of energy when my fingertips connect. Tyler's eyes follow my hand. "What do you have there?"

I look at him for a few seconds, wondering whether to tell.

"Can I trust you?"

He nods. "'Course."

I lower my voice so that Benicio won't hear. "It's a bracelet—from the ancient civilization that founded Ek Naab. My dad had it with him when we met on Mount Orizaba. He gave it to me before he died."

"Huh? I thought Ek Naab was Mayan."

"Not exactly. Itzamna was a time traveler. He copied the writings of an ancient civilization called the Erinsi. What he wrote became the four Books of Itzamna. One of them was the Ix Codex, the one we were searching for."

Tyler takes a moment to consider this. "You never told me that. About the time traveling."

"I don't tell you everything," I tell him. "I'm not sure if it's safe."

"You can't do everything by yourself, Josh."

I don't respond to that.

"What . . . does the bracelet do?"

I rub my eyes briefly. "It travels in time. Or at least it would—it's broken."

"Whoa. Does Montoyo know you have it?"

"Not a clue." I hesitate. "Well, maybe just a part of a clue."

"Yeah, well, he wants it, I bet."

"He's been after it from the beginning, since the day I met him. Ever since my dad took it from Ek Naab. Actually, a strange old guy gave it to him."

"Blanco Vigores? Isn't he the blind guy?"

"That's him. I told you about him—the one who lives in some weird, creepy, deeper-underground part of Ek Naab."

"The place with all the hibiscus flowers that grow in the dark? Yeah, you did. Think we'll see him in Ek Naab?"

For some reason, at the thought of meeting Vigores again, a tiny shiver of excitement runs through me.

"No idea."

The truth is, I'm dying to see Vigores again. There's something I've been wondering about, something I need to ask him. Vigores knows more than he's telling—that's how I see it. Dad used the Bracelet to get from wherever he was being imprisoned to the slopes of the volcano. Which means that before Dad lost his memory, the Bracelet was working, and Dad knew how to use it.

Someone told my father how to use the Bracelet of Itzamna. That someone is Vigores.

Somewhere in the jungle of Campeche, a vault in the ground opens up and swallows the Muwan whole. I'm back in Ek Naab.

The medical team is waiting with a stretcher. They take Tyler straight to the military hospital that's attached to the aircraft hangar. While they operate, I'm told that he'll be kept lying down for at least a day. "But it doesn't look complicated," a white-coated medic tells me. "No major organ damage. He's young. He'll be okay in two, maybe three days."

They let me stay in a room in the compound so that I can be close to Tyler. Benicio shows me to Tyler's room and stands in the doorway for a second, preparing to leave.

He seems to struggle for words, which is rare for him. "I'm sorry," he begins, speaking stiffly. "For what I said about you . . . being the cause of the kidnappings."

I point out, "In a way, I was."

"It's not your fault. It's ours. We should have protected you better."

The look we exchange says it all. He's trying to apologize for blaming me about Ixchel. But the words just won't flow.

"The Sect is everywhere," I say eventually, "with members all over the world. I guess we finally get that now."

Benicio nods, stiffly. "Yeah. I think we do."

When he leaves, I sleep. Just like the other night in Natal, I'm woken by the vibration of my UK cell phone. This time I'm really annoyed, because I made a point of turning it off. Or thought I had. I miss the call, but when I try to see who phoned, no number comes up. It's weird: the phone doesn't register any missed calls.

In the morning, I check on Tyler. He's still out—they tell me he'll sleep for hours. As ever, Benicio has been appointed to escort me around Ek Naab. Today, he doesn't even pretend to be pleased about the assignment.

"Babysitting duty again?" I say as we stroll down the corridors toward the chairlift.

"You got it," he agrees.

"So. Montoyo still doesn't trust me to get around Ek Naab by myself."

"It's not you," Benicio says with a touch of irritation. "Like I told you last time you were here, it's other people. You might be surprised at how many people in Ek Naab would like a quiet five words with you."

I stop walking and look at him. "All right," I say loudly.

"Enough with the *mystery*. What would they say? What's Montoyo trying to hide?"

Benicio takes my arm. He steers me back down the corridor. "Keep walking. Don't make a scene. Keep your voice down." We move on, and he continues. "You said it yourself last night. The Sect is everywhere. Even here, Josh."

Now that he's said it aloud, I realize that deep down, I've suspected for a long time. Ever since Ixchel and Benicio told me about the secret gatherings and people who are afraid of talking to Montoyo, I've wondered. I thought maybe I was being paranoid, seeing the Sect everywhere, but maybe not.

"And you know who they are?"

"Me?" Benicio sounds shocked. "Of course I don't. There are enough people in Ek Naab who don't like Montoyo. It wouldn't be impossible for the Sect to find someone willing to betray him."

"But what would be in it for them? Won't the Sect destroy everything that Ek Naab stands for?"

"Well . . ." He pauses. "We don't exactly know what the Sect wants."

"Huh? We *do* know! They want to get hold of all that ancient Erinsi knowledge that's in the Books of Itzamna. They want our technology, they want to know how to use that chamber Ixchel and I found. The one that's written about in the Ix Codex—the Revival Chamber. And when they have all that, they'll be able to figure out how to stop the galactic superwave in 2012. Except—they won't stop it. They'll make sure that it happens. And all over the world, civilization will collapse."

Benicio gives me a curious look. "That's what you believe?"

"That's what Ollie told me, when she was trying to persuade me that I'd be better off with the Sect."

Slowly considering, he says, "But . . . it doesn't make sense."

"I know! They're insane! You should hear how they talk about the human population harming the planet and needing to be wiped out and everything . . . they're psychos!"

"I don't know what you heard, Josh, but people don't behave like that. Soldiers, maybe—obeying orders, getting indoctrinated to believe they're doing the right thing."

"That's what I said—they're crazy."

Benicio shrugs. "I don't know . . ."

I can't put my finger on it, but there's something funny about his voice. He actually seems pretty uncomfortable talking to me about this. "The people at the top of the Sect, they will have their reasons. You can be sure of this: their reasons are things that even you and I can understand. In the end, it always comes down to wanting the same thing—power, money, influence."

We reach the chairlift station, from which suspended seats whisk travelers through the underground tunnels to Ek Naab. We ride through more slowly than I remember doing in the past. I guess that like me, Benicio is in no mood for fun.

When we arrive in Ek Naab, sunlight floods the underground city through the wire-mesh ceiling. I follow Benicio as he strolls to the plaza, crosses it, and reaches the outdoor café. But he doesn't take a table or order anything. Instead he grabs the waiter, who whispers something into his ear. Then he's back with me, leading me toward the building with the fancy marble lobby and an elevator. We ride to the top of the building, to the jewel of Ek Naab's camouflage—the surface-level eco-resort.

Then we're strolling through the tables of the restaurant under a giant palm-thatched roof. Citizens of Ek Naab are enjoying a typical Mexican buffet breakfast. My mouth waters at the sight of plates of sizzling-hot spicy dishes, stacks of pancakes, and heaps of fresh tropical fruit. When Benicio actually stops at a table, my stomach starts to rumble. I sigh with relief.

"Let's have a quick breakfast," he says, turning over a coffee cup. A waiter approaches and fills up the cup. Benicio and I approach the buffet and pile our plates high with scrambled eggs, black beans, chorizo sausage with fried potatoes, shredded tortillas, and chicken in green tomato sauce. I fill another plate with warm, crusty muffins topped with crushed pecans.

"I'm starving," I murmur. We don't talk for several minutes as we pack away the food. It's delicious, but I can't let myself think too much about how great it is. I have to steer

139

my thoughts away from any of the horrible things going on with my mother and Ixchel, or I start to lose my appetite.

Which would be a bad idea. You never know when you'll need energy.

"So, Benicio, where are we going?"

"To see the Bakab Kan, Blanco Vigores. Remember his instructions—every time you visit Ek Naab, he wants to be the first to see you."

"Yeah," I say. "You mentioned that last time I was here. But my dad's funeral—Vigores wasn't there, even though everyone else was—all the others from the Executive."

Benicio just looks at me, his irritation obvious. "Well, Josh, the members of the Executive don't tell me everything. I'm just trying to help out here."

The ruling Executive. One day not far from now, I'll replace Montoyo on the Executive. When I turn sixteen I'll have that right, as the Bakab Ix.

"Things will be different when I'm on the Executive," I tell Benicio. "It's not right, all this secrecy. It makes people uncomfortable."

But even as the words are coming out of my mouth, I'm aware of the Bracelet, covered up, high on my arm under a sleeve.

I'm as bad as any of them. With me, it's secret after secret after secret.

Vigores doesn't know I'm here, Benicio tells me. That's why Benicio had to ask the waiter at the café—his brother works for Vigores in his apartments in the "Garden." Vigores doesn't often emerge from the hibiscus-lined labyrinth in which he lives. But when Benicio put in a call this morning, it turned out that Vigores was on a rare visit to the surface. Not to sunbathe or swim in the shimmering blue pools of the eco-resort; he was actually at the church near the cemetery.

I freeze a little when I hear that. The cemetery is where my father is buried.

"So is he very religious?" I ask Benicio. We're striding down a shady avenue lined with tall palms, their thick trunks painted white.

Benicio shakes his head. "I don't really know much about Vigores, Josh. I keep telling you that. I've seen him just a few times in my life, and hardly ever spoken to him."

"Why not? Does he creep you out?"

"Not even a bit. If anything, he's the one who avoids me."

"Huh? Why?"

Benicio shrugs. "You're asking the wrong person."

We emerge from the palm-lined avenue and into the outlying orange groves near the cemetery. The path slopes gently upward toward the hill, on which sits the small, perfectly white Spanish-style church. But before we even reach the gravestones, I notice a white-enameled bench under a tree dripping with oranges. On it sits the figure of an old man hunched over in his cream-colored linen suit and panama hat. The hat casts a light shadow across his features, but I'm struck by how pale he is: a sharp contrast to Benicio's tanned, olive-colored skin. Vigores is all milky white, the flesh on his face stretched thin over his cheekbones, like paper.

Benicio clicks his tongue. "There he is."

We approach from the front so that the blind Vigores will have plenty of chances to hear us.

"Señor Vigores—it's Benicio. I have a surprise for you . . . Josh Garcia is with me."

The old man looks up, reaches for his white stick, and then rises unsteadily to his feet. Blue veins stand out on the hand that grips the stick.

Benicio shakes his hand, and then I stand in front of him and reach for his hand. His bony fingers grab one of my arms and then the other. I notice that his hand hesitates

142

slightly as he touches the Bracelet of Itzamna under my sleeve. I freeze, waiting for him to say something, but he doesn't react in any other way. He moves his hands up my arms to my shoulders and then my neck. Through his fingers he constructs an image of me. It brings a smile to his face.

"You've grown so much! Hah—much stronger now! Are you a 'monitor' yet, Josh? Or still a 'student'?"

I gasp and glance at Benicio to see his reaction. He gives an appreciative wink. Like me, Benicio is impressed that Vigores knows about the capoeira grading system. Someone must have told him about my interest in capoeira—I don't remember telling him myself.

"I'm still a student, sir."

"Your *apelido*?"

"They call me *Mariposa*."

He grins broadly. "*Mariposa!* That's a wonderful move. You've mastered it?"

I nod silently, then, reminding myself that he's blind, I add, "Yes, sir."

"That's marvelous. I wish I could see you do it."

I just stand there, not knowing what to do or say. Vigores sits back down carefully, pushing away a low-hanging branch heavy with oranges.

"Sit down, Josh. Benicio, please leave us."

Benicio backs away slowly. He shrugs at me as if to say

You see? Vigores doesn't move or change his expression. We sit in silence for perhaps two whole minutes. Finally he says, "Is he gone?"

"Yeah . . . a while ago."

"I want you to feel that you can talk freely, Josh. This time above all."

"Okay . . ." I hesitate. It's hard to know what small talk to make with this strange old guy, but anyway . . .

"Do you remember what we talked about last time we met?"

"Umm. . ." I cast my mind back. The answer actually surprises me. "I think we talked about . . . girls!"

Very gently, he corrects me. "We talked about love."

"Right." I'm already uncomfortable.

"I asked if you'd ever been in love."

"Uh-huh."

"And . . . ?"

"I don't know . . . I'm too young for all that."

He chuckles. "Now I know you're hiding something. No fourteen-year-old thinks he's 'too young' for anything."

A flush of heat rises inside me. Even hearing the word "love" disturbs me. It's like being poked with a stick in an old, deep, and still-tender wound.

"The girl in question . . . is in danger, isn't she?"

I gape. How does he know?

"Montoyo told me," Vigores says, almost as if he'd read

my mind. "He's noticed what's happening with you two. Now she's been abducted. And your mother too. This is very painful for you." He lifts his face as if to look at me, but of course his eyes look straight past mine. There's a sadness to his expression. Real sympathy.

My lips tremble slightly—and for a moment I'm grateful that he's blind. It's always hardest to stay calm when people show me sympathy.

"I'm going to give you some advice now, young Josh, that may surprise you."

"Uh . . . Okay. . ."

"In the matter of this kidnapping, you *must* trust your instincts."

"What?"

"You've begun to doubt them, no? Hardly surprising, given the way your father died. But instinct consists not of magic or 'the Force.' It's simple intuition based on lightning-fast data processing. With you, young Josh—the power of intuition is strong."

He faces me again with those watery blue eyes, and actually winks.

"Data comes in through all your senses. Much more than you're aware of. It is processed by your conscious as well as your subconscious mind. Intuition ignores nothing. Everything is given the appropriate weight of importance. Some things are *just so*."

"So . . . you're saying that what I think is jumping to a conclusion . . . might be the right thing to do?"

"Data comes in through all your senses," he repeats, this time even more solemnly. "Some senses that you perhaps aren't aware of." Then he leans forward, whispering, "Ignore nothing!"

I peer at him closely, watching his expression change from secrecy to determination. He seems to stare out through the foliage of the orange trees, past the clean stone of the graves and even beyond the glistening, whitewashed walls of the church.

I follow his gaze, but I can't see anything special. Yet it strikes me then—with a strange rush of what I guess I'd have to call *intuition*—that this is a moment I'm going to remember for a very long time. Elements of the memory become solid, each piece falling into place: chinks of blue sky behind dark green leaves, the faint scent of oranges, the sharp blades of grass beneath my feet.

Ignore nothing.

It's as though I can almost grasp what he's saying. Somehow it's still just out of reach.

Then I speak. "Can I ask you something?"

"You may."

I pick my words carefully. If he's talking about me to Montoyo, then there's a chance that anything I say might be reported.

"Montoyo once asked me to find out whatever I could

146

about the Bracelet of Itzamna. He figured that my dad stole it when he visited Ek Naab."

Vigores wags a finger. "That's incorrect. I *gave* it to him."

I knew my dad was no thief, but it's a huge relief to hear it from Vigores's own lips.

"Why?"

Very simply he says, "Because he asked me for it."

"What—you gave the Bracelet to him, just like that? Did you know what it can do?"

Vigores nods. "Indeed I do know, and did then too. It's a highly dangerous object."

"You told him that?"

"Naturally. I warned him that operating the Bracelet can cause you to materialize inside a rock. A painful way to die, I'm certain."

I gasp. "It can do *what*?"

"The Bracelet of Itzamna is thought to be a time-travel device, Josh, as I'm sure you know. What travels in time, however, must also travel in space."

"Why?"

"Because the earth flies through space. And spins on its axis—constant motion. Wherever you are on the earth at a given point in time, if you are to travel to the same place at a different point in time, you must also shift in space."

I consider this. "So the Bracelet is also a teleportation device?"

"Correct."

Dad jumped in space—but not time.

I ask, "Have . . . have you ever used it?"

Silently, he nods. "But I've also seen what can happen when the Bracelet is used without . . . due care." It sounds like he was going to say something else, but stopped himself.

"You've actually used it? What happened?"

There's a deep sigh. "Yes. I was lucky—I survived. I was a young man. It happened soon after I first came across the Bracelet of Itzamna."

I interrupt. "*You* found the Bracelet? That's news to me . . ."

Why didn't Montoyo tell me any of this?

He hesitates, like he doesn't want to admit something. "I did."

"Where?"

"In a place called Izapa."

Again I gasp. "Izapa, near Mount Tacana? Was it anywhere near the Temple of the Inscriptions—where Itzamna copied . . . ?"

"The ancient Erinsi writings that became the four Books of Itzamna? Yes, Josh, I found the Bracelet not far from that temple."

I lean back. "Wow! I mean—sorry, I never thought of you as a *Tomb Raider* type."

Drily, Vigores says, "It wasn't a tomb."

I guess he's never heard of the computer game.

"The Bracelet that I gave your father—it's broken,"

Vigores tells me. There's no doubt whatsoever in his voice. "Or more strictly, the Bracelet is incomplete. It lacks the crystal that—presumably—controls the time circuit. Without that, there's no way to know where the Bracelet will send you. Chances are, you'd end up in outer space and die."

"And my dad knew this?"

Vigores nods. "He did. He wanted to find a way to repair it. I tried to tell him that the crystal has never been found. Still . . ." Vigores seems to be searching for the words. "Your father . . . he insisted."

I fall silent, wondering. If Dad knew that using the Bracelet might kill him, why did he use it anyway and end up on the slopes of a volcano?

Vigores breaks across my thoughts. "You're thinking about your father again, yes? The Bracelet of Itzamna and why he wanted it, whether the Bracelet sealed his fate."

"Yes," I tell him slowly, "'sealed his fate' . . . I think it did. My dad lost his memory after using it. He ended up on Mount Orizaba. And later . . ."

"Later he sacrificed himself to save you," Vigores says firmly. His tone becomes sharp. "So don't you think you should visit your father's grave now? To pay your respects?"

With that, he stands up and makes to shake my hand good-bye.

There's one final question I'm itching to ask.

"You showed him how to use the Bracelet. Didn't you?"

149

Vigores looks sad. "Yes. As a precaution—so that he didn't activate it by accident."

I'd do anything to ask how to use the Bracelet of Itzamna. But I can't think of a single way to do *that* . . . without giving away that I actually have it.

The Bracelet can be activated by accident.

One wrong move, and I could suffocate in the vacuum of space.

18

Benicio is waiting for me when I finally leave my father's grave. The old man is nowhere to be seen. I get the feeling that Benicio wants to ask me about my talk with Vigores. Maybe because I've just been visiting my dead father, he lets me be.

I'm lost in thought all the way back. About the Bracelet. About my dad. Could it be that Ixchel was right, telling me that maybe I shouldn't meddle with the way things turned out? Perhaps that cemetery is where he's meant to be.

Yet, that doesn't make any sense. Ever since it happened, I've had the feeling that there was a reason Dad made the effort to leave me the Bracelet. It's like he was asking me to fix it, to come back in time to rescue him. What else could he have meant by those last words—"*This isn't over*"?

Then there's Vigores. I'm so disoriented after meeting him. Not for the first time; he has this way of getting to me, every time we meet. I've never hung on to someone's words the way I do with his. I can only understand half of what he says. The other half, though, seems to worm its way deep inside. Words that just idle away, quietly. One day maybe they'll make sense.

As we're approaching the elevator in the thatched-roof restaurant where we had breakfast, overlooking the pools and the gardens decorated with banana palms, pink oleander, and purple bougainvillea flowers, Benicio gets a call on his cell phone.

"Your friend is awake now," he tells me. "Feeling much better too."

I want to be with Tyler all the way from the beginning of his first visit to Ek Naab. So I go back to the aircraft hangar to pick him up. Benicio leaves me there and gets back to his own work.

Montoyo is with Tyler in the medical room. He's trying to act like we're the focus of his attention. But after only a few seconds his phone rings, and he stands quietly in the corner, talking. Tyler is dressed in some clean jeans and one of Benicio's T-shirts. Poor Benicio—he's always having to hand over his clothes. Tyler looks about a thousand times better than he did the last time I saw him awake. He even manages a broad smile.

"Hey, man," he says.

"You all right?"

"Right as rain," he grins. I know he's lying. When I was shot in the leg last December I was in pain for days, even after Susannah St. John stitched me up.

Susannah. Where is she now, I wonder? Back in Tlacotalpan? Or did Montoyo let her stay in Ek Naab? I decide to ask him.

"How is Susannah St. John?"

Montoyo puts his phone away. "Susannah St. John," he repeats, very slowly.

"Who is Susannah St. John?" Tyler asks.

"She's the old lady I met in Mexico last time I was here," I tell Tyler. "Last December. The one who sent the postcards . . . remember?"

Tyler nodded. It had been a crazy few hours, I recall. Phoning Tyler at all hours of the day as Ixchel and I traveled through Mexico by bus. Getting him to read aloud the coded messages on the backs of a bunch of postcards that kept arriving at my house. With his help we'd deciphered a code that the mysterious letter-writer Arcadio told Susannah St. John to send me. Susannah must have wondered what kind of strange message she was carrying—since Arcadio had her wait over forty years before she mailed those postcards.

Montoyo says, "Well, Josh, why don't you ever write her a letter? Then you'd know."

"I'm not much of a letter-writer."

"On the contrary, you're a tremendous correspondent. What else is a blog?"

"But letters . . . to, well, someone older like Susannah, you know, with all the 'I hope you are well' and 'I have been very

153

well myself' and all that . . ." I wrinkle my nose. "I can't be bothered, honestly."

"I'm sure she'd be grateful even for something written in that strange text language you youngsters use," Montoyo comments.

"Do you write to her?"

"No," he admits. "But I use the telephone. She's well. Back in Tlacotalpan, most of the time."

"Why did you let her come here? Why tell her about us?"

Montoyo smiles briefly. "It's nice to hear you say 'us' when you talk about Ek Naab."

I hadn't even noticed, but he's right; I think of myself as part of Ek Naab.

"I told her, Josh, because, well . . ." He pauses. "Because she already knew!"

I say nothing. Ixchel and I had tried hard not to talk about Ek Naab in Susannah's presence. I guess we hadn't been careful enough. Then my mother arrived in Mexico after the avalanche and my father's death . . . At that point, I have to admit, the beans had to spill. Yet Susannah had taken it all in stride—and Montoyo let her.

Meanwhile, even though in a couple of years I'll be on the ruling Executive, I still have to be escorted around. I don't understand Montoyo.

We begin the tour. It feels so odd—wrong, almost—to be having such an interesting time with Tyler when Ixchel and my mom are going through something so nightmarish. Neither of us mentions them, and neither does Montoyo. I really want Tyler to enjoy his first day here. Looking back, I hadn't really been able to enjoy my first sight of Ek Naab. The day before I'd arrived, I was in a car crash with my half sister and saw her drown. So I understand how Tyler must feel as we get into the chairlift and swoop through the tunnels, zooming past pools of phosphorescent water, stalactites, and stalagmites.

Just like me on my first day in Ek Naab, Tyler will be grateful for the distraction.

A short while later we stand on the steps of the chairlift station as they lead into Ek Naab, looking out over the gleaming mixture of modern, Mayan, and Spanish architecture.

Tyler gives a low, soft whistle. "Man, that is amazing!"

Montoyo watches him with a wry smile. "We don't get many visitors, as you know." He pats Tyler on the back. "You have excellent taste, my boy."

Montoyo walks us through the city, from the stone staircase down to the path that leads to the *cenote*, through the main town square where the daily market is in full flow, traders selling hot tortillas, fresh tropical fruit, dried chilies, warm bread, ice cream, clothes, paintings, and today, even books. We wander around, being given the spiel by Montoyo. Then he leads us back to the *cenote*—the ancient sacrificial sinkhole—the "dark water" for which Ek Naab is named.

After his initial whistling, Tyler actually doesn't say very much. He looks around mostly in silence, asking a question now and again, and that's all. Noticing how thoughtful Tyler has become, I take him aside slightly for a quiet word out of Montoyo's earshot. Staring at the smooth surface of the water, I poke his arm.

"So . . . what do you think?"

Tyler turns to me. There's a light in his eyes, but his expression is sad. He shakes his head. "I don't know, man. This is . . . it's like . . . so random. There's this. There's the world, and that superwave thing coming in 2012. The end of the world and whatnot. All these people here trying to stop it." He raises a finger and slowly pokes me back. "And then there's you."

I grin slightly, puzzled. "Yeah . . . I know . . . I told you all that."

Tyler shrugs. "Seeing it, though, that's different. It's like . . . some impossible secret. Yeah. Something impossible. This is too much, Josh."

"Too much, I know! It's am-a-zing."

Tyler looks down and shakes his head. He turns away from Montoyo, and speaking in a low voice, he says, "No. That's not what I mean. This is too much for you to handle alone. This Montoyo guy is *connected*, man. This morning in the hospital, when you were out? Never off his cell phone. People coming to see him. But you, you want to travel in time, change the past. You ever think about all the things you might affect?"

I take a step backward. "What are you saying?"

Tyler can see he's gotten to me. He steps closer and whispers, "I'm on your side, Josh, you know that. But just think about it, okay? Maybe you should hand the Bracelet over . . ." He cocks his head toward Montoyo. "Maybe he knows what he's doing."

Horrified, I whisper, "Did you tell him I have it?"

Emphatically, he shakes his head. "No way! I'm thinking about *you*. We've got real problems here and now—with the kidnapping. Montoyo is busting a gut to save your mom and Ixchel. All I'm saying is . . ."

"Maybe I should trust him?" I glance over my shoulder at Montoyo. He's on another phone call. Slowly I breathe out, releasing some of the tension. "Okay. I'll think about it."

At that minute, my UK cell phone goes off. It vibrates against my left thigh. I pull the phone out, turn off the keypad lock. All I can do is stare.

It's a text message.

Nothing so unusual there, perhaps. But the sender? On the screen flashes a name I typed into my phone during a fateful car trip down Highway 186 to Becan. The drive that led to my sister Camila's death. Moments before the agent of the Sect turned up and started shooting at our car, Camila and I had had a moment. A real connection, me with the sister I didn't even know I had. "Next time you feel like you're missing our father," she'd told me, "call me. Put my number in your phone. 'Camila, Call Me!' or 'Call Me! Camila!' Either way, it's with a C."

The number of times I'd seen her name come up on my phone, when I'd been browsing through the Cs. I never had the heart to delete it. I even thought I'd seen it the night we went out with Camila's husband, Saul, after it was all over and I'd found the codex. It seemed impossible to me then that so much could be left of Camila except Camila herself. But that's how it is when people die, as I've come to realize. The person is gone, yet you're surrounded by all their stuff.

It's so hard to accept that they're not just a phone call away. That the phone will never ring again because of them— the telephone that rings, but who's to answer? That's what I told Camila about our dad, that exact thing. Now it looks as if I'm being haunted by her phone number.

It wasn't easy to let go of Camila. Maybe it's because I'd only known her for a few hours. It just didn't seem fair that life could give you something amazing like her, only to snatch her away again.

Yet staring my cell phone, there's no doubt—I don't even need to pinch myself to see if I'm awake. Incredible, impossible, and yet there it is, plain as day. My dead sister's name.

Camila Call Me.

I press the "call" button and hold the phone to my ear. "Number unknown." I'm still gaping at my phone when Montoyo finishes his call and interrupts us.

"We need to get on the Internet right away. Ixchel's made another post."

Hurriedly, he leads us past the church to a very narrow little lane. Decorative hanging baskets drip flowers from the apartment windows above. The lane is so narrow that it seems that the petals might almost meet across the gap. Montoyo disappears into a doorway about ten yards down the alley. Tyler and I follow him to a second-floor apartment. It's almost empty—three small rooms, one a kitchen and the other two with hammocks. In one room there's a shiny new laptop computer, the box and packaging strewn around the room.

"I put you in this building," Montoyo says, logging on to

the computer. "It's small, but the best we have right now. Your things—and your mother's—are in the bedrooms."

I take in my surroundings—the newly whitewashed smell and four bare walls. The floors are covered with hard, glossy sisal carpeting. The windows are empty, still covered with the builders' dusty handprints. They face a balcony across the lane, bursting with orange and yellow potted flowers.

"This is . . . my place?"

He nods. "For you and your mother."

"We never said we were coming to live here . . . ," I say with a flash of anger.

Montoyo looks up suddenly, genuinely astonished. "Josh— at this point, the debate is over."

I stare back at my phone. We rushed off so quickly that I still haven't had time to check the actual message. While Tyler's looking over Montoyo's shoulder at the computer screen, I sneak a peek at the text.

So you visit the old man, but how about me?

There's nothing else. Every single sound in the room is drowned out—by the sound of my own heart thumping. I can almost feel it in my throat.

How on earth can I be getting a text message from Camila?

On the computer, the familiar sight of Ixchel's new blog pops up. We all lean in to read.

MESSAGE TWO FROM IXCHEL

Well, you've probably heard from Tyler by now that our new friends aren't your usual gold-digging kidnappers. In fact, they traded all the other hostages yesterday for a very reasonable sum.

But not us. They want us for something else—as a trade for you. The kidnappers have a simple offer—just like they told Tyler. I'm guessing he's still alive? I really hope so.

A trade—one of us in exchange for Josh. If you agree, they'll arrange for a place to swap hostages. If you don't agree, they'll shoot one of us. Then maybe you'll see sense and save whoever is left. (That's what Gaspar told me to write.)

You choose who to swap. They'll choose who to kill.

You can't begin to imagine what it feels like to write something like that about what might be my own death. How weird. It just seems unreal. I can't quite get it into my thoughts.

So now you know. That's what they say.

There have been a lot of threats. We haven't been hurt so far. Unlike Tyler, we haven't tried to escape.

Josh's mom has been having panic attacks. They're getting more tranquilizers for her . . . it seems she has a very nervous disposition.

What I've been told to tell you is this. We've been moved. I don't have any idea what country we're in now. They took us out of that empty building in Natal and into a van. We drove for many hours. Then we stopped, they drugged us, and we moved on.

We have to spend all our time handcuffed together and locked in a room. They've offered us some books to read. It's not easy to concentrate, though. It's slow going. I've been trying to read a book called *Fictions* by Jorge Luis Borges. You'd like it, Josh, I think.

That's all from me. Sorry, I'm just not in the mood to write.
XXXXXX

This is straight from Gaspar: you have until 1800 hours Eastern Standard Time to decide. Let me know your decision by posting a comment here. We'll take it from there.

Ixchel's flat, empty tone breaks my heart. All the worries I've been suppressing for the past few hours suddenly tumble free. Ixchel is facing her own death again, like in the underground river where we almost drowned, like on the slopes of Mount Orizaba. Because of me—or because of how close she is to me. And my mother—she must be in some sorry kind of state if she can't even put down some words for her only son.

I check my watch. We've got a little less than six hours. By this evening, my mother or Ixchel could be dragged out of a darkened room to be murdered.

I can scarcely comprehend the full scale of the horror. It's like looking at a huge painting—your eyes can only take in small chunks at a time.

I realize that I'm breathing faster. Montoyo's hand rests on my shoulder.

"It won't happen," he tells me. "I won't let anything happen to them, Josh. Do you believe me?"

I blink as tears fill my eyes. I want to believe Montoyo, but there's a catch in his voice . . . this time even he sounds unconvinced. I glimpse Tyler, rigid, helpless, his face ashen.

They're both as scared as me.

I stand up straight and wipe away the tears. "They've really got us this time."

"No . . ."

I insist. "They're not going to kill me. Are they? Those genetic experiments they want me for—I won't die from them."

Montoyo shakes his head, appalled at what I'm suggesting. "We don't know that. And Josh—if this is the Sect . . . you can't expect me to deliver you into their hands."

"Yes, I can. You've got to!"

The tears begin to flow again. I know that deep down—*I'm lying.*

"Yes, yes," I say, trying to sound like I'm begging. "Let me go. Please! You can't let one of them die. We don't have a choice!"

Montoyo grabs my arms firmly. "Josh, calm down. This isn't the way, trust me."

But I get more agitated, pushing him away.

Even though the last thing I want is for him to stop.

"You have to let me go!"

Montoyo pulls me to him hard, buries my head against his shoulder. "I'm going to protect you, you hear me? That's my first duty. We're going to rescue them. Don't worry, don't be scared!"

Then I really let the tears go.

He's saying everything I want him to say. I know then that Montoyo will never put me in real danger. Which is how I want it to be.

All this time I've let myself believe I could be brave, heroic. But when it comes down to it, I'm nothing but a lousy, stinking coward. More worried about my own life than about my mother's or Ixchel's.

Worst of all, I'm a liar, making out to Montoyo and Tyler that I'm some wannabe hero.

I don't deserve to live.

The sightseeing tour of Ek Naab ends abruptly. Montoyo dashes off to plan the rescue mission, leaving Tyler and me in the apartment. There doesn't seem to be much to do there, so we wander out into the lane.

I realize suddenly that Montoyo's left us alone. Unsupervised, in Ek Naab.

"What do you wanna do?" Tyler asks. "And who was that text from? You went white when you saw it—like you'd seen a ghost."

Slowly and without a word, I take out my phone and show him. Tyler looks, baffled, from me to the phone. "What . . . you don't think . . . dude, don't be insane."

"What's your explanation?"

Tyler's eyes widen, astonished. "Josh, someone's pulling your leg. Someone's got hold of your sister's phone, okay? And they're messing with you. Did you try calling her back?"

"Great idea, man. Only, oh yeah, I already tried that."

"And . . . ?"

"Number unknown."

Tyler shrugs. "Huh!" For a moment he seems totally stumped. "But . . . your sister . . . ?"

"Read the text, Ty! I was visiting my dad's grave just before I got this. The 'old man'—she means our dad. How could anyone know that except . . . ?"

"A ghost?"

"That's right." I take a gulp of air and think back to the past two nights when I've been woken by my phone buzzing—calls from a mysterious, unrecorded number. There's some part of me that is somehow not surprised. "Yes," I say, more firmly. "A spirit—a ghost. I don't understand how it works, or why me and not everyone else. But Ty, stuff like this happens to me. The world isn't as simple as you imagine. With me, this is normal."

"I mean this as a friend, Josh, but you—are not normal."

I lick my lips, thinking. The kidnapping scenario has escalated into something so scary that it's too painful to think about right now. Montoyo's taken total command . . . I'm in the clear.

There's only one thing I can think of that will help now—apart from handing myself over, which Montoyo will never allow.

I can fix the Bracelet. I can go back in time, save my dad, and make sure that none of this nightmare that I'm living ever comes true.

"Come on, Ty," I tell him, turning around in front of the church, trying to get my bearings. "We're gonna go find a Crystal Key . . ."

With that, I head off toward the Tech—where I'm guessing Lorena the Chief Scientist must have her lab. Tyler follows, asking, "Find a what, now?"

"It's not a key made of crystal, exactly . . . ," I begin. "But a crystal that *acts* as a key . . . to unlock some special activity in objects with Erinsi technology."

"A crystal," Tyler repeats, a little skeptical.

"A crystal made of chemicals—and I know the formula."

"How?"

"It's complicated to explain right now . . . but the formula was written in code, in the books that Montoyo brought to me in Brazil."

As we walk, I bring Tyler up to date on everything we found out about the Crystal Key—how it's mentioned in the first few pages of the Ix Codex, how it's one of the objects needed to activate the Revival Chamber that Ixchel and I discovered.

"And this Revival Chamber does . . . what?" he asks.

"No clue. It's got something to do with stopping the galactic superwave in 2012, though."

I tell him about how the Crystal Key has to be made in zero-gravity conditions, which is tricky. That it seems to be some key to using the ancient Erinsi technology that Itzamna, the founder of Ek Naab, managed to resurrect.

Tyler comments, "And Itzamna got all that ancient technology working again because he's a time traveler, right?"

"At least, that's what I think. Hence the Bracelet of Itzamna—a time-travel device. Only it's busted; it teleports you in space, but not in time. I have to find that Crystal Key and fix the Bracelet. And then I'll find Blanco Vigores and make him tell me how to use it. Go back in time, save my dad, and none of this will have happened."

This is beginning to sound like a plan I can get behind. I'm already feeling less sickened by my own cowardice.

This is dangerous too—but at least it's not suicidal.

"But how will you find your dad? You don't know where he is."

"I can go back to the volcano, way before the avalanche hits. Spend more time helping Dad get his memory back. He arrived on that mountain *months* before we found him near Christmas. Maybe even before I found the Ix Codex in Catemaco. In fact . . . I could take him to the codex. Then Dad will bring it back. My dad will be the Bakab Ix, not me."

I'll be home free.

Tyler gives a long, low whistle. "You've really got it all figured out, haven't you?"

"Yeah," I tell him. "That's right."

He stops walking. "And in this new timeline, you and me, we'll never become friends. Right?"

I try not to notice the disappointment in his eyes. "We'll still see each other in capoeira."

"Josh . . . we only became friends because of what happened to your dad and everything."

I don't hide my impatience. "Ty—what do you want me to do? Wait until Montoyo botches another rescue attempt? Let my mom or Ixchel get killed?"

There is one thing you could do. Find a way to give yourself up.

But that thought remains unspoken. Maybe even unthought—by anyone except me.

Tyler shakes his head. "I just don't know. Playing around with time travel to sort out your own personal problems . . . I mean . . . is that allowed?"

"Allowed? What do you mean? Do you see anyone making any rules about time traveling? 'Cause I don't."

"But Josh, where does it end?"

I shrug. "I fix this, and it ends there."

"What if it doesn't?"

"Huh?"

Tyler stops again. We're right in front of the main entrance to the Tech. I look up at the imposing glass-encrusted building. Next stop, Lorena's lab.

"What if whatever you do doesn't fix things? What if it messes up something else—something you hadn't thought about? Are you going to keep going back in time, trying to change one little thing?"

What Tyler says makes me uncomfortable. He's right—I haven't exactly planned the details.

"This feels right," I tell him. "I'm supposed to go back. My dad as much as said it—his last words to me were 'This isn't over.'"

"That could mean anything."

Irritated, I say, "*Anything* could mean anything!"

"Josh, hold on, wait a minute. You're losing it. One minute you're telling me that your dead sister is texting you from the afterlife, and the next you're talking about changing time . . ."

My eyes light up. "Yes, and Camila too."

"What?"

"If I change the past, I'll save her too. Tyler—it's the only way. Fixing the Bracelet—that fixes *everything*."

We breeze past the reception desk in the entrance lobby of the Tech. Of course, so do at least five older teenagers, students carrying books. With an embarrassed reluctance, the guy working the desk sidles out from behind it and catches up to Tyler and me just as we're about to enter the main corridor to the labs. I'm trying to act like I know what I'm doing, because all the place-signs are written in Mayan—meaningless to me. But the reception guy stops us anyway.

"Josh . . . Josh Garcia, yes?"

I nod, trying to look like I have no reason to be surprised that this total stranger recognizes me.

"Uh-huh. Carlos Montoyo sent me to meet with the *atanzahab*. Can you tell me the way to her lab?"

The receptionist looks shy, and then once again embarrassed. "I'm really sorry, sir, but . . . Montoyo hasn't notified us. I can't let unauthorized visitors walk right into the *atanzahab*'s department."

"Well, maybe it slipped his mind to call," I say, bristling slightly, "because he's dealing with a serious kidnapping situation. My mother and Ixchel—you know Ixchel?" He gulps and nods. "They've been kidnapped by the Sect of Huracan. We have less than six hours to rescue them before one of them is killed. Montoyo sent me to get some supplies from Lorena. Now if you want to delay things, call him out of a meeting and all that, then okay. But no one's going to be impressed."

The receptionist visibly shrinks. I'm amazed that my bluff is being taken seriously, but I try not to show it. He stands to one side.

"Of course, Josh, sir, I'm sorry. I'll call the *atanzahab* and tell her you're on your way. It's the second floor, two turns to your left."

I nod and keep walking.

Tyler hisses. "He's warned her you're coming! What now?"

I guess we'll have to get a little creative.

171

"I've been to university science labs before," I tell him. "We'll snoop around before we get to her office. We'll say we got lost."

We bypass the elevator and bound up the stairs.

"He called you 'sir,'" Tyler mutters, impressed.

But there's no time to reflect on how radically the world changes for me in Ek Naab. All I can think about is using the two or three spare minutes we might have to swipe the Crystal Key.

Beyond that, I'm clueless.

Following the receptionist's directions, we quickly reach a department with two sets of doors. Between the two doors is a small sink, plastic bags to put over shoes, and an air dryer. There's no one else around. I hesitate for a second and then go through the first set of doors, grabbing a fistful of the blue plastic shoe covers. I pass a couple over to Tyler, then begin to wash my hands with pink liquid disinfectant soap.

"What's all this for?" he mutters. "We gonna be performing surgery?"

"It must be some kind of superclean area. Just go with it—we need to blend in."

We're through the second set of doors minutes later. Still no sign of anyone in the corridors. I peek behind the glass window of the first door we come to. It looks like a lab. We walk straight past. Then we hear voices. Someone's coming. I grab Tyler and rush toward a big fridge-type door. We're inside just in time.

Inside it's pretty cold but not quite freezing. Metal shelving is covered with boxes of lab supplies, plastic petri dishes filled with cloudy jelly, boxes of test tubes scrawled over with handwritten labels. There is a workbench about two yards wide on which several chunky pieces of lab apparatus sit. Glass plates stand in liquid, with a brilliant blue stain across the middle of the plates.

Tyler clucks in appreciation. "Hey, man, a walk-in fridge!"

"It's a cold room," I say. "My dad's department has one too—for storing specimens. This would be a good place to store the Crystal . . ."

"Okay . . . so what are we looking for?"

My heart sinks at Tyler's question. Looking around this slightly messy cold room, I doubt that it would be used to store something quite so significant. Surely Lorena would keep something so valuable somewhere special . . . perhaps in its own fridge?

Then my eye falls on something I recognize. A box of pens—the exact same type of pen that I was given before my mission to find the Ix Codex. An instrument to secretly deliver a dose of a drug. I was supposed to use it to give myself short-term memory loss—in case I was captured by the enemy. But like all the other gadgets they gave me for the mission, I never got to use it.

I grab a handful of the pens. "These could be useful," I tell Tyler. "They inject you with an amnesia thing . . ."

Tyler looks baffled. "Amnesia? What do you want to forget?"

I glare at him flatly. "They're not meant for me, bozo."

I'm still scanning the room when the door begins to open with a loud clunking noise as the air seal is broken. Hurriedly I stuff the pens into my back jeans pocket. Tyler and I glance at each other wildly for a second.

There's nowhere to hide.

The door opens.

Standing in the opening is Lorena—the *atanzahab*, the chief scientist of Ek Naab. Wearing a stiff white lab coat, she looks more imposing than she did the first time I met her, the night I was installed as the Bakab Ix. From behind stern-looking black-rimmed glasses, she gives me a beady glare.

"Joshua Garcia . . . what the devil are you doing in here?"

I lift my hands to where Lorena can see them. "I just wanted to show Tyler a cold room! He's never seen one—he didn't even believe me that they existed."

Lorena looks doubtfully from me to Tyler, who gives a goofy nod. "He thinks there's hot rooms too."

I give Tyler a sharp glare. Hot room—what's he talking about? But turns out it's a good guess.

"There are," she says coldly. "But the 'hot room' isn't actually hot."

I step forward, looking straight at Lorena, as though nothing in the room could be of the tiniest interest. Innocently I ask, "Why is it called a 'hot room,' then?"

Lorena stands aside to let us out of the room. "Because of the radiation," she says, now impatient. "Josh, what are you doing here?"

"Montoyo is organizing a rescue mission to get Ixchel and my mother back from the kidnappers. We thought you might be able to help out with something for weapons, gadgets . . . you know, that sort of thing."

Lorena's eyes narrow. "Montoyo sent you? Because I can't get hold of him—he's not answering his phone."

I'm all wide-eyed innocence. "He's in meetings now, planning the rescue. He didn't exactly send me . . . but only because he's got too much to think about right now."

Lorena begins to nod, still a bit suspicious. "There are some things that might be useful, yes. The usual stuff—sedative drugs . . ." Her voice trails off, as though she's not supposed to say more. "We have a nice little dart delivery system now."

"Poison darts?" Tyler says. "Why don't you just use guns?"

Her attention turns to Tyler. "Guns? When people are killed, there has to be an investigation. A secret like Ek Naab doesn't stay secret very long when it starts murdering people. Look at the Sect of Huracan; they're really sloppy. We're picking up news stories linked to them every few months now."

"It's true," I tell Tyler. "My mom showed me one. Simon Madison killed this scientist woman in the Middle East. And he stole the Adapter from someone in the Middle East too."

"That's right, from a collector in Beirut," Lorena confirms.

"What's in the Middle East?" I wonder, almost to myself. "'Cause Madison keeps cropping up there."

Lorena seems surprised. "You don't know?"

I give her a blank stare. My comment was just offhand—I hadn't expected for a second that Lorena would be able to answer my question. "No, I don't. What's there?"

"I'm sorry." Lorena frowns. "I assumed, with you being the Bakab Ix . . . and the fact that you're the one who found the Revival Chamber . . ."

"Huh? What?"

"There's a second Revival Chamber in Iraq, Josh. Just like the one that you found under Structure X in Becan."

I'm too excited at the news to be angry at yet more evidence of Montoyo's secrecy. "Another one? Wow! How do you know? What does it do?"

"Well . . . we know from the Ix Codex. There were five Revival Chambers, spread throughout the world. One of them was in the ancient city of Eridu, in modern-day Iraq."

"Five chambers! Wow! This is huge!"

"In answer to your second question—we don't know what they do. The one here in Becan is empty."

"Empty; what do you mean?" From what I remember, the Revival Chamber was an octagonal stone room filled with what looked like sarcophagi.

"Well . . . we activated it," Lorena continues, still puzzled that I don't know any of this. "All the receptacles are empty."

Now I really do gape at her. "You activated the Revival Chamber? You got the Adapter to work in the Container . . . you have the Crystal Key?!"

They must have followed the instructions in the Ix Codex and succeeded where I'd seen the Professor, Marius, and Madison fail . . .

Lorena shrugs. "We didn't need the Crystal Key. The Liquid Key works fine, as long as it's used very soon after it's made. The minute we had the amino acid sequence from the Ix Codex, we had it made here in our peptide synthesizer and took it right over to the Revival Chamber."

Then I remember that line from the first few pages of the Ix Codex: the Key is unstable; it must be used within sixty minutes . . .

Lorena's words don't fully make sense to me. Amino acid sequence . . . peptide synthesizer . . . but what I do get is this: Lorena doesn't need the Crystal Key to activate the Adapter. She can activate it with something that is way, way easier to make.

So if Lorena doesn't need the Crystal Key—maybe she'll let me try it.

I repeat, "You don't need the Crystal Key?"

Lorena frowns. "No, Josh—once we cracked the code in the Ix Codex, we realized that the fifteen letters in that sequence represent amino acids. After that it was easy enough."

"So you've got the Crystal Key just sitting there, then . . . ?"
Doing nothing . . .

She shakes her head. "We haven't made the Crystal Key . . .

it's actually very difficult to make. We're still some time away from having a big enough crystal. Anyway, there's no need now. The Liquid Key works in our Revival Chamber. Whoever used to be in there . . . has long gone."

"Whoever?"

"Whoever, yes. Josh, you need to speak to Montoyo. I don't understand why he hasn't told you these things. Really, it's your birthright."

I feel a wave of such gratitude toward Lorena right then that I regret making plans to steal the Crystal Key from her.

There are five Revival Chambers . . . I guess those ancient Erinsi really got around. I shouldn't have been surprised that one chamber is in Iraq, now that I think about it. The clues were there all along—the news story about Madison stealing the Adapter did mention that the object was first found near Eridu in Iraq. Some of the ancient Erinsi stuff is written in Sumerian, the language of ancient Mesopotamia—now mainly in Iraq. Then there's the phrase itself—*Erin si*—ancient Mesopotamian words meaning "People of Memory."

So where are the other chambers? If Lorena expected people to be inside them, then what exactly are we talking about here?

Reviving the dead?

Lorena doesn't want to say any more. She's quietly angry with Montoyo, I can tell, and bewildered. But even she has her limits. "Go talk to Carlos," Lorena insists.

179

I'm angry too, but not surprised. It's typical of Montoyo to keep stuff like this from me. What's almost a million times worse than anything Lorena's telling me is a truth that dawns on me only later.

There is no Crystal Key in Ek Naab. I can't fix the Bracelet.

Ixchel and my mom are going to be slaughtered by those kidnappers. Montoyo will never find them, I know it. He'll never, ever give up his prize Bakab Ix—me.

The Sect of Huracan needs me to play some part in their top-secret world-changing plan. Well, so does Montoyo.

The Sect or Montoyo. When it comes down to it, I don't have much idea what either of them have in store for me.

Without the Bracelet of Itzamna, there's nothing I can do about anything. I'm stuck here, helpless. Just a kid waiting at home for news from the war.

Lorena gives me a case of stuff to take for Montoyo—the tranquilizer-dart guns and some darts, and also some tubes of a new "greasy glue" made of carbon nanotubes, which she tells us helps with climbing. I can't focus on what she tells us about what's in the case. Tyler at least seems focused on what she's saying, but I just keep nodding. I just want to get out of there. This is no place for me now.

Tyler and I walk back. In my daze, I make a wrong turn and we wind up in the marketplace. It's dense with stalls selling delicious-smelling food. Tyler stops at a juice bar, where a smiling girl in a crisp white apron stands in front of a mountain of fruit. Tyler points to some golden-ripe mangoes and fleshy guavas. The girl slices up the fruit, throws it into a juicer, and pours the pinkish-yellow juice over ice in two glasses.

We take our drinks and sit at one of the tables at the side of the square. I watch rocks of ice clink against the edge as I nervously push the glass around the table. Try as I might, I can't help but think back to that night on the beach at Natal. Ixchel with her goblet of frothy juice, me with the purple grape. How much it stabbed at me to see her laughing and dancing with Benicio. What an idiot I was not to give her a hug and kiss hello.

I take a sip, try to swallow, almost choke.

I think about the time Ixchel fell asleep against my chest on the bus to Tlacotalpan last December. Long moments of actually holding her. In my memory, I can still feel her breath ruffling the hairs on my arms. Just before she fully woke up, she squeezed me. I hadn't dared to move.

Why didn't I think about this at the time? It's like some horrible time-delay bomb. As if every detail was logged that day by a secretive part of my mind. It's being slowly released into my system, like poison, to torture me.

Every time I touched her, or looked into her eyes, or, even more heart-stopping, every time she touched me. It's all flooding back. Now that I can't see, hear, or touch her. Now that she might be about to die.

When I remember that as well as Ixchel there's my mother, my stomach lurches.

I wonder then—is this what Montoyo is going through? Is he thinking about my mom the way I'm thinking about Ixchel? I actually feel sorry for him for a minute. I wouldn't wish this on anyone.

I was so horrible to Mom, to Ixchel, that day on the sand dunes. What if that's their last memory of me?

Tyler says very quietly, "What's wrong?"

I lift my eyes to meet his and actually can't speak.

"Ixchel," he pronounces, watching for my response. I nod miserably, feeling my eyes fill with tears. Tyler looks at me for a few seconds, and then he nods too. "Figures."

Not for the first time, I ask him, "What am I going to do?"

Tyler doesn't have an answer to that one. But I can feel the answer forming inside me. It's not as easy as I thought to be a coward, interested only in self-preservation. It takes more nerve to hold out than I've got.

All this and it's only been a few hours. How will I get through the rest of my life, knowing that I let one of them die instead of me?

We finish our juice and wind our way back to the apartment where Montoyo's thrown my stuff. I can't think of it as "my place" yet. But being the one who leads Tyler around Ek Naab—even if I do make a couple of wrong turns on the way—makes me feel strangely at home.

No one tries to talk to us. Sometimes, when people don't think I'm looking, I notice them staring at us—especially me. It makes me wonder what sort of information is out there about me. What have they heard?

Back at the apartment, I open my suitcase and take out the two books by John Lloyd Stephens that Montoyo gave me. Tyler has been asking me about how I solved the code with the chemical formula of the Crystal Key. I show him how the cipher works, and talk him through the solution.

"So that's it, then? Those fifteen letters?"

"Lorena said 'amino acids.' That's some kind of chemical,

isn't it? We did it in biology. I guess each letter means a different amino acid."

"But why? Why is Arcadio putting that in this book?"

I shrug. Right now I'm off the whole idea. If Lorena—with all her labs—can't make the Crystal Key, what hope do I have? "I don't know, Tyler. I don't even know who Arcadio is."

But Tyler won't let it go. "He's written this same thing in all those other books? That's what Montoyo said, right?"

I nod. Tyler looks down and touches the final page of the book where Arcadio scrawled the quotation.

"And he's got a quote, right, from this Calvino guy, from 1979?"

"'I would like to swim against the stream of time . . .' That one, yes."

"But what this says, right, is that he wants to go back in time and change something, something that went wrong. But new things keep happening in his life . . . and things change. And he can't figure out which is the moment he needs to go back to . . . the zero moment . . . the point in time where . . ."

". . . where his fate changes," I finish. "Yeah . . . that's what he's saying."

It's not the first time those words set off a tingle inside me. Interesting that Tyler should notice something too.

"So he's talking about time travel, isn't he? This Arcadio— he's another time traveler!"

I nod. "It looks that way."

"You think he's actually . . . Itzamna?"

"Great minds think alike, dude," I tell him with a slight grin. "That's my theory, anyway. Arcadio disappears, we know that much."

"Disappears?"

"Uh-huh. Susannah St. John met Arcadio when they were both young. They had a 'thing.' Then one day, he never came back."

"What would happen, Josh, if that Bracelet thing broke? If the crystal got busted. You'd get stranded in time, right?"

I feel a crackle of excitement. "Unless . . ."

Tyler looks as excited as me. "Unless you could make a new Crystal Key. And to do that . . ."

"You'd have to keep the formula handy."

Tyler looks doubtful. "But writing it in a book . . . ? You could lose a book."

"Yeah, it would make more sense to, like, tattoo it on your body. Like in that movie about the guy who keeps losing his memory, *Memento*."

Then Tyler says something truly brilliant. "Maybe Arcadio never saw that movie. Or had other reasons why he couldn't write everything on his own body. So he wrote it in these books. Maybe other places too. All in code . . ."

"Someone must have been after Arcadio," I say suddenly.

I can understand how that might feel—pursued through time and space by the Sect of Huracan. You'd need every trick in the book to stay ahead.

"But then he disappears," Tyler says, closing the book. "Arcadio takes off one day and . . . that's it."

We stare at each other. A stranded time traveler from the future? Sounds a lot like Itzamna. . .

I sigh deeply. What's the use in sitting around an empty apartment, discussing the identity of Itzamna? It's not going to help anyone. Even now the superwave is on its way through space, bringing the end of civilization in 2012 and everything. But compared to the fact that in just a few hours my mother or Ixchel might be killed, it might as well be happening in *2112*. It doesn't seem relevant at all.

I stare despondently at the blank wall next to the kitchen. That's when I remember my phone, and the text from *Camila Call Me*.

I take the phone out and show it to Tyler again.

"This is from your sister's cell, right? What happened to it?"

I never found out. It was with Camila when the car went into the swamp next to Highway 186. "Maybe the police found it?"

"They could have dried it out. Someone else has it now."

I scowl. "Someone in Mexico is sending me texts in English? About visiting a grave?"

Tyler raises an eyebrow and smiles wryly. "What's up with you?"

"Huh?"

"Your life is off the hook, man. Here's you, thinking you've got a text from a dead person . . . you don't think that's insane?"

"It would be typical of Camila to mess with my head like this. She finds a way to get a message to me from the spirit world, and all she does is make a dig about how I visit Dad but not her. It's not like she's telling me something useful like *I know where the kidnappers have your mom* . . ."

The instant the words are out, I stop talking. My mouth freezes open.

"It's not like she's telling you that . . . ," Tyler says slowly. I can see that he's on the same train of thought.

"But . . . what if she could?"

I leap to my feet. Why didn't I think of this before?

Camila. The buzzing phone . . . was she trying to contact me back in Brazil, even before the kidnappers struck?

Was Camila trying to warn me?

Tyler smirks. "*Someone is trying to get in touch with you.*" He waggles his fingers mysteriously in front of his eyes. "Woooo! From the spirit world, maybe . . . ?"

This is all a joke to him.

"Trust your instincts," Blanco Vigores told me. "Ignore

nothing." I was so busy getting wrapped up in the fixing of the Bracelet, the secrets of the Ix Codex, and even Arcadio's book cipher, I totally ignored the chance that this Camila thing might be real, not some weird hoax or coincidence.

Tyler thinks I believe everything and anything, but the truth is—I'm not sure that I do. Even now I wonder: was it really the ghosts of those teenage lovers from Ek Naab, Chan and Albita, that saved Ixchel and me when we were lost in the labyrinth under Becan? The subconscious mind can do amazing things with information you think you've completely forgotten. Just as Vigores said. So it feeds back the information through a dream—what's the difference?

But, *what if*? What if Camila really could contact me from beyond?

It's got to be worth a try.

"We've got to get hold of Montoyo," I say. "I need to get out of Ek Naab and go visit my sister's grave."

From my left jeans pocket I take my Ek Naab cell phone and call Montoyo. It rings only once.

"Josh! It seems I can't leave you alone for a minute. Lorena called to say you have something for me, yes?"

Looking at the cardboard box of objects that Lorena gave us for Montoyo, I say, "We just wanted to make ourselves useful."

"Good work. We're about to take a break in the planning here. I'll come over and meet you boys for lunch."

I take a deep breath. Then I ask Montoyo for something I

can hardly believe he'll allow—an escort out of Ek Naab and down to Chetumal. As I expect, he's not happy.

"Please," I insist. "We'll be gone less than two hours."

"I can't spare the Muwans," Montoyo explains. "We need them all on standby in case we get a chance to make an early rescue."

"Have you found out where the kidnappers are?"

There's a momentary silence. "Not yet."

"Then get me a driver! There must be a way out of Ek Naab from the surface."

Montoyo pauses again. "There is. It's a tiny private road, mostly. Takes over three hours to get to Chetumal."

"Forget lunch," I say angrily. "I want to visit my sister's grave. Is that too much to ask?"

His voice grows cold. "Right now, yes. I'd expect you of all people to understand that. Josh, I'm going to send Benicio. This is tough for all of us. I'm doing everything I can."

Without another word, the phone goes dead. I'm left staring at it in my hand. I've heard Montoyo speak to people like this—his minions. Now I've been given the same treatment. Surprisingly, it really hurts.

Benicio turns up within twenty minutes. His face is drawn, pinched. He can hardly meet my eyes.

He's really angry.

"Okay, Josh, babysitter's here," he says sardonically. "What would you like to do?"

"You can get lost with that attitude, man," Tyler tells him. "We didn't ask for you."

"I want to go to Chetumal," I tell him. "To visit my sister's grave."

Benicio shakes his head. "Why?"

What can I possibly tell him? That I've had another crazy hunch? But, what else?

"I think Camila's been trying to contact me."

I tell him the rest of the story. Benicio rolls his eyes. "This is far-fetched."

I nod once, slowly. "Yeah."

He stares at me for a second. Far-fetched it may be, but Benicio's not a complete skeptic. Living in Ek Naab has taught him that there are places in the world where just about anything can happen.

And then, as if it only just this minute occurred to him, Benicio asks, "What will you do if your sister tells you where they are?"

My answer is every bit as spur of the moment as his. "We'll go straight there. And I'll give myself up. They promised us one hostage in return. You can bring back Ixchel."

The atmosphere intensifies. I can see from his eyes that Benicio doesn't share Montoyo's attitude toward my safety.

At least not when it's a matter of my safety versus Ixchel's.

Benicio starts to breathe quickly, eyes darting around. Thinking. He places his hands on his hips and stares at me for a long time.

"You'd do that?"

I'm defiant. "I said I would, didn't I?"

Tyler's said nothing so far. He puts the box he's carrying on the floor. Like Benicio, he looks into my eyes.

"You're crazy. You know that?"

I laugh. I'm literally laughing in the face of danger. It feels scarily good—makes my skin buzz, makes the hairs on my arms stand on end.

"Then I'm coming too," Tyler says. "Benicio can fly the Muwan. And I'll watch out for you."

The grin drops from my face. I bite my lip, hesitating, then throw an arm around Tyler. Fiercely, he hugs me back.

"Thanks, Ty," I mumble. "You're the best."

Benicio walks us straight to the aircraft hangar, where blue-suited engineers are making final checks to the entire fleet of Mark I and Mark II Muwans. Benicio goes over to one of the guys and has a few words. Then he comes back to us.

"There's no way we're getting out of here without some-one noticing. The best thing is just to go for it, nice and calm, no fuss. I've told him that your buddy Tyler wants to see the inside of the cockpit. So just climb in like it's no big deal."

With that, he leads the way to one of the Mark IIs. I guess if we're pursued—either by pilots from the National Reconnaissance Office with the stolen Muwan technology, or even by guys from Ek Naab—the Mark II gives us the best chance of getting away.

We climb in and strap up. Benicio takes the pilot's seat, roughly fitting a headset and eyepiece over his face. The anti-gravity engine starts up. From outside I hear a couple of shouts.

"Hold on," Benicio says grimly. The Muwan rises, hovering

only yards above the ground. A brilliant streak of sunlight opens in the ceiling above us. The Muwan lifts even higher, hovering just under the opening skylight until it's wide enough. Another couple of seconds and we're through.

Then we're above the canopy of the Campeche jungle, skimming just yards above the trees.

Classic UFO style.

My cell phone buzzes. I go to answer it immediately—another text.

Hey, hotshot, still waiting for you down by Highway 186.

Reading it, I gasp. "Wait!"

Benicio doesn't hear me, so I yell louder, beating on the back of his chair.

"Not Chetumal! I made a mistake! She wants to meet on Highway 186!"

The place where the car came off the road, shot by Simon Madison. Where Camila and I crashed into the dark swamp; where Camila died.

Benicio seems irritated. "This gets stupider. I can't believe I listened to you."

He's annoying enough to make me spit out what's been on my mind since he agreed. "Why *did* you listen to me?"

It bursts out of him. "Because Montoyo is nowhere on this. I've never seen him so panicked. Who do you think he'll let them shoot first, Josh? Not your mom, not Eleanor. Never her." Benicio pauses and breathes out, shakily. What he's admitted has shocked even him. "Who knows if your hunch will pay off? But when *you* are finally convinced that there's no other way . . ."

Benicio really wants me to give myself up to the kidnappers. He's expecting it.

He's doing this to save Ixchel.

Tyler and I stare at Benicio in stunned silence. It takes me several seconds to recover the power of speech. "Just get me to Highway 186!"

"Do you even know where? It's a long road."

"About an hour before Becan . . . a big swamp."

The Muwan changes direction in a long, smooth sweep. Within five minutes I see Highway 186 ahead, a bold asphalt-gray slash in the green forest. As we approach the road, Benicio takes us up high, so high that no one could observe us from the ground. He hits a button and the air before me bursts with light—a holographic projection. It's something I've never seen in a Muwan. Tyler breathes out in appreciation.

"Man, that is cool . . ."

It's an image of the terrain beneath us. "Touch the top right to zoom in, the top left to zoom out," Benicio informs us. But touch what? Experimentally I poke my finger into the air around the top right of the image. Immediately the image narrows its focus on the ground. I keep touching it until we can see a small patch of the road below.

"Find me your swamp," Benicio says.

The field of vision is too small and changing too quickly

for me to focus, so I zoom out until we can sweep enough of the ground at once.

Then I see it—the biggest swamp we've seen so far, but it's still much smaller than I remember.

"That could be it," I admit. "It seems small, though . . ."

"You were here in the rainy season," Benicio says. "It's the only time of year that you could drown in these swamps. Usually they're not deep enough to swallow a car."

I look at the image, feeling a stab of sorrow. So if it had all happened a few months earlier—or later—Camila wouldn't have died. "Then that's it."

Benicio takes us down in a wide spiraling movement, making it difficult for any observer to track our landing. He lands the Muwan in a meadow behind a thick wall of trees.

"Your swamp is about five minutes in that direction," Benicio says, pointing. "I'm gonna stay here and guard the bird. Tyler, go with him and see he doesn't get into trouble. Hurry, or we'll have Montoyo's people to deal with."

Tyler looks into the box of tricks from Lorena. "We should take something from here, just in case."

I unbuckle. "In case what?"

Tyler picks up what looks like a tiny silver-gray handgun. "This one shoots tranquilizer darts, Lorena said. That should be enough, right?"

I don't answer. It's actually started to hit me what a crazy escapade this is.

I'm on my way to a meeting with a ghost.

Until now it's all seemed like a sort of fantasy. Once the reality of what might happen actually sets in, I start to shiver. Uncontrollably.

Tyler notices. "You're shaking."

Pressing my lips together, I nod.

"What, Josh . . . you afraid of a ghost?"

Tyler's lazy attitude actually makes me laugh.

"And you're not?"

Tyler climbs out of the cockpit. "If only, man! I'm practically wetting my pants. But you gotta do what you gotta do, right?"

We make our way through the dry, scrubby vegetation, through a tangle of lean trees, and finally emerge near the edge of the swamp, right next to the road. A haze of warm air shimmers above the hot asphalt, like a mirage. In the far distance there's the whine of an approaching car.

Under the dazzling mid-afternoon sunshine, the swamp is utterly unrecognizable. I can hardly believe that I've been here before. Behind the reeds the water is as black as tar, its surface littered with insects, tiny leaves, and pollen. Small frogs rustle, hopping in the grass. There's a background chorus of tiny, high-pitched croaks.

All signs of last summer's car crash have disappeared. I glance to my right and see the beginning of the thicket into which I plunged right after the crash. Even by day it looks daunting, dark, impenetrable.

There's a constant drone as mosquitoes hover around us. Absent-mindedly I slap at an itch on my face. I walk to the road, gazing in both directions. It's empty and straight as far as the eye can see. Up and over hills; a horizontal line across the state, slicing through the jungle.

We stand fidgeting under the bright glare of the sun. The road surface hums as a vehicle approaches. The engine's roar shatters the air as the car shoots past. Within seconds we're back to the crackle and buzz of insects and frogs. A cloud of yellow butterflies hovers around us for a second or two before moving toward the road.

Time passes.

Tyler shuffles closer and looks down for a moment, uncomfortable. When he looks up he seems surprised.

"There's blood on your face."

I look down at Tyler's raised hand. I'm puzzled, then confused, then kind of appalled.

"Stop pointing that gun at me."

His voice seems to come from far away. "What gun? I'm not holding the gun."

"That gun, the dart gun," I say, wiping my brow. I can't understand why Tyler's messing around like this, pointing the gun. "Put it away. There's no one here but us."

His reply, when it comes, is confused. His speech is slurred. "Dude, I'm not the one with the gun . . ."

I turn back to face the road. It's empty apart from the

yellow butterflies. They float around the edge of the road, like a single creature made of fluttering autumn leaves, dipping in and out of the foliage.

Sweat trickles down my neck. A sense of desperation builds within my chest.

No one's coming.

This has to be rock bottom. Let's face it—I'm clutching at straws.

I'm at the point of admitting that it's all been a waste of time; I'm actually opening my mouth to say the words. Then I look closer at the butterfly cloud. There are no more gaps between the yellow, only a solid block of color.

It's coming closer, purring. Seconds of confusion pass. I realize that I'm no longer staring at the butterflies, but a car.

A yellow car: a VW Beetle. It draws up alongside me. The driver's window slides down.

"Come on, baby brother, get in the car."

I have to grip the edge of the car to stop myself from staggering.

"Camila . . . ?"

She nods, the woman, the ghost. I don't see how she can be a ghost when there's nothing even slightly ghostly about her. She looks exactly as I remember her that day—the only day I ever saw her. Glossy dark hair falling straight down her back, a lime-green tanktop, skinny white jeans. Lots of jewelry and lipstick.

I force myself to tear my gaze away from the all-too-lifelike apparition of my dead sister. Where the heck is Tyler? But he seems to have vanished.

"Your friend," Camila says with a jab of her manicured finger, "has fallen asleep. Right there."

I follow her pointing finger and see to my astonishment that she's right. Tyler is fast asleep, nestled just out of sight beside the swamp.

"How long have we been here?" I say aloud, but mainly to myself.

The ghost shrugs. "Your guess is as good as mine, sweetie."

We stare at each other. "So you *are* a ghost?"

She doesn't answer, but purses her very real-looking lips. "Jump in."

Somehow I do, without any serious thought for Tyler.

The next thing I'm aware of is that we're driving. We're far down the road, the swamp long behind us. I gradually notice that the air is filled with Brazilian jazz. I know this song—it's another of my dad's favorites, by Tom Jobim.

"So close your eyes, for that's a lovely way to be
Aware of things your heart alone was meant to see."

I hear my own voice say clearly, "What's going on?"

The ghost doesn't take her eyes off the road.

In a soft voice she says, "How did you think this was gonna work, hotshot?"

I'm even more confused. "How what was gonna work?"

"*Hermanito*, there are no happy reunions here."

"But you are Camila . . .?"

I'm actually still not sure. She looks and sounds so real . . .

The ghost says, "I'm an echo; a last breath. A sigh."

"Why am I here? Why are you here?"

"Because there is something I need to show you."

"My mother's been kidnapped!" I yell, only now remembering. "And my friend! Do you know where they are?"

It's amazing, but for a few long moments, I'd actually forgotten all about them—and Tyler. There's something very wrong with my thought processes, but I can't tell what.

"All I know is that I need to tell you something. Something I should have told you that day . . ."

Even the ghost seems to have trouble talking about the day Camila died.

"So now, well—now it's time to tell you."

"There's something you want to tell me from that day? But why now?"

"Actually . . . I don't know," she tells me thoughtfully. "It never even occurred to me to wonder."

"What do you mean?" I ask. "Where are you taking me? What about Tyler? And . . . who are these people walking along the road? They look like . . ."

Then I flinch in horror. I've just realized that the people we pass every so often, limping along the road with arms and legs at strange angles—are the walking dead.

Zombies.

"The worst thing about all this," Camila's ghost tells me, "are the ones who don't know they're dead. Believe me, they're everywhere. You can't imagine what a pain they are."

I want to scream. The more I look around, the more I see them. Crawling out from the edges of the roads, sometimes staggering around in the middle of the roadway. At least one every five hundred yards. Sometimes she has to swerve to avoid them.

"They can't hurt you," Camila says grimly, "except maybe by boring you to death. You'd think they'd get over it, but no. Telling you all the details of how they got hurt, asking you to take them to the hospital, every detail of their tragic lives."

I stare at her in horror. When I look very closely, I notice that she's got a thin stream of blood trickling from her head.

"You're dead."

"It's kind of rude to remind me."

My own voice sounds hollow when I ask, "Where am I?"

I can't even tell if she heard the question, because she keeps talking. "I was so happy to meet you that day, Josh. All I wanted to do was to look at you and talk to you and hear about our daddy. But we had that mystery to solve . . . can you understand how I was torn?"

Before I can answer, we suddenly arrive at a junction, which seems to have appeared out of nowhere. There are more people wandering. I watch as one obvious car-crash

202

victim stops to buy a bag of fresh pineapple from a street vendor. But the vendor just ignores him, until the zombie starts
to wave his arms in despair.

"He can't see him . . . ," I say. "Why doesn't the dead guy
know he's dead?"

"Car-crash spirits," she says, "are the worst ones for not
knowing they're dead. Must be the shock."

I look around in steadily mounting horror. The road does
seem unusually crowded.

"How many of these people are dead?"

"Oh . . . as many as half," Camila says.

I want to throw up. My skin actually crawls with revulsion.
My lips move but no sound emerges.

I am so not cool with this.

We turn off the main road and down an isolated side road.
The trees open out in front of us to reveal a long expanse of
shimmering water stretching to the left and right as far as
the eye can see. So many shades of blue—everything from
midnight blue to aquamarine.

"What is this place?" I ask, unable to drag my eyes from
the impossibly blue water.

"It's Lake Bacalar," Camila says. "Very popular for real estate.
It's become fashionable to own some nice lakeside property."

Slowly I ask, "Why are we here?"

"It's like I said, Josh, there's something I should have told
you the day we first met. That guy in the blue Nissan—I'd

seen him once before. I'm pretty sure I told you he was stalking me . . . but until the day I met you, I just thought he was a regular stalker, you know? The kind that wants to date you."

I struggle to grasp what she's saying. "You're saying you met Simon Madison before?"

It's not clear that she's even heard me as she continues, "I showed him around a house. On Lake Bacalar. Well, to be accurate, him and a woman. A woman he called 'Professor.'"

"Madison and *the Professor* looked at a house? A house, around here? A house near Becan?"

"Lake Bacalar is less than two hours from Becan," she says. "A few weeks before he chased us off Highway 186, that blue Nissan guy was about to rent a house."

She slows the car to a crawl outside a broad, carved mahogany gateway polished to a gleaming finish.

"It's right here," she says. "Don't you think I should show you?"

Then we're walking up an empty driveway. Me and my superglamorous sister.

My dead sister.

We've been together for what—an hour? I've started to see dead people. And the strangest thing is happening: it's all starting to feel almost normal.

Camila opens the main door without a key. The house is a large two-story villa, pure white with narrow pillars, arches on the balcony. There are high arched windows in every wall. A wide stretch of deep green lawn leads to the edge of the water, where a wooden jetty extends deep into the clear azure waters of the lake. Inside, the house is almost unfurnished, just a gray marble floor with a few pieces of white furniture. The walls are also white, decorated with an occasional piece of abstract art.

Camila leads me to the second floor, the heels of her golden shoes clicking on the marble. We pass open doors that lead to yet more scarily white rooms containing only beds (made up in white bedclothes) through to a room that looks like an office. The arched window looks out over the back garden down to the lake. It's a stunning view, all those shades of blue against a stretch of unspoiled green wilderness on the opposite bank.

The desk is clear except for a pad by the (white) phone. There are three numbers written there. All begin with 55.

I look up from the desk. "This is the Professor's office?"

She shrugs. "Go figure. None of this was here when I showed them the house. But you can be sure of this—that Professor woman is the one in charge. I thought maybe the guy was her son."

I run a finger along the top of the flat-screen monitor. Not a trace of dust.

"He works for her," I say. "His name is Simon. He's an idiot."

She allows herself a smile. "I knew you'd get the better of him. Good for you, li'l bro."

I force myself to look straight into Camila's eyes. That's when I know for sure that she's not alive. When she looks back at me, I see nothing—no depth of expression. It's like gazing into a hard, frozen space. After a second I can't bear to look.

Why has she brought me here? If this isn't about finding my mother and Ixchel . . . then what?

A horrible thought occurs to me. Hesitantly I ask, "Do you need me to . . . get revenge for you?"

She shakes her head with an ironic grin. "Oh, you think you're Hamlet now? Of course not."

I breathe a sigh of relief. I'm not sure what she means with the Hamlet thing, but I know this: I can't handle a revenge quest on top of everything else.

"Then why bring me here?"

"Those numbers, Josh."

I stare at the numbers by the phone. "What . . . ?"

"Remember them."

"Huh?"

"Memorize them. Now."

"Why?"

She stretches out a hand. Gently she says, "Will you let me touch you?"

I freeze. The ghost withdraws her hand. "I'm sorry, kiddo. Some impulses don't completely go away."

I feel suddenly cold, as if the air conditioning has just kicked in.

I stare at Camila's ghost. When I speak, I can actually see my breath in front of my face. "If you're just an echo, then where's Camila?"

She takes a deep breath. "Josh . . . this is only one part of existence."

"I miss Camila," I blurt. "And my dad too."

The ghost's eyes glisten, brimming with expressionless tears. She backs away.

"The numbers, Josh. Remember."

I force myself to look down at the numbers, obediently memorizing the digits.

When I look up again, I'm all alone. Yet somehow I'm very calm. My fingers trace the numbers on the pad by the phone. I can still hear the strains of jazz from Camila's car stereo.

"So close your eyes, for that's a lovely way to be,"

And then he sings,

"The fundamental loneliness goes whenever two can dream a dream together."

I'm still hearing it when I wake up.

I'm lying in the scratchy undergrowth, face up, no shade. Tyler is next to me, still snoozing. It takes me a full thirty seconds to realize that Benicio is stabbing at me with his shoe.

"You idiots!" he's saying. "Wake up, wake up now! Montoyo's guys are gonna be here any minute. What's wrong with you? What kind of stupid game were you playing?"

I sit up, still woozy. "Game?"

Benicio shoves the tranquilizer-dart gun into my face. "Playing with this. You shot each other! Idiots!"

He pushes Tyler hard until, like me, Tyler struggles to his feet.

"What's going on, hmmm?"

"Less talking, more moving," Benicio says. He leads the way back to the Muwan, hurrying. I follow in silence, thinking. Mainly about numbers.

"Did you shoot me?" Tyler asks. He doesn't sound angry, only fascinated.

"I might have," I admit.

I open my palm to see a streak of blood there. My last clear memory is of wiping my cheek, where a mosquito was gorging itself on my blood.

Truthfully, I don't know or remember who shot who, or why. But like Tyler, I had a tiny tranquilizer dart in the back of my hand when I woke up.

Numbers.

When we get back to the Muwan, Benicio calls in to Ek Naab. In the background of my thoughts, I hear him telling Montoyo that he's very sorry, that I made a big fuss about the Camila thing, that we'd be back in a bit.

"Can you check a number for me?" I tell Benicio the second he finishes the call.

"Can I *what*?"

I tell Benicio the first number. "Just check it. Does it mean anything?"

He doesn't even bother to type it into his computer.

"It's a telephone number. In Brazil."

I struggle to keep my voice calm. "Can you tell where in Brazil?"

"Of course."

"Benicio. Check it."

He's silent, tapping the numbers into his keyboard. "It's a place called Gesolo. Never heard of it."

"There's another number," I tell him. He checks that too.

"Gesolo again."

The third number is for somewhere in Natal.

Without a trace of doubt, I say, "They're in Gesolo."

Benicio looks at me hard for what seems like forever. Then he says, "You saw your sister."

I nod.

"She gave you these numbers?"

"She showed me a house she sold to the Sect. On the shore of Lake Bacalar. The numbers were by a phone."

"Bacalar. We knew the Sect had to have somewhere local. All that time they spent visiting the Revival Chamber under Becan . . . We never found it, though."

"I know where it is. I could take you there."

Benicio considers this. "That's a good idea. But it's a little soon. It would be smarter to wait. To let them believe their house is still a secret. Anyhow, Montoyo wants you locked up until this kidnapping situation is over."

I say nothing, too stunned by the idea that Montoyo would actually do that.

"Are you still willing to trade yourself for Ixchel?"

I can't speak, so I just nod.

Benicio looks thoughtful. He settles into the pilot's seat. "Then let's go to Gesolo."

I lean back into my chair as the Muwan takes off. It takes some effort to avoid Tyler's anxious stare. I really try, though.

I want to be alone to think. This might be my last hour of freedom.

Eventually Tyler breaks his silence. "What does he mean— you saw your sister?"

"I don't know how, Ty, but she came to me. It was like a dream. But it felt totally real."

He groans. "Pure insanity. Your sister's ghost spoke to you in a dream?"

"It was pretty messed up," I admit. "Like in that movie, *The Sixth Sense*. I could see dead people. They were just wandering around among the living people. Most of them didn't even know they were dead."

Tyler hesitates, then, voice heavy with doubt, he says, "You're not giving yourself up to those Sect people. For real, I mean?"

I stare out the window, watching as the craft plunges deep into the stratosphere. In a tiny voice I say, "What choice do I have?"

Tyler glances in Benicio's direction. His voice drops to a whisper. "We could try to rescue them."

"How?"

"Just you and me, man," he breathes. "With Benicio as the getaway guy. We've got these tranquilizer darts. We've got your memory-wiping injection pens. We've got this climbing-nanotube stuff from Lorena—she said you put it on your hands and it forms some rubbery bond thing with walls. Plus, if we have to, Josh, we use our capoeira."

Now I can't help staring at Tyler. "Are you serious? You're walking around with a three-inch gunshot wound and, like, fifteen stitches."

Tyler lowers his voice. "Look . . . what's the worst that can happen? The way you want to run things, they're already getting *you*."

I gasp. "It can get plenty worse. You could get caught too. They might not keep their promise to free Ixchel."

"Think it through, Josh. They're after *you*. Once they have you, we're no use to them."

"Yeah—what if they kill you all?"

"I don't think so. Why? They haven't done much killing so far, have they?"

I'm indignant. "My sister? My dad?"

"Your sister and your dad—they both died by accident. At least the way you explained it to me. Madison could have killed you, plenty of times."

"I think they *have* killed people," I tell him. "There was a story in the paper about this scientist from Oxford—from the same college as my dad. They killed her."

Tyler takes a deep breath. "Look, man. If you think I'm just going to let you hand yourself over . . ."

We exchange an angry glare.

"You agreed."

"No, I never did. Benicio's the one who wants you to walk in without a fight. Not me."

What can I say? I can't believe a friend would risk his own life for me. Do I have the right to stop him?

Then he leans close to me and hisses, "You don't fool me, anyway; I know you want to rescue them. You were glad that Montoyo wouldn't hand you over—I saw it in your eyes. You want to be free to help with the rescue. Then she'll *like* you, right?"

Astonished, I stare at Tyler.

"It's only natural," he murmurs, stretching as he settles back into his seat. "If my mom and my girl had been taken, no one would stop me from getting them back."

Just then, a map of Brazil appears in the air before us. The image zooms in on a region near the center, by the border with Colombia and Peru. A thick stretch of river dominates the area.

The Amazon?

The zooming continues as detailed satellite images layer through the air. In the middle of dense green jungle, a tiny town appears. I can't even see any roads leading to or from it. The town itself is nothing more than one street, a picturesque square, and a few houses. Including one large hacienda-style mansion set in a lush tropical garden.

"Nice little town, this Gesolo," comments Benicio. "Very pretty to be so far off the beaten track. My guess is that the owners of that hacienda run the whole town. Nowhere will be safe. You'll need to get right into the hacienda."

"Is that where they're being kept?"

"The numbers you gave me trace to phone lines on the hacienda estate. If you're right, Josh, that was some amazing information you got from that house at Lake Bacalar."

"What was it like to see your sister again?" Tyler asks. "Was it like in a dream?"

I consider. "It wasn't really her. I could tell. Something was missing in her eyes." A heavy sigh escapes me. "She was like an echo. Not like a dream."

What had been missing was in me, just as much as in the ghost-Camila. I'd felt numb around her. Cold, distant—no more alive than a ghost.

Seeing Camila, I'd felt nothing . . . not like when I saw my dad again on the volcano.

"We'll be in Gesolo in thirty minutes," Benicio announces. "It should be dark when we get there—it's two hours ahead. I'm gonna find somewhere to land in the jungle nearby. We'll use headsets to communicate. I'll guide you to the hacienda. Once you're in there, guys—you're on your own. I have no clue where they're being held."

Benicio overheard our plans.

Puzzled, I ask, "So . . . you're with us on the rescue plan?"

From the cockpit comes Benicio's languid voice. "You win,

214

Josh. You get to be the hero—or be captured trying. As long as we get our friends back."

My mind is already thousands of miles away, in Gesolo. I'm helping Ixchel into the Muwan. I'm climbing in after her, flying away. There's only me and Ixchel.

In my mind, she's clinging to me, filled with gratitude.

From way above the clouds, Benicio lets the Muwan drop into the jungle. It's over so quickly that we don't see anything but a rush of fluttering greenery lit by the craft's landing lights. We ruffle leaves all the way down. Amazingly, Benicio's used the satellite navigation system to locate a tiny clearing in the jungle. Still, it's not much more than the width of the Muwan.

This isn't a rainforest jungle like in Mexico; it's fully tropical, with enormous broad-leaved trees and a canopy so thick that underneath it's almost pitch-black, even with the last rays of sun still glowing purple in the sky. In a few more minutes the real dark will set in. I check my watch—there are just two hours left from the deadline to agree to hand me over.

Two hours to rescue Ixchel and my mom.

We can do this.

When Tyler and I clamber out of the Muwan, we're hit by a wall of sound—rushing water. Benicio checks his map.

"Guys . . . I'm sorry about this. Looks like there's a
you gotta cross."

Tyler and I follow the sounds of water through som
and find the source of the noise. We shine our flashlight
the water. It's not a stream—more of a whitewater riv
least three yards wide and running very, very fast. We
back to the Muwan, guided by its faintly glowing lights.

"You have to put us down on the other side of that ri
There's no way we can swim across."

Benicio sounds annoyed. "You think I didn't think of tha
There is literally nowhere to land on the other side. Unless yo
want me to put you into the garden of the hacienda?"

I pause. "That's actually not a bad idea. Not that garden,
though—they'd see us there. But how about the roof?"

Benicio nods. "That could work . . . to get you in. I could
turn all the Muwan lights off and go in on stealth mode. Even
in the dark, they might still spot us. I won't be able to stay
long—it would have to be a lightning drop."

Tyler says, "So how would we get out?"

"You'd have to meet me somewhere. Right here. We're
almost exactly due east of the house—no more than one mile.
Take a wrist compass—look in the compartment under your
seat. Without a compass, you'll never find your way through
that jungle."

Tyler leans into the Muwan and rummages in the drawer.

He pulls out a compass on a cloth wristband with velcro fastening and starts wrapping it around his wrist. "And the river?"

"I'll hover . . . you can all hang onto the rope ladder and I'll fly you over here so you can actually climb in."

I frown. "Sounds risky. It's a lot to ask of Ixchel and my mom—running a mile through the jungle in the dark, probably being chased. And then dangling from a rope . . ."

Tyler remarks, "I'd say it beats where they are right now."

We climb back aboard. I like the idea of the lightning strike. I'd kind of like an option for a lightning getaway too. But with just one Muwan, our options seem limited.

Have I made a huge mistake by not handing this whole mission over to Montoyo?

I push the thought out of my head. At least my plan has a backup possibility—if we get caught, I hand myself in. Something that Montoyo would never allow.

Benicio flies us in low above the trees. The hacienda is just visible under the glow of light from the windows and a few ornamental lamps in the garden. He lands as softly as a feather on the flattest part of the tiled roof. When we climb out, we realize that the Muwan's landing gear can adjust to a sloping surface, but of course we can't. We immediately struggle to stay upright.

Just then a huge beam of light appears in the garden. It's a searchlight. It swivels into the air, sweeping the sky. Tyler and

I hold our breath as Benicio lifts the craft two yards into the air and then shoots off vertically. The searchlight sweeps the empty air a fraction of a second later, only yards above our ducked heads.

I'm elated by our narrow escape—but at the same time horrified that we were almost caught so early into the rescue.

Got to stay positive. We can do this.

I adjust my headset. In the earpiece I hear Benicio say, "Okay, gentlemen, I'm clear. Now get going. Your window is on the lower roof level. As long as there's no guard there, that's your way in."

Tyler and I sidle carefully down to the edge of the roof. About two yards below is another level of sloping tiles, and five yards along there's a window. From our vantage point, we can see that there are two guards in the front garden. I can just spot them under a low coconut tree that's lit by a string of blue fairy lights. They're carrying semiautomatic rifles slung casually over their shoulders as they chat.

All it would take is a single flashlight beam in our direction. But their attention is focused outward—toward the entrance of the property. Meanwhile, the searchlight continues to crisscross the sky, a dramatic sword of light in the darkness.

I guess they anticipated that someone from Ek Naab might just drop by . . .

East is behind the house, I note. So when we hightail it out of here, we'll be headed for the backyard. It backs right onto the jungle. Presumably there's some kind of fence to keep wild animals out. I try to push away worries about how we're going to escape—for now.

First we have to get in.

Tyler and I easily lower ourselves to the window. It's slightly open—a trivial job to get in. We're in a bedroom with an attached bathroom. Silently, I indicate to Tyler that he should almost close the window, the way we found it. Just then I hear the sound of the toilet flushing. Tyler and I bolt toward the main bedroom door. We escape just before the bathroom door opens.

Then we're in a corridor. This house is huge. I realize now how hard it might be to find them.

Voices approach—two guys. It sounds like one of them is ordering the other around. We hunt for somewhere to hide, and duck behind a carved wooden shrine covered with votive offerings and a statue of the Virgin Mary.

They're muttering in Portuguese. After all the time we spent in Brazil, I've finally started to tune in to the language. It's sort of like Spanish spoken through some weird filter; once you get the phase shift, it's possible to catch the gist of what people are saying. I can just understand enough to figure out that the younger guy has been told to take food to the prisoners.

The second they're out of sight, we follow. They make their way down the main staircase and then keep going toward the basement.

But we're stalled at the ground floor level—there's an armed guard by the front door.

"I think he could do with a nap," Tyler whispers. He takes careful aim from behind the banister. The guard barely even reacts to the sound of the tranquilizer dart flying through the air before he collapses in a heap. We're down in an instant, taking his weapon. We can't leave him, though—lying in the middle of the entrance hall, he'll be discovered any minute now. So we drag his crumpled body into the cloakroom and stash him inside.

"Lorena said it lasts for ten minutes, no more. We'd better move," Tyler says.

We descend the last flight of stairs, Tyler carrying the guard's pistol, me with the tranquilizer gun. Stealing a gun wasn't part of the plan, and I find myself wondering if Tyler would really be able to use it.

Any minute now we're going to find Ixchel and my mom. It's the first time the reality of our situation has really sunk in.

The stairs lead to a corridor that was clearly once the servants' quarters. In contrast with the heavy wood and freshly white-plastered walls of the rest of the house, these walls are bare concrete, and we're stepping on brick-tiled floors. There's no sign of anyone in the corridor, but we hear voices in a room filled with the noises of laundry equipment. In the far end of the corridor there's a door slightly ajar. As we pass the laundry room, one guy emerges, shortly followed by another, from the doorway at the end of the hallway.

They see us right away and call out in shocked voices.

Before I'm aware of what's happened, I've shot the front guy in the leg with a tranquilizer dart. He stares at me in amazement, then down at his leg, and then he topples over in front of the other guard.

"Don't move," Tyler shouts. He points the pistol at the remaining guard.

The second guard slowly lowers his gun. Aiming at his thigh, I shoot him full of a dose of the tranquilizer.

Then, chillingly, we hear another voice, this time from inside the room.

"Whoever you are," the woman says, speaking English with a heavy Brazilian accent, "you're gonna drop your weapons and come in here with your hands up. Or I'm gonna shoot one of the hostages."

We both stand absolutely still.

In our headsets we hear Benicio say, "She's bluffing. If she's just a foot soldier, she doesn't have the authority to shoot a hostage."

But what if she isn't just a "foot soldier"?

I get an idea. Using hand signals, I send Tyler along the corridor so that he's right next to the door. Pressed against the wall, he'd only be seen once someone was all the way out of the room.

"I'm Josh Garcia; I've come to give myself up," I announce. "I'm alone. But Carlos Montoyo doesn't know I'm here with his rescue team. They're outside right now, taking out your guards in the garden. If I don't see my mother and Ixchel right now, I'll give the signal to move in."

There's a pause, and then a chuckle.

"I just spoke to the guards on my radio. They're fine."

Then I hear Ixchel, loud, almost hysterical. "Josh, she doesn't have a . . ."

Abruptly, Ixchel's voice is muffled.

What was she going to say? "She doesn't have a gun?" "Or she doesn't have a radio?"

I guess that the guard does have a gun—or else why would Ixchel and Mom even stay quiet?

But maybe no radio. She's cut off, for now.

I step forward. "I'll give myself up, right now. But you need to bring them both out, Ixchel and my mom. I want to see that they're okay."

"Josh, do you think I'm an idiot? If you want me to come out, it's so you or one of your team can shoot me. You have five seconds to come in here or I'll shoot the girl."

"Get in there, Josh," Benicio hisses over the headset. "Distract her; then Tyler, you follow. And shoot the guard. Don't hesitate."

I stride over to the doorway, being careful to avoid a sideways glance at Tyler. Standing there, I see the three of

223

them. A dark Brazilian woman in her twenties with her thin hair in a ponytail points a gun at my mother. Mom and Ixchel are tied to chairs, both hands behind their backs. Their eyes light up for just a second when they see me, but both looked exhausted and scared.

"Drop your gun," the woman says.

I let the tranquilizer-dart gun clatter to the floor. My eyes sweep the room as discreetly as possible. It's a small room, hardly more than three yards square. Hard to think of any distraction I could create in here . . .

"Step forward," she says, slowly moving away from my mother. She raises the gun, now pointing it at me.

Then commotion breaks out—the woman cries out as Ixchel kicks her hard in the shin. She staggers for a second, still vaguely pointing the gun at me. But I drop into a *ginga*, shifting my body from side to side. Tyler squeezes into the gap between me and the door.

It's just enough to distract the guard; for one second her attention flits from me to Tyler. In that split second, I use a hooking *gancho* kick to knock the gun out of her hand, then a low *ponteira* kick to topple her. Then Tyler is standing over her with the tranquilizer gun. He shoots a dart into her leg. We watch as her eyes close.

Without a word, we start cutting Mom and Ixchel free. They look disheveled, still scared, but incredibly relieved to be free. I'm not prepared for the rush of emotion I get when I see them both. It's actually pretty hard to speak. Even though I'm dying for a chance to hug Ixchel, there's no time to talk, or even say hello. I pick up the second gun.

"Where's everyone else?" Ixchel says hurriedly, glancing at the door.

"It's just us two," I say.

A mixture of bewilderment and dismay crosses their faces. I'm horribly aware that we've already used two or three of our ten minutes before the first guard wakes up from the sedative.

We have less than seven minutes to get out, and at least a mile of jungle to get through. And, on top of everything else, whatever dangerous wild animals we might encounter out there, prowling around in the dark.

Tyler takes the lead, tranquilizer gun in his right hand. Mom and Ixchel follow; I'm at the back with my own dart gun. Both Tyler and I have the guards' pistols in our back pockets too, just in case. I guess we're all scared, but there's no time to think about that. Time is running out; every second counts.

"We're on our way out," I tell Benicio over the headset.

"Go carefully," he replies. "You're a long way from safety."

Approaching the laundry room, I'm grateful for the heavy thumping noise from the equipment. So far, it seems to have saved us from discovery.

Just as we're past the door, it springs open. Two dark-skinned, muscular guys in their late teens rush toward us. I try to turn and take aim, but before I know what's happened, the nearest one has thrown himself into a handstand, his feet aiming right at my shoulder.

226

With one swift and deadly capoeira move he's knocked the gun out of my hand. I bend to pick it up; he follows with a sweeping *queixada* kick to block my path. Tyler moves back to protect Mom and Ixchel from the second laundry guy. They clash in the middle of the corridor, a high kick meeting Tyler's blocking movement. Then with his left fist, Tyler punches him in the face. The guy reels for a second, dizzy. Tyler follows up with a tranquilizer dart to his chest. His opponent is out cold.

The guard attacking me throws a punch. I duck, grab him around the waist, and throw my full weight onto him, pushing him to the floor. We land almost two yards from the others.

Tyler maneuvers around to get a clear shot at the guy underneath me. He fires the tranquilizer gun.

Nothing. Struggling to hold my opponent down, I glance up to see Tyler pulling the trigger over and over.

"I'm out of darts, man!"

"Get mine!"

Ixchel, Mom, and Tyler all scramble for my tranquilizer gun. Tyler reaches it first, aims at the guard's leg, and shoots. Two seconds later the guy stops struggling.

We all breathe a massive sigh of relief, still shocked by the encounter. I check my watch.

"The first guard is going to wake up in four minutes."

We file out of the basement, up the stairs, and through the empty entrance lobby, looking for a way out around the back or side of the house. We stay as close to the walls as possible, treading lightly, but even so we make some noise. Following the corridor through the east wing of the hacienda, we come finally to a door. There's no light from under it—the room beyond is empty.

Tyler pushes the door open. There's a large room, sparsely furnished with a round table and some chairs of dark, heavy-looking wood. Against the wall is a small bar counter and a shelf full of bottles.

"The windows," he says, and makes straight for the opposite wall.

I close the door behind us and follow Tyler and the others to the windows. They're already opening them, pushing aside the wooden blinds behind the glass. I stick my head out. It's a short drop to the grass below. Tyler swings himself through the window with one smooth leap. I help Mom and Ixchel out, and listen to them land softly in the garden. Then I follow.

We're on the east flank of the yard. To the east, the edge of the jungle begins more than seventy yards away, across an almost-clear expanse of lawn. All the larger trees are lit.

Due east is way too risky.

Behind the house, I can see from the encroaching darkness that the perimeter is much closer.

"We need to cross the fence behind the house," I whisper. "And make our way through the jungle."

"We'll lose lots of time," Tyler says.

I point across the lawn. "We'll never make it without being seen."

Mom and Ixchel glance from me to Tyler.

Mom says, "Josh, where's the rest of the rescue team?"

"Benicio? He's waiting in the jungle."

Ixchel says, "Tell him to come get us!"

I hesitate. But the searchlight keeps streaking across the sky.

"He can't land without being seen."

Ixchel sounds annoyed. "Then we head for cover. Don't you boys know anything?"

Before I can stop myself, I say, "I know . . . that's what I said!"

She starts moving toward the back of the house. "Well, let's get going!"

Mom and I follow, staying low and away from the light spreading from the house and trees.

Tyler hangs back for a second, and then he follows too.

As we pass a window, there's an exclamation from inside. We rush past, but inside I hear scrambling for the door and window. When I turn my head to check, I see the shadows of two figures leaping out of the window and sprinting straight toward us.

Behind the house, the fence beckons, less than ten yards away.

Tyler rushes forward and throws himself at the fence. He

screams in agony. Thrown backward, he lands on his back, groaning.

"It's electrified," Ixchel says.

"Oh no," Mom murmurs, her voice quaking.

I take aim in the shadows. The first shot misses; the second dart hits the closest guard just as he's about to leap at me. When I fire a third time, my gun is empty.

"I'm out," I say, tossing the gun away.

Tyler is momentarily shaken, but starts to struggle to his feet. I reach into my back pocket and take out the pistol. I aim it at the second guard.

"Shoot him!" Tyler yells.

I hesitate, and then fire at the ground. As the gun goes off in my hand, everyone seems to leap. It's so loud that I almost jump too. The second guard doesn't stop running, though. He pulls out his own gun and shoots. I hear a bullet whistle past me, somewhere close to my left ear.

His voice comes from out of the shadows. "Drop the gun."

Ixchel draws a rapid breath. "That's Gaspar," she whispers. "He's in charge."

Behind me, I sense Mom and Ixchel shrinking farther into the darkness near the fence.

I shout, "Take another step and I'll fire again."

Gaspar laughs, still walking toward me. He's almost completely in shadow, but slightly silhouetted by the faint glimmer from the lights on a tree about thirty yards away. I can't see clearly whether his arm is raised. "Not a good idea to take shots at each other in the dark, Josh."

I let rage flood into my voice. "Stop moving! If you think I'm gonna let you hurt my mom or my friends, you're wrong."

I fire again, this time aiming into the air only slightly above his head.

He stops, less than four yards away.

"Relax! I've stopped moving. I could kill any of you from here, Josh. And you know it."

I point the gun straight at him. "Better make sure it's me, then. Or it'll be the last thing you ever do."

Gaspar chuckles. "Tough talk from a boy. Ollie told us you were brave. And Madison will never admit it, but I think he's a little afraid of you, Josh. You got him into a *lot* of trouble."

"He's flattering you, Josh," Mom warns. "Be careful, he's good at that."

He mentioned Ollie and Madison. These Brazilian guys really are part of the Sect of Huracan.

I tighten my grip on the pistol, trying to psych myself up to shoot.

"How do we get over that fence?"

"You don't. Face it, you're stuck. Put the gun down and we'll talk. We only need you, Josh. I'm still happy to trade."

"There are concrete supports," Tyler yells from behind me. "We'd have to use Lorena's climbing grease . . . but I think we can get over."

In the darkness, I nod. "Do it." There's a rustle as the three of them head for the fence.

In a low voice Gaspar growls, "Drop the gun, Josh. Or I'll shoot them."

"No," I say. "You and me, we're gonna stand right where we are. Until they're over. Maybe a bit longer too, until I'm sure they're safe."

There's a long pause. I can't make out anything but the silhouette of Gaspar's shape: tall, well-built; but standing perfectly still, I aim my gun at his chest.

"You won't shoot me," Gaspar says. But he doesn't sound too sure. "You're just a boy. What do you know about killing?"

I'm silent, not moving.

Gaspar tries again. "You'll never make it out of here."

I say nothing.

Somewhere behind me, Mom and Ixchel gasp with effort as they climb over the fence. I hear one, then another, land heavily in the thick jungle beyond.

"We're over," calls Ixchel.

"They're bluffing," Gaspar says. "I heard only two . . ."

"That's 'cause I'm here, man," yells Tyler. He emerges from the darkness from where he's doubled back and crept up behind Gaspar. Gaspar swivels and shoots. He shouts as Tyler tries to disarm him with an upward kick.

I falter. I'm scared to shoot now in case I hit Tyler. In the gloom, there's no way to be sure which of the two grappling shadows is Gaspar.

They're wrestling, a close hold. I hear Tyler shout, then gasp for breath, wincing in agony. Gaspar must have jabbed Tyler in his gunshot wound. I leap in closer, swinging for Gaspar's head with the pistol.

I connect with the back of his head. He gasps for a second or two, then grabs my gun arm and yanks my hand all the way to the ground. He's freakishly strong, holding both Tyler and me at bay. Gaspar twists my wrist until I'm forced to drop the gun. My right leg is close enough to get near the gun; I slam the back of my heel into the pistol and kick it far away.

Meanwhile Tyler and Gaspar are still struggling over the weapon in Gaspar's right hand. I try to reach it—it's impossible. With his free arm, Gaspar has my right arm in such a painful hold—one twist and my wrist will snap.

All three of us breathe painfully. I can hear more guards approaching from the east side of the house.

This is not going well.

Into my headset I mutter, "Benicio . . . you gotta help us. There are too many guards . . ."

Abruptly, I relax so that Gaspar falls against me, carried by his own momentum. Just as he's about to crush me, I move away, a classic defensive roll. In the confusion, Gaspar drops his gun. In the dark it's impossible to see where it's fallen. Before Gaspar can reach for it, Tyler kicks him hard in the abdomen.

233

Gaspar releases us both, rolls away, and leaps to his feet. His shadowed figure takes up a *ginga* stance. I hear the smile in his voice. "Come on now, boys. Show me your moves."

We're thrust into the capoeira fight of our lives.

Gaspar flies at us, head low to the ground, legs swooping through the air. His raw power and speed are devastating. I duck and dodge, but not before his foot catches me hard in the back of the thigh. A second kick rips away my radio head-set. Tyler manages to sidestep; he follows up with a series of rapid *queixada* kicks, whirling around and around like a dervish between each one. But Gaspar's moving so fast, he's no more than a shadowy blur. I throw myself into the melee, aiming *ponteira* kicks, dodging low, rolling. Nothing but the most basic moves. Zero elegance.

This is capoeira, street-fighting style. It's more my style, too. Elegance easily escapes me, but survival, I can do. Whatever was missing at the tournament, I've found it now.

The other guards are close now, less than ten yards away. In the sky, there's a loud humming from the east. Instinctively, I glance up to see two sizzling red beams streak across the sky toward us. The ground between the guards and Gaspar,

Tyler, and me explodes—clods of soil and lumps of grass fly in every direction.

Benicio's here—giving us laser-fire cover from the air.

We don't stop fighting—we're all arms and legs and energy. Every so often someone lands a kick, and there's a yell or a groan. But with adrenaline roaring through me, I don't feel any pain beyond the first blow. For the first time ever, I know what bloodlust is.

I want to get Gaspar. I want to land a kick that lays him out cold, or even breaks a bone.

The laser fire stalls the guards for a second, but then some of them turn and start firing at the Muwan. Benicio's zipping all over the place. It's dark—I can only hope it's enough to keep the Muwan from serious damage.

The Muwan fires two more bolts. A guard falls screaming to the ground.

Hearing that, Gaspar's energy seems to double. It dawns on me that Tyler and I can't take him.

I need an advantage. On my next dodge, I roll to the ground. From my back pocket I pull one of Lorena's drug-delivery pens. Meanwhile Gaspar flies at Tyler with a cartwheel attack. Tyler manages to duck, so Gaspar sails right over him and crashes to the ground right in front of me.

I roll the pen in my fist, preparing to surprise him with a stab.

As I'm getting up and he's landing, I swing back, then hurl

myself at Gaspar: a high kick followed up by a tremendous punch as I throw my whole body around, leading with the pen.

It lands against the hard muscle of his shoulder. Gaspar gasps in shock as the spring-loaded needle punctures his skin. His momentum carries him forward, but by now he's out of control. He reels, falling against me and dragging me to the ground. Holding my pen arm hard against the ground, he tries to punch me in the face. But his aim is off, his reactions are slow, and I easily dodge the punches. Then Tyler comes up from behind Gaspar and lands an immense kick to the guy's ribs.

Groaning slightly, Gaspar slides to one side, a hand clutched on his shoulder. He slumps onto all fours, more disoriented by the second.

The Muwan's lasers are still walloping into the ground between us and the guards. Benicio isn't trying to kill them—he's just holding them off. I hear Tyler mutter into his headset, "We're going for the fence. Hold them off a little longer, then meet us at the rendezvous."

Tyler grabs my arm and pulls me toward the fence. We stop in front of a smooth concrete support post. It's about three yards high and no more than six inches wide.

"Give me your hands," Tyler urges. When I open my palms in front of him, he squeezes two dollops of Lorena's grease from the small tube he's been carrying. Then he applies some to his own hands. "You have to slowly peel your hand away from the surface," Tyler mutters, trying it out. "Like this.

Don't just yank it away." I watch, breathless with urgency and seriously relieved that Tyler actually paid attention to Lorena's instructions, unlike me. I slide my palms along each other in upward strokes. I place both palms as high as I can reach on the concrete post, taking care not to touch the electrified wire.

It works. I can hold my whole weight with my palms. The skin on my hands stings and stretches with the effort, but it holds me. I peel one palm—then another—off the post and slap it on a few inches higher. It's incredible. When my hands are actually in contact with the post, I can't imagine that anything will unstick them. But after a second or two I can feel the glue weakening—after just enough time to move along.

Moving up the post like that, I'm over in a just over a minute, and so is Tyler. We land on the rough ground beyond, under a thick canopy of leaves. From the shadows, deeper inside the jungle, I hear Ixchel calling out to me.

I throw a last quick glance to the guards on the other side of the fence. They can't climb over. But they're not going to stop. Someone else is barking out orders: "Shut down the electric current."

Any minute now they'll be chasing us. I reach inside my pocket for one of the slim, powerful flashlights Lorena gave us. I shine the light into the trees until I pick out Ixchel and my mom. They're dazzled by the beam. Tyler and I join them, and then we're all running—due east.

Around five minutes later, we hear the buzz of the Muwan flying overhead.

Five minutes is a good lead. But the jungle is so dense in places that it's slow going. We're about as quiet as a herd of elephants. Between that and the beams from our two flashlights, I can't imagine we're hard to locate.

Our only chance is to reach the rendezvous first. Then Benicio can throw down the rope ladder, we can all hang on, and he'll fly us to safety.

Amazing. Me, Tyler, and Benicio will have done what Montoyo couldn't: rescued everyone.

I'm flushed with confidence as we make our way through the jungle. Ixchel doesn't need any help at all. She's just as nimble and agile as she was the very first time we met, when she guided me through the rainforest to the ruins of Becan. I'm relieved that this time I'm less of a liability—back then I was soaked through, terrified, and nursing a snakebite in my ankle.

I can already feel a few nasty bruises from Gaspar's heavy capoeira kicks . . . but other than that, for once—incredibly—I'm in good shape!

What worries me, as we keep crashing through low branches and thick undergrowth, is Tyler. I can hear it in his breathing—he's in agony. Gaspar caught him more than once in the stitched wound. I can guess how painful that is, remembering my own bullet wound.

I slow down to wait for Tyler. He's bringing up the rear, lighting the way for Mom. He pauses for a second, leaning against a tree. Ixchel stops too. She turns around.

Agitated, she cries, "Don't lean against the trees!"

Tyler pulls away in alarm.

"There can be snakes hanging from trees," she continues anxiously.

From behind us there's a scream. It's just a shocked yell at first, the kind you might make when you trip and fall. But it's followed by the most blood-curdling scream of terror I've heard for a long time . . .

Abruptly as it started, the scream stops.

Tyler, Ixchel, and I stare at each other, horrified.

Mom.

We race back, flashing beams of light all over the foliage. When we see her, we stop hard in our tracks.

She's on the ground, thrashing among dry leaves. Three thick, muscular coils of a giant snake are wrapped around her. Mom's eyes are wild with panic, but she hardly makes a sound above a whimper.

Ixchel says in a loud but steady voice, "Eleanor . . . breathe shallow . . . try not to struggle. It's gonna be okay, we'll kill it."

I'm not so calm; I push past, throw myself onto the snake, and grab its head. With the sharp end of one of the drug pens I stab it in the throat, dragging the tip of the pen down in a slicing movement to tear open its flesh. I grit my teeth the

240

whole time; I don't flinch when the snake's blood spurts out onto my hands.

I've never wanted to kill something so badly.

The coils are still rock-hard for several seconds, until finally they begin to slacken. I pull the beast off my mother and pick her up, hugging her tightly. Not surprisingly, she's still shaking.

I am too. The violence of what I've just done takes me by surprise.

Ixchel puts a hand on my shoulder. "Josh," she urges. "We really need to go."

I wipe the snake blood on my shirt and take my mother's hand in mine. She grabs a few deep breaths and gives a flustered laugh. "Jesus, Mary, Joseph, and all the saints . . . I thought I was dead for sure," she says, which makes me laugh too.

I love it when Mom's Irish side comes out.

We press on, slower now, being even more careful to check everything in our path. It's nerve-racking to make such painstaking progress, knowing the kidnappers are only a couple of minutes behind. I keep pausing to listen for any signs of them. But every time I stop, all I can hear is my own heart pumping, ready to burst.

Every now and then I steal a glance at Ixchel. It's weird, being with her again yet managing not to look at her or think about her (much). I've somehow blocked the thoughts I was having about her—I have to, if I'm going to get through the

241

next five minutes alive. But now I'm confused. Maybe I don't like her so much after all? Maybe she's just a girl running through a dark jungle beside me again?

The next few minutes are pure concentration as we maneuver through a tangle of trees, vines, and leaves. With who-knows-what gross kinds of insects and spiders underfoot . . .

When we hear the rushing water of the river, we begin to breathe more easily.

Tyler speaks to Benicio, telling him to get the Muwan ready. We're sticking like limpets to the compass bearing. Any minute now we'll break through the jungle, onto the narrow riverbank. Anxiously, I look at my mother. She's hardly said a word, not even glanced at me since the anaconda. Is she scared? Or still angry with me for what I said that day on the dunes?

I mean, she can't still be angry. Can she?

We arrive at the riverbank. We're just in time to see the Muwan slowly lowering to a few yards above the river. A rope ladder hangs from the side. I have no idea how we're all going to fit inside the craft—there are only two passenger seats.

I guess Ixchel and I can share one . . .

Under the blue-white landing lights of the Muwan, I spot another problem—Tyler. He's bent double with exhaustion, barely able to stand. His side is soaked in fresh blood; just looking at it makes me shudder. He's fading fast.

From about thirty yards upriver, there's a sound: the rustle of leaves. Then footsteps. I shine my flashlight to see four men rushing toward us. Gaspar's among them—I catch the glint of his fair hair in my flashlight beam.

One of them begins to shoot.

We break out in panic. Mom leaps up and grabs the end of the rope ladder. Tyler tries to reach but staggers, and Ixchel has to catch him.

"That's it, Tyler, get over here," Mom instructs. I watch her in amazement. Despite the fact that she's hanging from a rope for dear life, Mom's voice sounds pretty steady.

"Get your arms around my neck. Hold tight. Now don't you worry, I'll hang on for the both of us."

If Tyler even thinks about grumbling, he doesn't. My mom can be pretty tough to argue with.

The guards are almost upon us. Bullets zing into the river and trees around us. Benicio's already starting to float the Muwan away. There's only enough room on the ladder for one more pair of hands. I grab hold and tell Ixchel, "Do like Tyler. You hang on to me."

Rushing footsteps tell me that the kidnappers are almost here. Ixchel wraps her hands tightly around my neck, clinging to me as the Muwan begins to climb. Glancing up, I'm dazzled by a stream of light. I can see the effort in Mom's face as she struggles to grip the ladder. And Tyler looks ready to drop.

Just a few more seconds.

Then there's confusion. Ixchel's grip becomes a bone-breaking tug around my neck, a deep pain in my shoulders.

Ixchel screams. I can feel her fingers loosening around my neck. I clench my jaw, trying not to yell from the effort of keeping my neck muscles rigid. My head's bending from the weight: Ixchel's being tugged hard from below. I lower my eyes, terrified. There are two guys grabbing each of Ixchel's legs, pulling her back down to the riverbank. And with Ixchel, me.

The Muwan lifts slightly, wrenching another agonized scream from Ixchel. Mom and I are yelling at Benicio to stop lifting the craft.

There's one last, wrenching cry from Ixchel.

Then her fingers unravel, sliding over my neck and shoulders. Ixchel drops.

She drops, and I'm still hanging in midair. I'm yelling at the top of my voice, back for one terrible second in the chill of that moment, gripping the ice claw, feeling the weight of my father's body suddenly vanish as he falls to his death.

Below us, something unbelievable is taking place.

One of the guards grabs Ixchel and holds her, screaming with terror, at the brink of the river's edge. I glimpse flashes of white water under the lights—the river crashing over her feet.

A voice shouts in the darkness, staccato words, like gunfire. It's Gaspar. "The girl goes into the water, Josh. Unless you let go. Now."

"No, Josh, no," Mom shouts desperately. "Please . . ."

I stare directly ahead. Then slowly, down.

My fingers slacken. There's a tight ache in my knuckles. I open my hands, head ringing with Mom's imploring cries.

I can't let them hurt Ixchel. That would be simply . . . impossible.

So I drop.

Arms catch me, hands muffle me. There's a cold bite of pain—a needle slamming into my arm.

A drowsiness washes over me. I sway, trying to catch sight of Ixchel.

The last thing I see before my eyes close is the silhouette of my mother and Tyler, dangling from the rope ladder. Around them, a halo: the glowing lights of the Muwan.

They sail lazily upward, like a hot air balloon. I can't hear them any longer—there's a roaring in my ears. Even the air slows down.

Everything fades.

I open my eyes from what feels like a long night of broken
sleep. There are flashes of dreams left in my memory—but
nothing that makes any sense. For the first few seconds of
being awake, I'm aware of fading images of people carrying
me, of smooth, curved metallic walls, of an almost deafening
roar. Another needle is pushed into my arm the minute I open
my mouth to scream.

I was drugged. We were taken somewhere—where? I
woke up at least once, I'm fairly sure of that. But now there's
no sign of Ixchel. The last I remember seeing of her is her
drugged body, tied up next to mine in . . . where were we?

Then the image-memory makes sense to me. We were in
the cargo hold of an airplane.

Now I'm alone in a room; it looks like a hospital room.
Could be anywhere. I seem to be wearing a hospital gown. I
try to sit up and immediately, something chafes hard against

my wrists. With steadily mounting terror I realize that I'm strapped to the bed. I can't move either arm.

The second I realize that, I begin to struggle. I don't care how much it hurts. There's something absolutely electrifying about being strapped to a bed. I struggle, I yell for help.

Within minutes, the door opens. A nurse strolls calmly toward me, totally ignoring the fact that I'm making a racket. She grabs my shoulders and forces me to stare into her eyes.

"Josh Garcia. Yes? Be quiet now. You won't be hurt. The Professor is on her way to see you. Try to remain calm."

The woman speaks with a French accent. She has short red hair and pink cheeks—she doesn't look much older than me. But when she talks to me, she's expressionless. I gaze back at the woman, silenced by her words.

"Where am I?"

"I can't tell you."

I have an idea, though—a terrible idea. As time passes, I'm starting to remember things, to put everything together. The Professor—the woman from the Sect of Huracan. The one Camila told me was in charge . . . the woman whom Ixchel and I spied on in the Revival Chamber in the tunnels under Becan.

"The Professor . . . ," I repeat. "What's she doing here?"

For the tiniest second, the nurse's bland expression changes—she almost smiles. "Ah . . . so you do know who she is . . . ?"

Before I can answer, someone else comes through the door. A woman, probably in her late forties, very elegantly dressed in soft fabrics in gray, black, and white. Her hair is shoulder-length, light brown with amber highlights. All very stylish. She looks like one of the moms who pick up kids at the ritzy private schools near my house, in their massive cars. Good-looking, I suppose, for a woman that age.

Yet definitely familiar. *I've seen her before.* But where? Immediately, I start racking my brain.

She sidles up to the edge of my bed. She actually smiles.

"Josh," she says softly. "It's good to finally meet you. We didn't get a chance for a real introduction that day in the tunnels."

It's the Professor—the scientist who was with Marius Martineau the day that Ixchel and I stumbled across the Sect in the ancient Revival Chamber.

I scowl. I kind of doubt that meeting her is good for *me*. But I dare not say anything insulting. I mean, you don't. Not when you're strapped to a hospital bed.

"Where's Ixchel?"

The Professor makes a shushing sound. "She's fine. She's done what we needed—she led you to us."

"If you've hurt her . . ."

"I don't blame you for being angry with me," she drawls in her American accent. It's definitely *her*—listening to her voice, my memory goes right back to that morning in the Revival

248

Chamber. "After all, I did bring you here against your will." She gives me a meaningful stare. "I doubt you'd have volunteered, though, would you? Even in the interests of science."

I return her gaze with as much hostility as I can muster. But still I say nothing.

Then, to my surprise, she removes something from the pocket of her flowing gray cardigan.

The Bracelet of Itzamna.

Her eyes meet mine. "You were wearing this on your arm," she says lightly. "What is it?"

I roll my eyes. "As if I'd tell you," I say, after a long while.

"Well, sure, I didn't expect that you would. Even if you actually knew."

I feel sweat break out on my forehead. My breathing quickens.

She's not going to torture me for information about the Bracelet—is she?

The Professor rolls the Bracelet around her wrist for a minute or two. "It's Erinsi, isn't it? The ancients who were really behind the Books of Itzamna and all that incredible technology in Ek Naab."

I'm about to say something vague, when she continues, "Don't bother to lie, I can see perfectly well for myself that it *is* Erinsi. I've seen this kind of writing before. And you know where, don't you?"

Slowly she regards me, as if sizing me up. For a second or

249

two I remember Blanco Vigores's words about the Bracelet being activated by accident. I fantasize that the woman before me will suddenly vanish into a wormhole in space and be zapped into the molten center of a volcano.

But it's not that easy. I've had the Bracelet for months and never yet managed to activate it accidentally.

"I wonder how much you saw in that Revival Chamber," she muses. "Do you even know what the Chamber is for?"

I shake my head. It's the truth—I really don't.

"If you saw as much as I think, then you'll remember this: my colleagues and I in the Sect have been hoping to get your help with some experiments. For as long as we've known about you, in fact. It's not that we're short on males with the Bakab genes. As you must have realized by now, Josh, you're not unique. Except in Ek Naab, where they've been throwing away one of their greatest resources for hundreds of years."

"I don't know what you're talking about," I tell her stubbornly.

She smiles. "Josh, don't be silly. I know that you do. Your friend Ollie told me—you had quite a discussion with her about the Sect, didn't you? And she told you that all but the firstborn Bakabs were eventually exiled from Ek Naab, before they grew old enough to learn the secrets of the city."

I find myself wondering if this woman has any idea how secretive Ek Naab really is. I doubt that even the Bakabs who stay really get any idea of the big picture.

I know I don't.

"What kind of society does that, Josh, to *children*? Can you imagine what those boys have gone through, throughout the ages? Being sent away when their older brothers became the Bakab? Do you think anyone in Ek Naab ever asks themselves what becomes of those boys and their families?"

She's confusing me on purpose. No one in Ek Naab's ever told me that it happened like that. I don't want to believe her.

"Well, they come to us; to the Sect. *I've* found them, their descendants. I'll tell you all about it, if you survive the genetic modification, Josh."

If I survive?

She stares once again at the Bracelet, and then at me. Carefully, she puts it down on my bedside table. "You'll get this back, don't worry. Then perhaps you'll be kind enough to tell us how it works."

"I have no idea," I tell her.

The Professor looks deep into my eyes. "You might be telling the truth, I suppose," she says absent-mindedly. "I guess we'll see."

Who is she?

It's seriously starting to annoy me. There's no doubt that hers is the voice that I heard in the tunnels under Becan that day with Ixchel. But when I look at her face, my mind keeps thinking of Oxford, strangely enough.

"Don't I know you?" I say.

For the first time, she looks slightly disconcerted. Like something might not be going according to some great plan.

"I doubt that. We hardly move in the same circles."

She's lying, I can tell. She's been in Oxford. I concentrate hard, trying to remember. It's something to do with my dad, and Oxford. Somehow, amazingly enough, there's a connection.

I remember. "You're Melissa DiCanio," I blurt. Too late, I realize my mistake. Her mouth hardens into a straight line.

She's Professor Melissa DiCanio—that scientist from Oxford who runs the pharmaceutical company in Switzerland. The one from the news story: I recognize her from the photo. She's supposed to be dead—killed by Simon Madison.

Her voice a low, menacing purr, she almost whispers, "Well, no one is as free as the dead . . ."

The Sect faked her death. Now she can do anything she wants.

She pauses, gazing at me with an unmistakable air of threat. "You've got lovely eyes, Josh. I hope they're as attractive after the experiment."

The blood drains from my face.

What are they going to do to my eyes?

I pull against the wrist straps again, even though I know it's useless. DiCanio keeps watching me, interested to see my reaction, but entirely without pity. As if I were just some lab rat.

I'd love to reply with some tough talk, but I can't find my voice. The sheer ludicrousness, the horror, of the situation is

252

nauseating. It's like some nightmare James Bond thing . . . I literally can't believe it's happening to me. Yet there's nothing vague, weird, or dreamlike about anything. It's all too starkly cold and real.

"I can't deny it's a risky procedure . . . ," she admits. "If you hadn't come along, we might have been forced to try it on one of our own people." Her eyes twinkle dangerously. "But imagine how unpopular that would make me in the Sect."

Finally, I bring myself to say it. "What are you going to do to me?"

DiCanio inhales deeply. "Nothing less than this, Josh: the genetic procedure will change the course of your destiny."

I wait, but she says nothing for a long while. I'm desperate to ask *Will it hurt? What are the chances of it going wrong?* But I don't. She's not getting the pleasure of watching me dissolve into tears like a terrified kid.

Eventually she concludes, "When you wake up, Josh, all being well . . . I believe you'll be more than happy to join us in the Sect."

Are they going to brainwash me—from inside my DNA?

It's a struggle to keep my voice from shaking, but I do it. "I will never, never help you, no matter what you do to me. Not after what you did to my dad, to my sister, to my mom, and to my friends."

DiCanio leans in close and puts her mouth next to my ear.

"We had *nothing* to do with your father's disappearance. But you're right to fear me, Josh; I'm relentless. The fate of the planet is at stake. I won't let a teenage boy stand in my way."

She pulls away and stares down at me, her expression dark and fathomless.

I look back at her, but can't answer.

There's a taste like ashes in my mouth when I wake up. For several seconds I have the strongest sense of déjà vu. I'm alone, strapped to a bed in a barely furnished hospital room.

Did any of that stuff with the Professor woman actually happen? Or did I dream it? The last thing I remember is that redheaded nurse approaching me with a syringe. I was literally rigid with fear.

I tug at the straps.

Amazingly, my wrists slide right through them. The straps have been unbuckled.

I'm free.

But who unbuckled them, and why? I'm entirely alone. The room is exactly as I remember it. Even the Bracelet of Itzamna is precisely where I remember DiCanio leaving it—on my bedside table. I pick up the ancient relic and slide it onto on my left arm until it won't go any higher.

In no time at all I sense the familiar surge, a sizzle of energy between my skin and the Bracelet.

It's definitely a specific thing, this weird electricity between the artifact and me. The Professor didn't seem to experience anything similar when she touched the Bracelet. At least, she didn't mention it to me.

But then, I guess she might not tell me anything . . . who knows?

Slowly, I climb off the bed and test my legs. They seem fine. I'm still wearing the hospital gown, but when I glance toward the end of the bed I notice a heap of blue and green clothes and sneakers. They're mine.

Needless to say, they weren't there before.

Someone has tried to rescue me. Were they disturbed before they could wake me?

I remove the gown and give myself a quick once-over. Pretty much as expected, my chest and ribs are covered with bruises from Gaspar's capoeira blows. But apart from the bruising, I seem to be okay. There's a bandage on the inside of my left forearm; when I pull it away there's a blood-soaked dab of gauze.

Okay, so needles have been plugged into my arm . . . but that seems to be all. Whatever they did to me, it doesn't seem to have caused any obvious damage.

Unless they haven't started yet. Or maybe the changes are

inside me—something I won't know about until I eat or drink or talk?

I test my voice, quietly. It seems all right. I check my face with my fingers. That seems okay too. Then I remember that she mentioned my eyes. I blink a few times. My vision seems unaffected. I don't seem to have x-ray vision or anything cool . . .

So what was DiCanio talking about?

Quickly, I get dressed. The door to my room has a small glass window. I peer through into the corridor before opening it. It's empty. I dart out and walk down the corridor until I come to what I recognize as the door to a cold room, similar to the one in Lorena's research department in Ek Naab.

I can't resist taking a look inside. I found some pretty useful stuff in Lorena's cold room. Who knows what I might find in here?

Inside, I'm shivering within seconds. I don't seem to be able to handle the cold as well as I used to. Is that a side effect of the genetic treatment?

Fear twists my guts. Is this how it's going to be for the rest of my life? Every time I feel some new or strange sensation, wondering whether something is going wrong inside me? Waiting and wondering when and how my body is going to betray me?

My gaze passes over some metallic shelving, on which sits a large glass case with a sliding door. I catch my reflection in the glass and metal, just for an instant. That's when I glimpse it for the first time.

There *is* something odd about my eyes.

I focus, staring hard at my reflection in the shiny aluminum. It's such a simple thing, but even so, it takes me seconds to figure it out.

My eyes have turned *blue*. Nothing too distinctive; not a deep or violet shade. Just everyday pale blue.

Carefully, I poke a finger into my right eye. I force myself to touch the eyeball. There doesn't seem to be a contact lens there.

My eyes are *actually* blue.

Now that's a real change. Just as I'm starting to feel elated that it isn't something grim, I wonder what else they've done. The Sect wouldn't have gone to all that trouble only to change the color of my eyes—would they?

Suddenly it's all shockingly real. They've changed the inside of me—altered my DNA. But *what* have they done? Will I ever really know?

It's a bombshell. I blink rapidly, now incredibly aware of my eyes. Leaning against the glass case on the metal shelving, I slowly focus on the contents—a bunch of plastic tubes with blue screw-cap lids, in a rack. Each one has a long label, handwritten in black marker.

I stare at one of the labels. Once my brain registers what I'm looking at, it's unmissable.

AGYLIHRPPREIKGR

The fifteen-letter sequence of the Key. Is the Sect still working on making the crystal version?

Very gradually, I begin to figure out where I must be. The newspaper story mentioned that Professor Melissa DiCanio ran a pharmaceutical company. I can't remember the name, but it was definitely in Switzerland. That must be where they would store the Crystal Key—in the company's top-secret labs.

So I'm in Switzerland, not the jungle of Brazil. That explains the airplane. If I can only find Ixchel, maybe we can break out of this place, escape.

Switzerland: organized, efficient. How hard could it be to get around such a country?

I'm at the point of turning away and leaving the cold room to look for Ixchel, when I turn back. I stare long and hard at the tube with the label **AGYLIHRPPREIKGR**.

Could it be that the actual Crystal Key is in there? The object I've been searching for, obsessed with during the past months—what if it's actually here, just inches away?

With a hand that trembles not only from the cold, I pick out the tube and unscrew the lid. Inside is a coin-sized piece of Styrofoam. I pluck it gingerly between two fingertips and pull it away.

Underneath, lying on a farther wedge of foam, there it is. It's beautiful.

They did it; the Sect actually did it. They managed to grow the Crystal Key.

A crystal: not particularly shiny like a diamond, yet definitely a crystal. It's about as big as a pea and roughly diamond-shaped, but with at least eight faces of different sizes.

I roll up my T-shirt's sleeve to expose the Bracelet of Itzamna. Holding my breath, I pick out the crystal with utmost care and position it over the dimple in the Bracelet. It's going to fit—more or less. But I have no idea how I'm going to keep the crystal in place. I'm still holding my breath when I push the crystal into the depression on the Bracelet.

I gasp. The metal of the Bracelet seems to melt around the edges of the crystal. Some of the symbols light up from some hidden power source. I didn't realize that the Bracelet had moving parts, but from the vibrations through my skin, I sense that it does. Parts of the outer casing slide over each other, revealing a smaller panel covered with symbols that start to flash. Another symbol, which seems to be made of what looks like mercury, actually changes shape before my eyes.

There's a scarily steady rhythm to the shape-changing. Like seconds counting down.

With a jolt of dread, I register the fact that the roaring noise in my ears isn't just my own fear. From outside the cold room, there's a steady noise like a siren. Somewhere in the lab, an alarm has gone off.

I've triggered something—maybe when I took the tube holding the crystal, or opened the glass case that contained it. Either way, I'm about to be toast. Judging from the commotion outside in the corridor, the security guards just sprang into action.

With a kind of fascinated horror, I stare at the Bracelet on my arm. It's counting down to something—but what? The newly exposed flashing symbols keep cycling through the same series of flashes. Am I supposed to press something?

The Bracelet of Itzamna can be activated by accident.

This must be what Blanco Vigores meant. He said it happened to him too, when he first found the Bracelet. The Bracelet of Itzamna is active now; it's going to transport me somewhere in time and space. Maybe I need to press some of the symbols . . . but I'm way too scared of making a mistake to risk it. Desperate, I try to unclip the Bracelet.

The release catch has vanished into the inside of the device. I can't move the Bracelet.

I'm trapped—going wherever the Bracelet of Itzamna decides to take me.

The door to the cold room clunks heavily, opened from the outside. Harsh voices reach me from the corridor.

"There's someone in here . . ."

I feel the rise of panic. This is unstoppable. Let's hope I don't end up inside a mountain . . .

There's no blinding flash or anything. It's as though a tear appears in the world around me, like a mask ripped off to reveal the true features underneath. The cold room vanishes, torn away in one gigantic sheet. Instead, I'm in a long, bare corridor, with a concrete floor and walls of bare rock. Faint strains of music drift from somewhere down the corridor. I can't hear much more than the soft, steady rhythm of a snare drum. Dim electric lighting flickers unsteadily overhead. I take a few steps forward and see a heavy metal door. It's slightly ajar. I push the door gently and peer inside. The music gets louder.

I know this song—but what's it called? Something about the tune drills deep inside my head. There's a sense of a dream half-remembered. It feels like something connected with my father, but also . . . with Camila.

I shiver from the sheer impossibility of what's just occurred to me. This really can't be happening . . . can it?

Not again . . .

I'm staring into a prison. Most of the room is separated off with floor-to-ceiling bars. There's a man sitting in a cell about ten yards square. He's wearing an orange-colored jumpsuit and sitting on a wooden stool facing away from me, reading a book.

He doesn't have to turn around for me to recognize him. I know my father from this angle—his head in a book, cool jazz on the stereo.

I clear my throat quietly. "Dad."

I try my best to stay calm when he turns around, but don't quite manage it. He turns around and meets my eyes with an expression of such joy that a lump forms in my throat. He leaps up, drops his book, and rushes to the perimeter of his cell.

"Josh! Josh!" He laughs, incredulous, hands gripping the sides of his face. Then I'm against the bars and hugging him, feeling his beard against my cheek. When I look at him again, he's so thrilled that tears have come to his eyes.

"*Hijo*, Josh, what"—his eyes roll with amazement—"what are you *doing* here?!" He laughs again, more dazzled by the second, and throws his head back. "This is incredible! Do you have any idea how much I've dreamed that I'd see you again? That somehow you'd just walk through my door one day? And now you have! God, it's unbelievable!"

Dad's joy is infectious. But I can't quite give myself over to it. I need to understand what's just happened. Because if my dad's alive, then . . .

I've gone back in time.

"Dad, Dad . . . where are we?"

He looks puzzled. "You don't know?"

I shake my head.

"Inside Area 51," he explains. "In a deep underground military base. But if you didn't know that . . . how did you get here?"

Silently, I roll up my sleeve and show him the Bracelet. That instant, his expression changes completely. He looks at the Bracelet for a long time, not touching it. Then, carefully, he runs a finger around the depression that holds the crystal. He looks back at me.

"The Bracelet of Itzamna."

I nod. "I fixed it—I found the Crystal Key! Now I'm going to get you out of here. You know how to use it, don't you, Dad?"

He takes a deep breath. "Yes, I do."

We both gulp, moved by the utter seriousness of what I'm suggesting. Instead of getting on with it, Dad takes a step back, his chin in one hand. He looks me up and down slowly, as if seeing me for the first time.

"You're older. Taller. Your arms, your chest, they're bigger. Even your face—you're getting a square jaw . . ."

"I'm fourteen," I tell him.

"But . . . there's something else . . . something very different about you . . ."

"My eyes," I say. "They're blue. From a genetic experiment. Long story . . ."

If he's surprised, he doesn't show it. In fact, he seems to be thinking deeply. Bluntly, he says, "You're from the future, aren't you? When did you get here?"

"Less than a minute ago."

My dad is speechless; he just looks at the ground, shaking his head.

"You found the Crystal Key . . . and fixed the Bracelet? When?"

I shrug, puzzled. What's he getting at? "Right before I used it."

Dad's expression intensifies. "No one used the Bracelet since you found it?"

Now I'm frowning. "Well, no. It was broken."

Dad starts muttering to himself. "He found it . . . fixed it . . . ended up here . . . which means . . ."

"We have to send you back into the past," I interrupt, pushing my face against the bars. "And stop the NRO from capturing you and bringing you here."

But when Dad looks up again, there's a sad smile on his face. "Why?"

"Because unless we do, bad things happen."

"'Bad things'? You look to be in pretty good shape, Josh. How's your mother? I miss her so much, you have no idea."

I swallow, nervously thinking of what my mother went

265

through when my father first disappeared, and then when he really died. How can I tell my dad any part of that? I decide to stick to the bare bones.

I don't want to have to tell my dad that unless we get him out of here, he's going to die.

"Mom? She's okay—now. It's been hard for her . . . really hard."

He nods thoughtfully. "I wish we had more time, Josh. But we don't. If I'm right—and I think I am—we have probably five minutes."

"Before the guards come?"

"Before I use *my* Bracelet."

Now he's completely thrown me. "What?!"

My dad lifts up his right arm and pulls back the orange sleeve to reveal the Bracelet on his forearm. "Your Bracelet is mine—but from the future. If you just used it a few minutes ago—that means that it was last used to leave this place about five minutes from now."

I stare at him blankly. "Huh?"

"You don't know how to use the Bracelet, do you, Josh? So listen carefully now. I'm serious. Your life and the lives of millions of others may depend on it."

Anxiously, I lick my lips. "What? No. You have to use my *fixed* Bracelet to escape. And I'll use the old Bracelet . . . to get to wherever it's going."

Which, I now realize, must be Mount Orizaba. Dad's

broken Bracelet would zap him from here to the slopes of the volcano.

Well, not in my new timeline. This is the *zero moment*. From here, everything changes.

I stretch an arm through the bars, trying to reach my father's wrist. "Give me your Bracelet. Show me how to use it. I'll be fine—come and look for me on Mount Orizaba. Dad, can you remember that? Orizaba."

My dad steps back. "Don't you know you can't trust your memory when you use that device?"

I falter again. "My memory?"

"Amnesia is a risk with the Bracelet. That's what Vigores told me. Use it and you risk losing your memory. Even worse, you risk ending up inside a mountain—or in space. There's only one safe way to use the Bracelet—that's the default."

"How do I do that?"

"It's simple. Press hard on the crystal. It triggers the safety mechanism."

I stare in astonishment. "Safety mechanism?"

"You just used it, Josh. It takes you back to the same place, ten minutes before you last used it."

"Ten minutes?" I'm so baffled by everything that I can't quite follow or believe what my dad is telling me.

My dad points to his own Bracelet and the empty crystal chamber. "You said you fixed the Bracelet. You used it and it brought you here. That means that the Bracelet returned you to the place and time it was last used. Don't you see, Josh? In a few minutes I'm going to use this Bracelet . . . If I don't, then you wouldn't be standing here."

I push forward, my voice urgent. It's all beginning to make a horrible kind of sense.

Amnesia.

"Not you, Dad, me! Take your Bracelet off . . . give it to me!"

He looks sad. "I can't. It's locked into position. When the NRO captured my Muwan, I panicked. I started the countdown . . . and then I stalled the countdown. The Bracelet is locked on my wrist now until it's used to transport me."

"You stalled the countdown?"

"Well, it was kind of a crazy thing to do in the first place. To use the Bracelet without the crystal is practically suicide! Without the time-control circuit, the most likely thing is that you get zapped into space!" He grins ruefully. "I decided to take my chances with those NRO bastards. So yes, I stopped the countdown."

I stare at my dad in sheer frustration. "Dad! You have to get that thing off your arm! It's not safe . . ."

Now I get it: if my dad uses the Bracelet, he's going straight to Mount Orizaba . . . he's losing his memory, and everything will unfold just the way it did.

My plan will be ruined.

My dad gazes at me curiously. "Where did you say to meet

268

you, Orizaba? You don't want me to use the Bracelet to go there—yet somehow you believe it's safe for *you* to go to Orizaba . . . ?"

I start to shake my head. "Don't use it." I've changed my mind—maybe the best thing is not to use the Bracelet at all. We'll both stay, tackle the NRO together, and change the timeline a different way . . .

Dad echoes, "*Don't* use it . . . ? Josh, what's going on here? Who sent you? Why are you here?"

"No one sent me. I'm here because I want to save your life. And Dad . . ." I stare at my father, dreading what I have to tell him. "If you go to Mount Orizaba, you're gonna die."

That doesn't faze him as much as I'd expected.

"I've faced death a few times since we last saw each other, Josh," he says, leaning forward suddenly.

He has no idea how literally true that is from where I'm standing . . .

"Death doesn't worry me," continues Dad. "But you . . . you do. What's been going on? Why are you involved?"

"I found the Calakmul letter," I say bluntly. "I found Camila. I found Ek Naab. I found the Ix Codex."

He staggers slightly, a smile spreading across his face. "You . . . you did all that?"

"It should have been you, Dad. Take my Bracelet and get out of here. I'll find another way out of this place."

"Josh," he laughs, "this is Area 51! They will *never* let you

269

out of here!" He faces me with grim resolve. "No. This is how it's going to be: I'm going to use my Bracelet—complete the countdown. I'll go to Orizaba, and everything will pan out just the way it did. You'll use your Bracelet—to go right back to where you came from." He winks once. "Except . . . ten minutes before you set out. Safety mechanism, okay?"

I shake my head in desperation. "No . . . Dad, NO! I came back here to save your life! To change the past . . . to stop everything from going wrong . . ."

"You think I'm going to risk the life of my own son to save my skin?" He shakes his head. "Josh, you don't know me very well." He grips my shoulder hard and makes me look him right in the eyes. "How do you know I die on Mount Orizaba?"

I stare back at him, lips trembling. "Because I was there. I saw it."

He nods. "But you didn't die."

"No, Dad," I whisper. "You died saving me."

That silences him. For a second or two, we just stare at each other. Dad's stereo is still playing the same song. It breaks across our silence, tugging at some part of my memory.

My dad takes a step forward, stretching an arm through the bars. An expression of fierce pride crosses his face. He pulls me close and presses his lips against my forehead. "That's good enough for me," he breathes.

After a few seconds he releases me, a quizzical, faraway

sort of look in his eyes. "You look so different with blue eyes. You remind me of someone I knew . . . a long time ago."

I stare at him, hardly able to believe what I'm thinking.

"I remind you of someone . . . ?"

He nods. "You do. A guy I knew when I was not much older than you."

My voice drops to a whisper. "Was his name . . . Arcadio?"

It's as though someone hit my dad in the face—he looks that stunned. "Josh . . . no . . . it can't be."

Am I Arcadio?

Dad keeps shaking his head. "No . . . no, Josh, please. That can't be your life. It's too dangerous."

"What . . . what's going to happen to Arcadio?"

I'm not getting through to my dad. He's still reeling from the implications of what I've said, talking frantically to himself.

"Arcadio . . . you? No . . . it can't be . . . You?" And finally he stops pacing the cell and stares at me. "It's true. You remind me of Arcadio. How do you know about him?"

Where do I begin?

"Dad . . . is Arcadio a time traveler?"

Dad presses his lips together, deep in thought. Then he says something that astonishes me. "Promise me you'll only use this Bracelet once—right now. Promise me!"

I'm dumbstruck. "What? Dad . . . why?"

Dad is becoming more serious and thoughtful by the

271

second. He doesn't speak again for several seconds. Then urgently he says, "Give me your arm, Josh."

Baffled, I stretch my left arm through the bars. He grabs a pen from his bed and then takes hold of my arm, scrawling something on my inside wrist. When he lets go, I stare at what he's written.

I am Josh Garcia from Oxford, England, son of Eleanor and Andres.

"Use the Bracelet just this once, Josh. Go back to where you came from. Then never use it again!"

I'm about to answer when there's a sound from somewhere down the corridor. Hurried footsteps, and they're on their way to us. Frozen, I stare at my dad. His eyes widen; he grabs my arm.

"Okay. This is it."

My mouth drops open. "What . . . ?"

With his other hand, my dad ruffles my hair. He smiles, his eyes shiny with emotion. "Good-bye, Josh."

I'm too astounded by the speed at which things are moving to take his words in. "Dad, don't go, please."

With a nod, he steps back. "If it's meant to be, we'll see each other again, Josh. Don't worry."

The footsteps are right outside the cell. I'm paralyzed, watching as my dad presses something on his own Bracelet.

"Press on the crystal, Josh," he murmurs. "It'll take you right back."

The door to the cell opens, but I can't take my eyes off my dad. A surge of white light emerges from the Bracelet and envelops him. For just a second he glows like some unearthly apparition. And then all that light seems to contract, as if it's suddenly been sucked down a drain.

He's gone—to Mount Orizaba. To a life fractured by a lost memory, a few months living like a hermit, and then to that final, fateful day of the avalanche.

Where he'll save my life by giving his.

When the three uniformed soldiers barge into the cell, I hardly even give them a glance. They all aim their guns at me.

"Get your hands up where we can see them," barks one of them, aiming a semiautomatic rifle at my head. Then he screams, "Now!"

I sigh despondently, shake my head, and raise my arms slowly. Another soldier steps forward to search me.

"What just happened to the prisoner?" shouts the first soldier.

I sigh again. "You know what . . ." Then I reach one arm behind my head and, through my sleeve, press hard on the crystal.

"Stop moving! Get your hands back in the air!"

It's too late. Already the soldiers are being ripped out of my field of vision. Instead, the surrounding air fills with the nearby walls, shelves, and lab equipment of the cold room.

Just like my dad said, I'm back where I came from—the

273

mysterious lab where the Sect took me and Ixchel after Brazil. Except that according to Dad, it's ten minutes in the past—ten minutes before I first used the Bracelet.

Well . . . ten minutes? In ten minutes you can change the world.

At a time like this, you need a watch. But I don't have one. I can almost hear the seconds ticking away in my head as I search the cold room for something that might help.

Ten minutes from now, the past version of *me* is going to walk through the door of this cold room. I don't know much about time travel, but that sounds a lot like *time paradox* territory; I'm pretty sure I want to avoid being here for that.

On one of the metal shelves I find what I'm looking for—a gray plastic stopwatch, like a kitchen timer. I set it for nine minutes. Not taking my eyes from the clockface, I begin to think.

Dad didn't have time to show me how to use the Bracelet correctly. But I can use it in safety mode. If I hit the crystal again, I'll go right back to Dad's underground prison . . . and probably meet myself!

But that's not what actually happened. I know because I was there. If I do try to go back, I guess I might even cross over into a parallel reality where I do meet myself. Yet another paradox . . . My head hurts just thinking about it. I can't risk something like that.

As I start to think through the possibilities, the potential power of this Bracelet begins to make me feel dizzy. I mean, it's incredible.

Time travel!

It was just a dream before. Now it's real. And I don't know how to control it.

Just one press of the crystal will buy me ten extra minutes with my dad.

Eight minutes to go before past-me comes crashing through the door.

In the past, Dad's in a secret base in Area 51. In the present, he's dead and buried. He died saving me.

For the first time, a shadow falls across my plan.

Past-me is going to come through this door. But only if someone frees me.

Ixchel is somewhere in this building. If I could find her, we could escape together. Right now, no one knows I'm free—for all they can see, I'm still lying in a hospital bed, until someone unbuckles the straps that tie me down. Until someone frees me—someone thoughtful enough to bring my clothes.

My heart begins to sink. It's me—I'm the one. Who else? *I'm the one who sneaks in and unties myself.*

If I don't do it, I won't find the crystal. I won't fix the

Bracelet. I won't get a chance to go back in time to see Dad. I won't even be here wondering what to do.

Seven minutes.

The way I see it, I don't have a choice. If I don't . . . this timeline might just disappear right now.

So I leave the problem with Dad to one side. I have problems to solve in the here-and-now. Like, where do I find the clothes to leave at the end of my hospital bed? How am I going to get out of this building?

Leaving the cold room is a tense moment. Behind that thick fridge-style door, there's no way of knowing if someone's in the corridor. Grabbing hold of the timer, I close my eyes, hold my breath, and push. When I see that the corridor outside is empty, I exhale.

There are some lockers a few doors farther down. I dash over and try opening them until one gives way. My clothes and shoes are heaped up in a pile. As I pick up the jeans, I notice some extra weight and bulk. In the back pocket is one of the drug pens I took from Lorena's lab. My Ek Naab and UK cell phones are in the front pockets.

Bonus!

I stash the drug pen and phones in my own pockets. Then, holding the clothes and shoes, I rush back to the room where they performed their experiment.

I'm inside the room in the next few seconds. I drop the clothes at the end of the bed, exactly where I remember finding them. I have to get this just right. No mistakes—or who knows what will happen . . .

I unbuckle the wrist straps, trying not to look at the sleeping body on the bed.

My own sleeping body.

That was me, about six minutes ago. Or even less. It strikes me then—this sleeping version of me still has to wake up, get dressed, find the cold room, and fix the Bracelet.

All in less than six minutes. A heart-stopping thought hits me. Did I really do all that so quickly?

I have to wake myself up now!

I put my mouth right next to my own ear and whisper loudly: "Josh—wake up! Go to the cold room down the hall. Find the Crystal Key, repair the Bracelet."

Anxiously, I stare at the closed lids of my own eyes. There's an agonizing second or two while nothing happens. Then they begin to flicker.

I glance at the timer. Five and a half minutes.

Time to leave.

I race down the corridor toward a group of doors. Something's pumping through me; it feels exactly like adrenaline, but it's just a single word, an idea.

Freedom.

It's so close that I can taste it. I only have to find Ixchel and we are out of here. For the next five and a half minutes it's as though I don't exist: I'm off the radar.

Passing the elevator lobby, I see I'm on the fifth floor of five. An elevator is on its way to this floor. I dive into the nearby stairwell.

Time to make a choice. Where would they be keeping Ixchel?

Some companies put their cafeterias on the highest floor—but not this place. I guess that a secretive pharmaceutical company puts its most secure facility on the top floor.

My guess is that Ixchel is somewhere on the fifth floor, too. But there are so many doors . . .

I take a deep breath. All I can do is try every possible door. I peer from behind the glass in the stairwell door, waiting for the elevator to arrive. Two passengers step out, both wearing white coats. They're deep in conversation. I don't recognize either one. I watch as they disappear down the corridor, then I push the stairwell door open. I'm just in time to see them vanish behind a door about halfway down the corridor.

A door only yards away from the one where by now past-me is awake and getting dressed . . .

That was a close shave.

I stride to the door nearest to the stairs, which are at the extreme end of the corridor. It's a solid door, with no glass window. There's a red light beside it, which isn't lit up. I open the door to find a room full of camera equipment and trays of vinegary-smelling liquids. A photographic darkroom.

The next door leads to a small lab—I can see that much by

looking through the window. Looks like it's unoccupied right now. The next door is solid, with a nameplate. Someone's office? I decide to pass it by.

The next door is also solid. But there's no nameplate. I push it open slightly.

Amazingly, a voice I recognize says, "Who's there?" Someone yanks the door wide open.

It's Ollie. Now that I see her, I'm not totally surprised—I guess she goes where the Sect sends her. Still, it's a bit of a jolt—for Ollie too. Seconds tick past on the clock as we stand, frozen, gaping at each other.

"Hi, Ollie," I say, trying to sound cool. Ollie stares at me as if she can't decide whether to yell for help or not. Her eyes and mouth are doing that whole *You? Here? Really?* kind of thing.

"Your eyes . . . ," she says, gazing at my face with an expression of wonder. "It works!"

She's obviously confused. The idea that I could have escaped seems simply impossible to Ollie. So I decide to play along. "The Professor told me to come to you. She wanted you to be the first to see."

Ollie gazes at me, now obviously moved. "She . . . she wanted me to be the first to see . . . ? So she's not still mad at me?"

The Professor was mad at Ollie . . . ?

Ollie takes a step forward. She looks older than I remember.

Her hair isn't as blond or lustrous; her face seems less rosy. I guess she's stopped making an effort to look sixteen; her clothes certainly look more grown-up: brown jeans, a white blouse, a long blue wool cardigan. She's still pretty, but looks tired and a little drained. All that confidence that used to burst out of her—it seems to have vanished.

Looking at her now, I don't like her even a bit. In fact, I wonder what I ever saw in her.

"Josh," she says, touching a hand to my hair. "Still so cute. Blue eyes suit you!"

I struggle not to push Ollie's hand away. For some reason, she's in the doghouse with the Professor—I'll have to find a way to use that.

"What about the other genetic changes?" Ollie asks suddenly. "Have they worked too?"

So there are other changes. Anxiety surges through me again, like a wave of nausea. What have they done to me? So far I seem to be okay. Is that going to change? Soon? Or do I have years to wait, worrying?

I just nod. "It looks like it, yeah. The Professor sent me down here to get you."

"She's going to make the announcement . . . ?" Ollie asks, eyes round, hopeful.

If you say so . . .

I keep nodding. "Uh-huh." I reach into my back pocket for Lorena's drug pen.

"And I'm invited?" Ollie continues with a smile of amazement. I try to smile, concealing the pen behind my wrist. I step forward, in what I hope is a friendly way.

"And Ollie, I just wanted to say . . . the Professor told me to say . . ."

I put a friendly hand on her shoulder. Ollie's face is a picture. The Professor's approval really seems to mean something to her.

"No hard feelings, Ollie, okay?"

Yeah, right.

Behind Ollie's back, I slide the pen into position. Just as I'm going in for an all-friends-again hug, I jab it against her neck, feeling the spring-loaded mechanism burst inside. For one still moment, Ollie's eyes stare directly into mine, with a look that's half-shock, half-betrayal.

She collapses through my arms and slides to the floor trembling as she falls into unconsciousness. I watch her drop, and can't feel any pity at all.

Softly I mutter, "But now I think you're really gonna get it . . ."

I'm standing in a windowless room that has floor-to-ceiling bookcases against every wall. Rows of bound science journals cover the shelves. In the middle of one wall is a door. I try the handle, but it's locked. From behind the door I sense movement. I lean against the door and put my mouth close to the surface. In a low voice I call, "Ixchel . . . ?"

There's a pause, then an amazed reply. "Josh . . . ?"

For a second, relief washes over me. Then I'm looking around for a way to open the door. From behind the door Ixchel says, "Ollie has the key, Josh . . ."

Right—of course she does. As Ollie lies sleeping on the floor, I go through her pockets until I find the key. I open the door to find Ixchel standing before a window through which sunlight streams. For a second I can't move. Luckily for me, Ixchel doesn't hesitate. She rushes forward and hugs me tight. After a second I squeeze her back. Over her shoulder, I gaze at the view.

A blue-green river glistens like a slug trail in the sun, right in front of the building. To the left, the river snakes off into a lake. Across the river a field of mountains rises from the ground, surrounding the lake. In the distance they're jagged, crooked, white.

"Switzerland," I breathe, releasing Ixchel.

Ixchel freezes, staring at me. I'm getting that look again—the one when someone I know first sees my eyes. A half smile. In Ixchel's case, it's followed up with a frown.

"Blue eyes," she says. "Uh-oh . . ."

Before I can ask her to explain, she continues, "So, hotshot, do you have a plan this time?"

I give her a sheepish grin. "Um . . . nope."

Ixchel pretends to sigh. "Well, your eyes may be different . . . but you're the same old Josh."

I *do* have a plan! It goes something like this: run down the stairs, get out of the building, then keep running . . .

Oh yes, and somehow find time to stop and call Benicio. Not sure exactly how he's going to get me out of this, though. Switzerland is a very long way from Ek Naab. Even with a Muwan.

We make it to the stairwell. We get all the way to the third floor when the commotion hits. An alarm goes off, followed by all kinds of running noises and shouting. I'm guessing that someone has found Ollie and the open door to Ixchel's room. Maybe even my own vacant hospital bed.

Which means that by now, past-me is hiding in the nearby cold room, about to discover the Crystal Key, about to activate the Bracelet of Itzamna, about to zap back through time and space into the underground military base in Area 51.

About to meet my father.

I get a little shiver thinking of that. For me, that's all in the past, but past-me is about to get one of the shocks of his life. Of *my* life.

I've experienced the past ten minutes of time *twice*. Is this what they call a time paradox, or a time loop? It doesn't seem paradoxical to me, though. Just like some more stuff I did to get out of a tight spot.

I stepped outside of time and helped myself to escape. Weird, but true.

Some of the guards are heading in that direction already. I heard them when I first lived through this moment in time. There could be others too. There usually are . . .

I've caught up to myself—my ten minutes are up. I can't help grinning as we almost tumble down the stairs.

I bought ten extra minutes. I think I spent them pretty well.

At the bottom of the stairwell there's a fire exit. It only opens one way—to the outside. It isn't guarded at all. I guess they built the place with the idea of stopping people from getting in, not out. Ixchel and I push heavily against the fire door, and we're into the company parking lot.

At least, I assume it's the company parking lot, which is

already packed. I spot at least two signs as we dash past: Chaldexx BioPharmaceuticals.

Yep—that rings a bell. It's the name of the company from that news story.

The Professor definitely *is* Melissa DiCanio. I'd say she's in pretty good shape—for a corpse.

From behind us, I hear the sound of the fire door being opened again. I risk a tiny glance over my shoulder to see two security guards racing toward us. They're led by a fair-haired, dark-skinned figure that I recognize.

Gaspar.

I flinch. Even in that split second I've seen enough to realize that Gaspar is very, very angry with me.

"Faster," I say to Ixchel.

She gets just one word out as we speed away from the building and down toward the riverbank. "Where?"

I can't answer that. Mainly because I have no idea. The river? There's nowhere else.

"Look for a boat," I yell, speeding ahead of Ixchel.

Staying to fight isn't an option. No more drug pens—and I don't imagine that Gaspar will let me slither through his fingers a second time.

There's a line of trees on the riverbank. We bound through them, desperate to get some cover in case Gaspar and his pals start shooting. Then it's along the riverbank, toward a nearby bend in the river. After that there's a small harbor lined with about ten pleasure boats.

With Gaspar and his men less than fifty yards behind us, we can't risk slowing down. I put my head down and run harder, pulling even farther away from Ixchel.

I only hope she doesn't think I'm abandoning her. One of us needs to get to a boat and get it started up—and fast. As the harbor comes into view, I start hunting for a boat that might not be locked.

I don't know what time it is, but my senses tell me that it's morning. There aren't too many people out on the boats. Over on the river I can just see the edge of a big cruise steamer heading for the road bridge. Beyond that, the river runs clear to the lake.

Scanning the line of white speedboats, something catches my eye. At the far end of the mini-harbor, a man is guiding his boat in between a dinghy and another speedboat.

Over my shoulder I call, "Ixchel . . . gonna head for that boat . . ."

If he sees me coming, the guy doesn't get suspicious until the last second; he's too busy turning off his engine and steering his boat. By the time I get close enough to jump for it, the boat owner is already fiddling with the moorings.

I leap off the edge of the pier and land smack in the center of his deck. The guy is so stunned that he hardly reacts—at first. Once he's realized that I'm actually daring to try to steal his boat, he makes a grab for my shoulder and starts to punch. He's in his late forties or so, quite a bit taller and heavier than me. When that first punch lands near my ear, the whole side of my face rings with pain. In fact, there's definitely something wrong with my right arm—it feels weak and slightly tingly. No time to wonder why, though—so I concentrate on ducking to avoid his follow-up punch. A tirade of what sounds like German streams out of his mouth. I recognize at least one swear word.

Well, yeah. I'd be mad too, if some scruffy teenager tried to steal my boat.

I twist free of his grasp and drop into a low defensive roll. There's just enough room to swing to my feet and fly at him with a couple of rapid *queixada* kicks. I land blows to his chest and gut. The second kick knocks the wind out of the guy, who is clearly out of shape. As he's doubled over, I shove hard and then high-kick him. Staggering in stunned bafflement, he topples and falls overboard into the river with an almighty splash.

I turn around just in time to see Ixchel flying through the air toward me. I don't even have time to step aside—she crashes straight into me, almost knocking me to the deck. Gaspar and his men are close. They've almost reached the harbor.

We have one chance to get this boat moving. I've never driven a speedboat before. But Ixchel has . . .

I don't have to ask her to get started—she pushes past me, goes straight to the engine, and yanks on something. The boat jerks into motion. Seeing that we're about to move out of range, Gaspar puts on a final spurt of energy. He leaps into one of the nearby boats and then jumps from boat to boat. We're still moving slowly, trying to navigate through the other boats. He's only one boat away by now . . .

"Pull away!" I yell as Gaspar jumps from the last boat in the row. Our boat moves away just in time to watch Gaspar crash into the edge. He lands in the water, but grabs onto the boat, gripping, and tries to swing his legs up onto the deck. I push all my weight against him and shove a hand into his face, pushing him back. We struggle for a few seconds, him trying to climb aboard, me leaning my whole weight against his face. The boat picks up speed and wobbles as we turn toward the lake.

With a final shove, I push Gaspar off the boat. By the time he hits the water we're already away.

But we still have a problem. The other two security guys from Chaldexx seem to have found another boat to commandeer. It's pulling out from the mini-harbor and sluicing around toward Gaspar. I gaze down the river toward the lake, trying to think.

The big river cruiser I spotted moments before is turning slowly, just ahead of the road bridge. In fact, if we don't make it to the bridge pretty soon, we're going to have trouble squeezing past the cruiser. Ixchel has seen it too—I can tell by the way she's leaning forward, urging the engine to go faster. But it just won't. Our boat has a top speed of . . . something not very fast.

I can't tear myself away from the front of the boat, staring out over the windshield.

"We've got to go faster . . . ," I say, feeling helpless.

"I know, I know, you wanna try?!" Ixchel says, exasperated.

I make myself look back, past Ixchel and toward the second boat. I almost freeze in panic when I see how fast it's moving. I guess they've picked up Gaspar by now . . .

The space between the fat paddle steamer and the road bridge narrows. The steamer doesn't seem to have any problem with taking up all the space on the river and making the smaller boats wait.

"We have to make it to the road bridge!" I yell.

"I know, Josh . . . hold on tight . . ."

Briskly, Ixchel steers the boat, almost knocking me over. We bank hard to the right and then make a headlong rush for the last remaining gap under the road bridge. I can see it getting smaller by the second.

"Keep going!" I urge. The second boat is gaining, no doubt at all.

The last few seconds are pure nervous energy. I'm helpless to do anything about it. Ixchel just stares ahead, her features tense with concentration. We head for the gap, the second boat now less than ten yards behind. I think we might just about make it . . . but will they get through too?

If they do, we've had it.

We spring through the gap with what seems like less than half a yard to spare between us, the boat, and the road bridge. As we pull through, I'm aware of a small crowd of people watching us from the deck of the steam cruiser. They look angry and hugely disapproving, some of them actually shaking fists and wagging fingers at us.

The second boat has decided to abort the attempt—it stalls with a crazy spin, sending a huge wave crashing into the air. Spray rains down on the deck. There's a chorus of outrage from the tourists.

We're clear to the lake. That river cruiser has bought us a few precious minutes. Even as I take out my Ek Naab phone to call Benicio, I can't help worrying.

Will we have enough time?

"Hey, Josh, what's going on?"

Benicio sounds deliberately cool. I'm a little surprised, given that I might have been dead and everything. His voice changes then, becoming urgent. "Is Ixchel with you?"

"Yeah," I reply, a bit miffed at his reaction. "She's driving the boat. I can hardly hear you 'cause of the engine. You're gonna have to shout, okay?"

"What?"

I have to bite my lip to stop myself from yelling angrily through the phone. This is a very bad time for Benicio and me not to make ourselves clear.

"We're in Switzerland," I tell him slowly, shouting.

"I know that, Josh, I can track your phone when it's on, remember? You're on Lake Brienz."

"Where?"

"Go to Interlaken," he says. "It's a city behind you."

"We're running away from there!"

"Oh . . . damn."

There's a silence. Ixchel and I look at each other, exasperated.

"What's he saying?" she calls from the back of the boat. I shrug dramatically and then point back to where we came from. "He says that's Interlaken."

"Can you stop the boat?" Benicio says. "I can't hear you very well."

"Can't stop!" I yell. "We're being chased! The Sect took us to Chaldexx BioPharmaceuticals."

Benicio goes quiet again. "What are you doing?" I ask, getting annoyed by the silences.

"I'm trying to find a place for us to rendezvous. My ETA in Interlaken is thirty minutes. You're lucky—we knew you were in Europe, so I've been flying around here. Someone must have turned your phone on at some point."

"Benicio," I tell him, now really shouting, "we can't go back to Interlaken! They. Are. After. Us."

"Cool it, buddy; I know. Okay. I've got it. You're on a boat, yes? You need to get off the lake and onto the road. Find a car."

"Find a car . . . ?" The idea of racing through the mountains sounds pretty cool, but I have to admit I've never handled a car in traffic . . . "Dude, I don't drive!"

"Of course not," he continues smoothly, "but Ixchel can. At the end of the lake is the town of Brienz. Find a car. Take the left fork on the road after Brienz. Keep going to Lake Lucerne. I'll find you, got that?"

"Brienz," I repeat. "Lake Lucerne. Got it."

I close the phone, slip it back into my pocket, and look back at Ixchel. For the first time since I rescued her, she smiles at me.

"Is he coming for us, Josh? That's so great—we did it!"

I nod, try to smile, and say, "He's coming, all right. But not for a while. We have to keep moving."

Behind us, the paddle steamer has totally blocked the river under the road bridge. It's too far away to see what's going on, but I imagine there's probably something of a quarrel with Gaspar and his men. The people on that steamer seemed pretty irate at our stunt; looked like they were ready to hand out a mighty telling-off.

Under a milky sky, our boat cuts a deep white V into the clear green depths of the lake. Forested mountains on either side of us create a dark, brooding atmosphere. In the distance to the right is a spectacular expanse of high, snowcapped peaks. There's a suggestion of mist on the lake, thickest near the bank to our left. Past the beach I can see a small town: a few stylish old buildings nestled among a cluster of log-cabin chalets.

Brienz.

Looking around, Ixchel says, "Josh, this place is beautiful!" She beams at me.

"Stick with me, babe," I tell her. "I'll take you to all the best places."

Wow. I can't believe I actually said that. But it's too late to take it back. I try to look like I'm concentrating on something else, but secretly watch Ixchel for a reaction. She just smiles a little and says nothing for a while.

"Well, life sure is a lot more interesting when you're around," she eventually says.

I turn away to hide my grin.

She likes me.

Behind us, the paddle steamer has finally cleared enough space to let Gaspar's speedboat through. I brace myself to watch them bursting free and ramping up the chase. But they're nowhere to be seen. I search the lake and river behind the steamer for any sign of them—but they really seem to have gone.

"Have they given up?" Ixchel asks. I guess she can sense that I'm puzzled.

"I can't believe it . . . ," I say. "But where are they?"

For now, it looks like smooth sailing all the way to Brienz. Anxiously, I eye the lakeside road, where a steady line of traffic zooms by.

Out here in the middle of the lake, we're not exactly hard to spot. The sooner we get to Brienz, the better.

"Josh," Ixchel begins, "how did you get free?"

I've been wondering when she'd ask that. I've realized that there's a limit to how much I want to tell Ixchel about the Bracelet—for now.

"The Bracelet," I say. "I fixed it, then went back in time by ten minutes and freed myself."

"You did *what*?"

"I fixed the Bracelet. The Crystal Key—the Sect has it! They made it—it's in their lab. I woke up in the bed after the experiment . . . I'd been untied. I picked up the Bracelet, snuck into the cold room nearby . . . and found the Crystal Key. Then I put the crystal into the Bracelet; I went back in time by ten minutes. I freed myself—ten minutes in the past." I pause, realizing that I'm breathless with excitement. "That's when I came to find you."

Ixchel stares at me in wonder. "You figured out how to use the Bracelet?"

I grin. For several seconds Ixchel says nothing, staring out over the water, seeming to concentrate on getting the most out of the boat's engine. I'm surprised that she isn't more delighted, but for some reason the news seems to have put Ixchel into deep thought.

"How did you figure out how to use it?"

I need to be careful—I'm not ready to talk about what happened in Area 51 with my dad. I don't want Ixchel knowing that I might be Arcadio . . . that's way too complicated. I mean, Arcadio gets together with the young Susannah St. John . . . which is too weird for even me to get my head around just now, let alone remind Ixchel about.

But it's tough to keep something this important from her.

Cautiously, I say, "I didn't figure out anything. I just pressed the crystal into place and—bam! There I was."

"There you were," she echoes doubtfully, "ten minutes in the past?" Ixchel lifts her eyes to mine for a long moment, and then turns the boat to avoid another boat coming the opposite way. The sudden movement sends a fine drizzle of spray into my face, but I don't wipe it away.

"Well, that's amazing . . ." She stares up at me again. "You traveled in time?"

"I didn't know what was going to happen," I say. At least that part is true. "I just wanted to see whether the Bracelet could be fixed. But it must have some sort of default mechanism . . ."

"A what?"

"A fail-safe," I suggest. "Maybe to use in emergencies. I guess if you're in danger, it's always safe to take you back ten minutes . . ."

"I guess," Ixchel says, but she doesn't sound entirely convinced.

Of course, it's even safer to take you to *where* and *when* the Bracelet was last used. I can't imagine how the Bracelet knows where it is—I can only guess that it has some kind of GPS, like a satellite navigation system. Only, with the added power to bend time.

Is there some ancient Erinsi satellite in orbit around the planet? Have I just activated a mechanism that hasn't been used for centuries? Did my dad activate it when he used the

297

bracelet? Or is Itzamna, the original time traveler, still wandering around the space-time continuum, doing who knows what?

No use worrying about it now, though, because unless we manage to get to Lake Lucerne before Gaspar and his goons catch up with us, we'll end up right back with the Sect.

This time, I imagine they'll be quite forceful about getting information regarding the Bracelet.

I peer toward the distance at the cars streaming along the lakeside road. Gaspar's in one of those cars. And there's not a thing I can do about it.

The town of Brienz rises up ahead, dwarfed beneath a rocky mountain face that drops sheer into the blue-green waters of the lake. Dark-timbered chalets and yellow-and-cream-painted buildings cling to the mountainside, their balconies decorated with baskets of red flowers. A red railcar chugs along a steep slope. There's a promenade at the edge of the lake, and beside that a little harbor of water that's crystal clear to the rocky bottom.

"So I've been meaning to ask," Ixchel begins. "What's that writing on your arm?"

I blush. "Nothing."

Ixchel gives me a curious glance. "It's not 'nothing.' In fact, I've seen it . . . I just asked to know why. Why did you write your name on your arm, Josh?"

I sigh. There's no easy way out of this. "Because when you use the Bracelet, you can lose your memory. Like my dad when we found him on Mount Orizaba. Remember?"

She's silent for a bit. "You really used the Bracelet, then," she muses.

"I said I did, didn't I?"

To that, Ixchel says nothing. As we get closer to the town, a high rustle of tinkling bells carries across the water toward us. It doesn't seem to be coming from the red-roofed church spire; this sounds like lots of little bells ringing at random.

Ixchel stands up for a better view. "Now what?"

I take a deep breath. "Well, now we have to steal a car."

"Steal a car," she says casually. "Is that all?"

I eye Ixchel closely to see if she's kidding—she's good at keeping a straight face.

Ixchel switches off the engine as the boat floats into the harbor. She looks up at me, and for a moment, we share an uneasy smile. I try not to think about the stress of what is about to come. Just twenty minutes or so . . . and we'll be meeting Benicio on the banks of Lake Lucerne.

If we manage to steal a car.

If the Swiss cops don't jump on us.

If Gaspar and his men don't catch up.

The way I see it, that's three big *if*s. I'm starting to get a really bad feeling; twenty minutes is stretching into a painful length of time.

The side of the boat clunks against the pier. A few bystanders throw us suspicious looks. Two young teenagers on their own in a speedboat may not be an everyday sight for the people of Brienz. Then there's the fact that we don't look very Swiss. Nervously, I help Ixchel tie the rope to the mooring. The bell-tinkling noise is much louder now. I keep looking around to see its source, but so far there's no sign.

An elderly woman pauses as she walks by. She fixes first Ixchel and then me with a glare. Then comes a garble of sharp-tongued German. I don't understand a single word.

"*Französisch*?" Ixchel replies hopefully. If it's possible, the old lady eyes us even more beadily.

"*Que vous faites*?" she says in a guttural accent.

Ixchel answers her with a stream of perfect-sounding French. I just gape. "How many languages do you speak?" I mutter.

"Languages . . . are what I do . . . ," she replies under her breath, still gazing sweetly at the Swiss lady. "You didn't notice?"

Whatever she said to the woman, it worked. She continues on her way, and we climb out onto the pier.

"I told her I was parking the boat for my father," Ixchel explains as we scurry toward the main street.

Finally I can see the source of the bell-tinkling. The streets are filled with cattle. Huge, long-haired beasts coated in toffee-colored fur, with their little cream-skinned calves. Brass bells hang around their necks, swishing back and forth as they walk, led by young cowherds.

I have to catch my breath. All the traffic is stalled—cars

paused where they stand as the cattle navigate around them. Pedestrians and drivers look on admiringly at the animals. Some people stop to take photos. The town is at a standstill.

How are we going to get out of here?

Ixchel turns to me. Outwardly she looks calm, but I'm beginning to wonder if it isn't something else: resignation.

In a flat voice, she says, "Okay, what now?"

"Don't give up on me, Ixchel," I say softly. "We *are* going back to Ek Naab."

With a tiny shrug, Ixchel turns away. I can sense that she doesn't believe me. My heart sinks. How can I blame her? This is the third time I've tried to rescue Ixchel. The idea that we'll get caught again is an almost choking fear.

I look once more down the cattle-filled street. The cows are processing through the main part of the town and then up a side street. Firmly, I grab Ixchel's hand.

"Let's go."

I probably look quite a bit more confident than I actually feel, striding along the narrow lanes of the lakeside town. Yet it's looking like we might be trapped in Brienz—and that's hitting Ixchel pretty hard. I have to do something to cheer her up; something to make escape seem possible.

A moment later, we're in one of the side roads and away from the cattle procession. As carefully as possible, we start trying the doors of the parked cars.

All locked.

A woman driving a small white Peugeot almost knocks us down as we dive across the road. She gets out in a rush, her face flushed with anger, hardly even looking at us as she dives into a nearby door marked "*Arztespraxis*"—something to do with a doctor's office, I'd guess, from the green cross.

Ixchel's eyes follow the woman and then trail back to her car.

"She didn't lock it."

Something tells me that this is our only chance. I dash across the road and test the car door—Ixchel's right, it's open. If the car is an automatic, I've got half a mind to insist on driving. One glance dashes that idea. Manual transmission—no chance!

But there's also some very good news: the keys are still in the ignition.

"I guess that lady's in a hurry," I say, helping Ixchel into the driver's seat.

I'm just belting up in the passenger seat when the woman reappears.

Ixchel starts the car and swerves out into the road, speeding toward the main street. Behind us, the owner's expression turns into outrage and astonishment. I can hardly believe my eyes as we approach the main street. There are still some cows straggling through; the traffic remains stalled. Ixchel drops the car into a lower gear and makes it mount the wide sidewalk. Even through the windows I can hear the angry shouts from pedestrians as they leap out of the way.

With all the lunatic driving I've made people do these past few days, it's a wonder I haven't killed anyone . . .

"You're . . . crazy," I say, impressed. "How come you drive so well?"

"Never really driven in traffic before," she replies, eyes fixed on the road. "Only around the ranches above Ek Naab."

One of the stalled cars we pass suddenly roars into action. I turn around to watch as it turns clumsily in the middle of the road, narrowly missing a couple of huge cows in the process. Then, like us, it mounts the sidewalk and heads out of town, against the traffic.

Chasing after us.

"It's Gaspar," Ixchel says. I can hear the tension in her voice.

I close my eyes, trying to think. This does not look good. We haven't even made it out of Brienz and we've already got Gaspar and his thugs on our tail. The Swiss police can't be far behind either.

Once we've passed the cattle, we join the main road. Luckily there's not much traffic in the out-of-town direction. Ixchel speeds up to sixty-five miles an hour. I glance behind to see that Gaspar's car—a red Mercedes—has also sped up.

"You need to go faster," I urge Ixchel.

She hesitates for just a second, and then slams her foot down. The engine roars as we approach a hundred. I have a sudden flashback to being in the car with Camila on Highway

304

186, just seconds before we crashed. For a brief moment, I can't breathe.

A signpost zooms up ahead—a fork in the road. Before I can open my mouth, we've followed the road around to the right. As we flash by, I notice the word "Luzern" on the sign.

"Um . . . ," I begin, then look over my shoulder. Gaspar's car is approaching the signpost too. In the distance I can hear a siren.

Ixchel says, "What?"

"I think . . . we should have turned left there . . ."

Turn left after Brienz . . . that's what Benicio said. I can't believe I forgot.

In disbelief she says, "Turn left?"

"You didn't see the road sign . . . ?" I say mildly. "To Lucerne?"

Ixchel explodes. "No, Josh, I'm the one driving the car . . . didn't you notice?"

There's no way around this. We can't turn around—not with Gaspar and now maybe the police behind us.

There's a slow-moving tractor up ahead, pulling neatly stacked bundles of chopped wood. Our car swings out as we move to pass. Ahead, an oncoming car squeals noisily, honking its horn—but Ixchel slots the car back into the lane just in time.

I murmur, "Nicely done . . ."

We approach a curve in the road. Ahead, the sky fills with

305

towering, snow-capped peaks. I check behind us—no sign of Gaspar. I guess it might take some time for them to get around that tractor.

I take out my Ek Naab phone and try Benicio. But there's no answer.

"Well . . . ?"

I swallow. "We may have a problem."

Ixchel resumes her stony silence. We churn through another few miles, zooming through a forest of pines. I stare ahead, feeling pretty useless. I can't tell if Ixchel is angry with me, too scared to talk, or just concentrating on driving. All I know is that we need to stick together through this. Ixchel needs to know she can count on me—but I've already messed up.

Maybe I should be the one driving—if I could actually drive—because it looks like I'm useless at navigating. I need to come up with something new, and fast. We're racing headlong toward a wall of mountain, cutting off any easy way to escape. Any minute now, Gaspar is going to pass the tractor. In that big Mercedes, it won't take them long to catch up.

There has to be a solution. One glance at Ixchel is enough to tell me that she's using up everything she has just keeping this car on the crazy mountain roads. It's going to have to come from me.

I don't know where this road plans on taking us, because we're running out of ground. A sign up ahead reads Sustenpass.

Softly I say, "A mountain pass."

"There's nowhere else to go," Ixchel says, "except up."

In the rock face that looms above, I catch glimpses of cars moving sluggishly, zigzagging back and forth. They're practically in slow motion.

"Oh no," Ixchel breathes. "We really are in trouble now."

So far there's still no sign of Gaspar's car. That tractor must have held back quite a line of traffic, because for a long way behind us there's no sign of a car.

We slow down, approaching a hairpin turn.

"Don't brake on the turn," I suggest. "Or we'll skid. And accelerate as soon as you're straightening . . ."

Ixchel shoots me a questioning look. "I thought you couldn't drive."

"I know the theory," I say.

307

"Sure, and I'm the one behind the wheel."

I flush. "Just trying to be helpful."

Ixchel says nothing. She's gripping the steering wheel so tightly that her knuckles have turned white. She takes the first few hairpins so slowly that I'm starting to get nervous. At this rate, Gaspar won't have much trouble catching us.

To take my mind off it, I try calling Benicio again. Still nothing.

Surely he's close to Lake Lucerne now? Why isn't he phoning me?

I put a hand on Ixchel's shoulder. "You're doing really well."

The encouragement seems to work, because she takes the next turn a bit faster. And the next two. In fact, by the fourth, my stomach is starting to lurch. Then I make the mistake of looking over the edge of the road.

It's a sheer drop of several hundred yards.

"Don't look down," I warn Ixchel.

"You think I'm crazy? I'm looking straight ahead . . . and nowhere else!"

My hand moves to my mouth, hiding a smile. Ixchel is even cute when she's scared.

At the next bend I look down again. That's when I see the red Mercedes. Gaspar and his men are only two curves away from us.

"Okay," I tell her. "I want you to stay calm . . ."

But there's an unmistakable edge of panic to her reply. "Gaspar?"

"Yeah. Just keep driving. You're doing great."

"Josh . . ."

"Yeah?"

"Look at the gas level . . ."

I follow Ixchel's paralyzed stare. The arrow is in the red zone. We're almost out of gas.

"Oh, you have got to be kidding . . ."

I gaze back over the road. We're most of the way up the mountain face, overlooking a forested valley cradled by mountain peaks. At this altitude there's snow piled high at the edge of the road in banks as tall as me. The temperature outside drops. The car windows begin to fog up.

Perilous mountain roads, an inexperienced driver, low on gas, and now we're having trouble seeing through the windows . . .

At that moment my Ek Naab phone rings. I almost leap out of my seat.

Benicio shouts through the phone, "Where the hell are you?"

"We're on the *Sustenpass* . . ."

"I know that! What are you doing there? I can't land in these mountains."

"We're almost out of gas, Benicio. The guys chasing us have almost caught up."

309

Benicio swears quietly a few times. Exasperated, he says, "What do you expect me to say? Keep going as far as you can. I'm getting a good lock on your location . . . I'll stay close. At the top of the pass there's a small lake at the base of a glacier, if you can make it that far, I can land around there."

"Okay . . . what if we don't?"

He's silent for a second. "Keep going. I'll call you when you're close to the lake."

But as I snap the phone shut, it's already too late.

The red Mercedes has just pulled around the last bend in the road. It bears down on us until I can see Gaspar's eyes in the mirror. He looks triumphant; he winks and gives us a little mock-salute.

Then their car rams ours from behind. We skid slightly; Ixchel pushes harder on the accelerator. They speed up, catching us at the next turn and slamming hard into the right rear. Our car goes into a tailspin. It looks like we'll twist too far to make the turn.

I shout, "Hit the accelerator—not the brake!" The car straightens just in time.

My phone rings again. "There's a place I can land up ahead!" Benicio yells. "At the next hairpin turn, there's a little place for stopping. I'll be waiting!"

We hit the first long stretch of straight road, thickly lined with snow and deep-green pines.

"Put the pedal to the metal," I urge.

"I'll kill us both!"

But when the Mercedes creeps up behind us again, she doesn't think twice. Even so, they match our speed, and then pull out to pass.

"Don't let them pass! We have to get to the rendezvous with Benicio!"

There's nothing we can do. Gaspar's car is already drawing level in the opposite lane. It starts to snow: a drizzle of thick, wet flakes. I flip the windshield wipers into action.

Ahead, a truck trundles around the corner, heading toward our position. For a second the Mercedes pulls even farther ahead, daring to go for the pass. Ixchel screams as the truck hurtles straight at Gaspar's car.

"Don't let them in!" I shout, grabbing hold of the wheel.

At the last second, Gaspar chickens out. The Mercedes's brakes squeal as it drops back in line behind us. The truck whizzes by close enough for us to feel the rumble of its wheels. As soon as the truck has passed, Ixchel swings our car out to block Gaspar from passing. I check the fuel level. It's right at the bottom.

Our car, the Mercedes, and the truck: we all shoot past the stopping place. I guess not one of us gives a second glance to the Muwan parked there . . .

Ixchel wails in despair. "Josh—what are we gonna do?"

"Don't let them pass us, Ixchel, keep driving . . . let me think . . ."

After the next curve, the terrain changes. The road clings to the edge of a slope, dropping off steeply to a forested valley on the right. There are hardly any trees up here, just snow-coated scrub. The snow falls more thickly. Heavy mist hovers over the road ahead. To the right we can finally see across the valley from which the mountains rise. They dominate our entire field of vision now, rising like an apparition out of the clouds: snow-smoothed peaks over ashen rock.

I check the fuel gauge. It's practically empty. We're running on vapor.

In the distance, I spot a pool of milky-green water. Behind it there's a long trail of gray ice flowing from somewhere high. It must be the lake and glacier Benicio mentioned—but I can't see a way down to it.

Our car enters a cloud slung low across the valley. We're enveloped in gray, damp mist so thick that we can't see more than a few yards ahead. Ixchel slams on the brakes. The Mercedes finally shoots ahead of us.

Then she groans. "Oh no . . ." We're almost at a standstill. Ixchel pumps away at the accelerator, but nothing happens.

"We're out of gas!"

Through the mist, I can just make out that the Mercedes has pulled off to the side of the road.

"We have to get the car off the road, Josh . . . or someone will crash into us . . ."

Eyes glazed, we both stare ahead at Gaspar's car. One

of their doors opens; a shadow appears at the side of the Mercedes as someone climbs out.

Our car comes to a halt. I look across at Ixchel. Her hands are still gripping the wheel. Violently, she begins to shake, her teeth chattering.

I put a hand on hers. Her muscles are locked rigid.

Gently, I say, "Ixchel . . . let go . . . we need to get out of the car."

Actually, we need to run for it. I have no idea where. We're almost out of options.

The gray figure of Gaspar walks through the mist toward us, slowly. From behind us there's another sound—a third car enters the cloud. It speeds just beyond our car and screeches to a halt.

The cops.

Two uniformed policemen spring out of their car, making a beeline for us.

I unwrap Ixchel's fingers from the wheel and squeeze her hand.

"It's okay, Ixchel . . . we're safer with the police than with the Sect . . ."

She can't stop trembling. The stress of the car chase has finally slammed into her. Ahead, Gaspar has stopped moving.

Both doors are yanked open. One of the cops starts shouting at us in German.

"I think they want us to get out . . . ," I whisper. Ixchel

313

nods slowly, still shaking. "Come on, Ixchel," I tell her. "It's gonna be okay now . . . we'll just let them arrest us . . ."

We're both about to step out of the car when from the direction of Gaspar's car there's a muffled, almost squeaky sound—a shot being fired. The cop at my side of the car slumps to the ground, stone-cold dead.

Lightning-fast, the second cop ducks behind our car. A second later he pops up again and fires a round into the fog. It's followed up by a barrage of bullets in our direction. Some of them hit the car, shattering the rear window, bursting a tire.

Ixchel and I cower in our seats, bent double, clutching our heads.

My Ek Naab phone rings. My own hand trembles slightly as I answer it. The gun battle isn't letting up. A bullet explodes into the back of the passenger seat, and I almost jump out of my skin.

"You have to get out of there!" Benicio's voice screams against my ear.

"Oh, ya think?" I reply. "*Where are you?*"

"I'm right next to you, buddy, I'm right here. I'm hovering under the road, at the edge of the mountain."

I gasp. "Hovering . . . ? What do you expect us to do?"

"Jump," he says firmly. "Move in a straight line from your car to the edge of the road. Jump off. I will catch you."

In this fog, there's no way I can check whether Benicio is right or not.

"Benicio is here. We have to run for it," I tell Ixchel. "Get over to this side—we need to crawl out together."

Ixchel hesitates for a second, then slides across my knee. We squirm around until we're both lying across the front two seats with our heads next to the passenger door. We're completely squashed together, but thankfully Ixchel doesn't seem too bothered by that.

Of course I'm not bothered by it either, not one bit . . .

I raise my hands above my head, getting ready to push on the door.

Right then, the windshield shatters. Crumbled glass rains down over us and scatters across the floor of the car.

My eyes meet Ixchel's. "It's gonna be okay . . . ," I murmur. "On the count of three, crawl out, stay low, and get to the edge of the road. You'll see Benicio there. He'll catch you."

Silently, she nods.

"One . . . two . . ." I push the door open, hard. "Three!"

We both drop to the ground, slithering out of the car on our bellies. The edge of the road is only a yard or so away—and we have the shelter of the car.

We crawl within inches of the dead body of the first policeman. I almost throw up when I see what the bullet did to his head. He's dead because of us—because he chased a stolen car.

The soggy air is filled with the sound of gunfire. One person has died because of us—and the second one has no hope

315

against Gaspar's men. We have to do something to help this guy. I can't leave this place with two innocent deaths on my conscience.

We slide under the guardrail that lines the edge of the road. The lights of the Muwan greet us, glowing white and blue behind the fog, hovering about three yards below the road.

Benicio—he really is here.

The cockpit opens and Benicio stands up. He's less than two yards away from the edge of the road. I can't quite make out his face, but I can see him stretching out both arms.

He calls, "I'll catch you . . ."

I nudge Ixchel forward. "You go first. Jump out as far as you can, and put your arms out so that he can grab you."

We look at each other one more time. With one smooth movement Ixchel gets to her feet and leaps off the edge of the slope, arms outstretched . . . flying. The Muwan dips slightly when she lands smack-dab in Benicio's arms. I hear her relief as she tumbles into the passenger compartment.

Behind me the gunfire is relentless. Abruptly, the cop stops shooting. Gaspar's men yell something; I hear them rushing forward, toward the edge of the road.

They start shooting at the Muwan.

"Give up, Josh," calls Gaspar, his voice coming from somewhere close. I'd guess he's just behind the car. "Hand yourself over, boy. How many people have to die?"

I watch in dismay as the Muwan drops out of sight under the cloud. When I look around again, Gaspar is right next to me. He gives me a smug grin.

"Okay, Josh. Game over."

Before I can budge, Gaspar grabs hold of my left wrist and twists it hard, into an armlock. I'm opening my mouth to gasp when he pulls me against him fiercely, wrenching my arm even further. An agonized yell leaves my throat.

He pushes me down to my knees and presses his foot against the back of my neck. Slowly, he forces me to bend all the way to the ground.

"I could snap your neck right now, you know that, don't you?"

My eyes water from the pain. I just nod.

"I'm not going to end up like Simon and that girl, Ollie, doing only the stupidest jobs. After all their training! No. The minute they put me in charge of hunting you down, boy, I told them: no problem. Okay? With Gaspar on the case, you got a deal. You cannot fight me, boy, I will always win. You hear me?"

I nod again, my face stinging as he pushes me harder against the gravel.

He shouts, "You got that, Josh Garcia?"

"Yes!" I groan in reply, voice muffled.

"You're gonna work for us now. You're a miracle of science, you know that? A walking Nobel Prize for DiCanio. You should feel honored!"

"What did she do to me?" I manage to ask.

He repeats, "What did she do . . . ? Man, what *didn't* she do? The whole nine yards. You've got it all, kid. You're wayyyy too valuable to lose now."

Behind us there's a sudden crunching sound—a body rolling on the ground. Then a single gunshot, followed by a scream of pure agony. Loud, uninterrupted groaning follows—I get a terrifying vision of pain. Gaspar turns away for a second, evidently shocked by what he's just heard.

It sounds like someone is dying. But is it Gaspar's man? Or the cop?

Gaspar loosens his grip just enough for me to get some wriggle room. In another second I'm out of the armlock, attempting a dodge roll. His attention returns with laser-like focus. He sweeps a foot into my ribs—it's like being kicked by a horse. I'm so winded that I can only lie motionless, gasping like a fish tossed onto the deck.

There's another gunshot; the bullet whizzes past above Gaspar, who stops moving. I tilt my head slightly for a better view. Like a ghost emerging from behind a veil of gauze, the figure of the second Swiss policeman appears. He holds his

319

arm rigid, straight, he and the gun merging into one shadowy killing machine. In the distance, the groans subside, replaced by an occasional pitiful whimper.

"In my country," the cop begins in halting, heavily accented English, "we do not tolerate child killers."

I whisper a prayer of thanks. Gaspar says nothing.

"Move away from the boy," says the cop.

Gaspar hesitates, then takes one step away from me. I finally manage to catch my breath and suck in a few freezing-cold gulps.

The gray shadow-cop waves his gun slightly. "Farther away."

Gaspar takes two more steps away from me. I struggle to my feet, still slightly unsteady. Gaspar and the cop stare at each other for a few seconds.

"Take out your gun," the cop orders, "and throw it to the ground, over here."

"I'm no child killer," Gaspar says slowly. "The boy is a runaway. Look what he did—he stole a car."

"You killed a police officer. My partner. This we also do not tolerate."

"It was an accident. If I wanted the boy dead," says Gaspar, "he would be."

But still Gaspar won't obey.

I can hear the policeman's breathing quicken. He takes aim and points the gun straight at Gaspar's head. "Boy . . . get behind me."

I shuffle around until I'm behind the cop. Another groan from Gaspar's man shatters the silence.

"Your friend is going to bleed to death," the cop tells Gaspar. "I shot him in the belly—not a nice death. Throw down your gun and I'll handcuff you; we'll take your friend to the hospital. Maybe he'll live. As for your other pal . . . a life for a life."

Gaspar doesn't move.

In my pocket, the Ek Naab phone buzzes.

"If you answer that phone," Gaspar seethes at me, "I'll kill this cop."

The policeman bristles. "Silence!"

I breathe quietly through my mouth. This cop has no idea how fast Gaspar can move. He might get one shot off before Gaspar's on top of him. Or Gaspar will throw himself into a wild, unpredictable capoeira move.

One thing is for sure: the longer these two guys keep staring each other down, the less I can believe that the cop is ever going to shoot Gaspar.

Chances are, Gaspar senses it too.

My decision's made. I bolt away, back toward the cars. The cop's gun goes off, and then I hear two voices, yelling. I keep running hard along the mountain road, past the cars, farther into the thick cloud. I can't see anything now but fog; fog and the solid line of asphalt beneath my feet. I'm running full tilt, the sounds of my footsteps squelched in the damp air, blood thundering in my ears, no sound but my own heartbeat.

Against my thigh, the Ek Naab phone buzzes again. I feel like yelling with rage at Benicio—*I'm a little busy now, think you could call back later?!*

Through a haze of adrenaline, I become aware of a sound behind me.

Footsteps, hard and swift, twice as rapid as mine. They're chasing me, coming closer. It can't be long now; any second. Fear surges within; I squeeze a last effort from my legs.

Then, to my right, there's a mist-muffled voice.

"Josh! Jump! I'm right with you, buddy . . . I got a lock . . . just jump . . . I'll catch you."

Run off the edge off the mountain—without even look-ing first? The idea fills me with terror. I keep running. Even to change direction would be too risky now. Gaspar is mere steps behind me—I'd run right into his grasp.

"You're coming to a bend in the road, Josh," Benicio calls. "Keep going! Jump! Jump right out!"

I put my head down for a final spurt. Without warning, I burst free of the cloud. Sunlight explodes around me. I can see everything—the road, the valley, the mountains. The sheer drop to the bottom of the valley.

Hovering in midair, just beyond the road, is Benicio's Muwan.

Immediately before I hurl myself at the road's fence I hear Benicio shouting, "Josh . . . trust me!"

I grab the fence with both hands and spring off into a

handstand flip. The valley spins around me as I turn in the air. I fly across the divide, the Muwan directly below.

The cockpit is open, but I don't quite make it. With a thud I land just short of the opening, clutching at the edge of the cockpit, scrabbling for a firm hold. For a few breathless seconds I hang one-handed over the edge. With a gasp, I swing my other arm over and grab hold with both hands. When I gaze up, it's straight into Ixchel's eyes. For once, they're filled with admiration.

"You did it, Josh . . ."

Benicio lowers the craft all the way to the floor of the valley. I relax my grip and crumple to the ground. From the front of the Muwan, Benicio's triumphant voice yells, "Nice flying, Batman!"

All the fear and tension vanishes, replaced by a surge of euphoria. We made it. Me, Tyler, Mom, Ixchel—we all escaped the Sect.

About fifty yards above I catch sight of Gaspar leaning over the edge of the road. He stares down in disbelief. I grin and give him a little wave.

Hasta la vista, baby.

BLOG ENTRY: SLEEPING IN A CITY THAT NEVER WAKES UP

Well, it turns out that I'm not done with the blog. I'm back where I started, with a whole bunch of things I can't talk to anyone about.

Most of the way back to Ek Naab I was semisleeping. I was thinking; I couldn't stop. More than anything I wanted to talk to Ixchel.

What is it about that girl that makes me want to tell her *everything*? Yet every time I open my mouth to speak about anything really serious, I choke on it.

Benicio being up in the front of the Muwan didn't make things any easier. He doesn't know about the Bracelet, so that topic is out of bounds. Luckily he didn't seem to notice my dad's writing on my arm. More than once, I caught Ixchel staring at it.

Was she wondering if it was my handwriting?

So much happened in the last couple of days, it's one big jumble in my head. The dream-visit from Camila, the genetic treatment they did on me, finding the Crystal Key, fixing the Bracelet. Meeting my dad again in Area 51. Having the power to travel through time.

Tyler and Ixchel kept making me explain what had happened in the Chaldexx labs, how I went back ten minutes in time and rescued myself. It's almost as if they sensed I wasn't telling them the whole truth.

"I just don't get how that thing works," Tyler concluded. "Why does it take you ten minutes into your own past as a safety setting? Isn't that just gonna send you right back into the same problem? And how come when your dad used the Bracelet he wound up on that volcano? It doesn't add up . . ."

Well, I agreed with him, of course! What else could I do?

Tyler was also a bit puzzled about the idea of two versions of me in the same place.

"You saw yourself on that bed? You rescued yourself?"

I told him I did.

"What happened to that other you, the one you woke up?"

"He's me, don't you get it? I'd already been him. I woke up, went to the cold room, found the Crystal Key, fixed the Bracelet, and—bam! I traveled back in time. All that happened was that I got to see myself from another viewpoint. I went back on myself, and then caught up."

I even drew a loop in the air with a finger and explained all about the time-loop thingy, just like Dad explained it to me.

Tyler still seemed doubtful. "Seems to me that's got to happen a lot, with the time traveling. How do you know it hasn't already happened? Maybe you've already met your future self—you know, yourself, but, like, older."

At which point I started to think about Arcadio again. In case Ixchel started to wonder about Arcadio too, I changed the subject.

Anyway. There may well be bad news waiting for me. Lorena and Montoyo are eager to find out what genetic changes the Sect introduced into my DNA.

It's kind of worrying . . . to say the least.

Benicio told me right away that Tyler had been rushed back into surgery when he got him back from Brazil. His wound had opened up again. All that fighting had made it worse. By the time Tyler reached Ek Naab, they even had to give him a blood transfusion.

Mom was fine—scared out of her wits about me and Ixchel, of course. If I were a better son, I'd probably worry more about putting Mom through all this stress.

325

It's not as if I go looking for trouble. I just want a quiet life.

Is that too much to ask?

Maybe I'll enjoy life in Ek Naab, after all. From what I've seen, it's pretty darn quiet.

I'm writing my blog on a brand-new laptop in my own room in my very own new apartment in Ek Naab. Tyler lies resting. I insisted on getting a bed. Hammocks are all well and good, but sometimes you need an actual bed.

There's a polite little knock on the open door. It's Montoyo. I turn around and meet his eyes. There's a half smile there, but he's looking solemn.

"Josh," he says with a nod. "It's time."

I snap the laptop shut and follow him out of the apartment and into the street, trying not to give away how nervous I am. I don't like blood tests at the best of times, so yesterday's session with Lorena wasn't much fun.

Today I get the results.

Today I find out what Melissa DiCanio really did to me. Apart from changing the color of my eyes to blue . . . which I wouldn't mind, except that the one person I want to like the new color is Ixchel. She doesn't seem that pleased.

327

"What were you writing in your blog?" Montoyo begins. "Your deepest, darkest thoughts?"

I try to chuckle. "Something like that."

"Ha! I wish we'd had blogging when I was a youngster. I think I'd have enjoyed having a secret diary."

"What stopped you?" I ask. "I mean, you had pen and ink, right? Or would that be a quill and parchment?"

Montoyo looks slightly irritated for a second. "Sure, I could have written a journal. I just always seemed to have other things to do. Scribbling away in a book . . . would have seemed kind of . . ."

". . . girly?" I offer with a grin. "I kind of felt that way too."

Montoyo laughs and shakes his head. "Not at all! I was going to say . . . earnest, serious. Very, very serious."

"That sounds like you, all right."

"Earnest and serious?" He seems surprised. "Not when I was a young man, believe me."

I look up at him. "What changed you?"

He turns away, shrugging. "So many things happen at your age. Don't you find?"

"Well, to me, yeah . . . ," I say. "But all I want is a quiet life."

Montoyo guffaws. "Absolutely not true! It's as I told you, Josh; for men like us, happiness comes at a cost. We're only truly happy when we're living life on the edge."

"Not me," I say, objecting. "I've got the soul of a poet, man!"

Montoyo laughs even harder. I'm enjoying myself now, despite my anxiety. I decide to take it further. "I could have been another Alex Turner! But instead I have to go on all these crazy missions for you . . ."

"Who's Alex Turner?"

I can tell he's being serious. Well, okay. Even my mom might not know.

"Only the coolest guy on the planet. He's a singer—a rock star."

Montoyo arches an eyebrow. "A singer? I'm sure he's making a tremendous contribution," he says. "But he's going to have to leave the important work to people like you and me." Then he frowns. "Anyhow, when have I ever sent you on a mission? As I recall, I forbade you from getting involved in rescuing your mother and Ixchel. Or have you forgotten?"

I haven't forgotten. Remembering how protective Montoyo was of me, I'm suddenly uncomfortable about deceiving him. The Bracelet is back in my bedroom, safely stashed in my luggage among my clothes.

"You sent me after the Bracelet," I tell him in a quiet voice.

He gives a dramatic sigh. "Ah, yes . . . the Bracelet of Itzamna. Since you raise the subject, Josh, I was thinking that we should have a conversation about that."

He stops and turns to face me. In that instant I see it.

He knows.

I pause, then try to continue walking. Montoyo grabs hold of my arm. Staring deep into my eyes, he twists my arm so that the inside wrist faces upward. I've showered since arriving from Switzerland, but my dad's handwriting is still there—faintly.

"You wrote this," Montoyo says, his eyes boring into mine. "You wrote this because you used the Bracelet."

Hotly I reply, "I *so* did not!"

"I met a man once," Montoyo says, his expression now deadly serious, "with a tattoo on his forearm—in the exact same place. Can you imagine what that tattoo said?"

I shake my head nervously. There's something about his tone that I don't like.

Montoyo's grip on my wrist tightens. "It said 'Incidents II JLS 195.'"

I struggle to return his gaze. A tattoo like that can only mean one thing. It's a reference to that book by John Lloyd Stephens. To *that* page of *that* book—the one with the coded message, the formula for the Crystal Key.

I can only think of one person who might tattoo that on to his arm.

Which means that Montoyo has met Arcadio.

I whisper. "Where did you meet him? When?"

But Montoyo brushes off my questions. "Surely the real question is *who is he*?"

I breathe, "Arcadio . . . ?"

330

"Precisely. Blue-eyed Arcadio Garcia, the forgetful time traveler. Now here you are . . . mysteriously, *miraculously* escaped from the clutches of our deadliest enemy, your eyes blue, your name inscribed on your arm . . . *in case using the Bracelet makes you forget.*"

He continues, and I'm almost pinned to the spot under the intensity of his gaze. "A strange thing to have tattooed on one's arm, wouldn't you agree? I thought as much back then when I met him. Imagine my surprise to find Arcadio's name in a book with the title *Incidents of Travel in Yucatan, Chiapas, and Central America* by a Mr. John Lloyd Stephens."

He's right; it's a strange thing to have tattooed. Montoyo's not the first person to have that idea. It's like I said to Tyler about Arcadio: why didn't he tattoo the formula on his body like that guy in *Memento*?

Well, maybe he did.

Montoyo and I stare at each other in silence. Citizens of Ek Naab stroll by, giving us a wide berth. Everyone knows who we are. Everyone would love to listen in, I'll bet. But nobody—*nobody*—dares to give away the tiniest hint of curiosity.

He walks away a few paces and sits down on a bench next to a small fountain. I listen to the water gurgle up and splash over the blue ceramic tiles. His shoulders slump slightly; he's exhausted from a long day's work. "You have to give me the Bracelet, Josh," Montoyo says, a little sharply. "Time travel is not a thing to be trifled with."

He's right, I know. I haven't forgotten that my dad tried to make me promise never to use the Bracelet again. But I don't want to accept it.

"If I'm Arcadio," I say quickly, licking my lips, "then it stands to reason that I keep the Bracelet. Don't I? One day in the future, I must figure out how to use it. And then I use it to travel in time. So I can't give it to you," I tell him, warming to my argument. "Or that would change the timeline. Wouldn't it?"

Montoyo laughs again, this time cynically. "A nice try! But Josh, see it from my point of view: you think I can leave a teenage boy running around with the power to change time itself?"

I ask him straight out: "Am I Arcadio?"

Montoyo shrugs. "Maybe."

"Do I look like him?"

He studies my face closely for a long time. "The truth is, I don't know." He sounds sincere. "It was a long time ago. I didn't exactly take a photograph."

I remember how Susannah St. John once told me that Arcadio didn't like to have his photo taken. Was he trying to avoid leaving evidence—a hostage to fortune?

I say, "How can I find out?"

"We can ask Blanco Vigores."

"Vigores?"

"He found the Bracelet of Itzamna, Josh. He knows more about it than anyone," Montoyo says with a sigh. "Don't pretend you don't know that."

"If Vigores tells us I can keep the Bracelet," I say, thinking rapidly, "will you let me keep it?"

Montoyo hesitates. "If you give me the Bracelet today," he says, "then you have my word: when we talk to Vigores, he can decide who keeps it; you or me."

"What if he wants it for himself?"

Montoyo shrugs. "He has the authority to do that. You and I, we had a deal. Remember?"

"That's right," I say with a touch of sarcasm. "My secret mission for you."

"I'll owe you, Josh. Don't dismiss it out of hand—many in Ek Naab would enjoy having me in their debt."

I know immediately the "favor" I want to ask Montoyo.

Stay away from my mother.

BLOG ENTRY: BLUE-EYED BOY

Mom was the first person to meet me when we arrived back in Ek Naab from Switzerland.

The minute she saw me, she burst into tears. Later she said it was because of my eyes.

"The day you were born, Josh, the first thing I noticed about

333

you was your eyes. Dark brown, just like your father's. That's rare, you know. Babies are usually born with blue-gray eyes. Yours were brown, from the very first minute."

I just stood there, blinking. It was hard to believe what she seemed to be saying. She gave birth to a brown-eyed boy. Now my eyes are blue.

I remember how my voice shook when I told her, "Mom, it's still me."

But is it? Deep down I've got a nagging suspicion that the Sect changed something important about me; something that will make sure that whoever I am from now on, it's not Josh Garcia.

At least, not quite.

Mom was already with Lorena when Montoyo and I got to her office. It was just getting dark outside, and the lights from the Tech poured over the quadrangle in the middle of the building. I stared through the window, watching the students—some of them the same age as me. They shuffled around, laughing and talking. I got a little stab of pain in my chest when I remembered goofing around at my own school, hanging out with Emmy, chasing classmates through the circular cloister.

I'll never go back there. That life is over for me now. Looking down at those Ek Naab teenagers, I knew instantly that I'll never fit in.

Not completely. The Bakab thing will always keep me apart.

I noticed Montoyo looking at me. He flashed me a quick grin, as if to say "hang in there." Then he took my mother's hand and squeezed it. Mom's cheeks flushed a little.

For a second or two I couldn't tear my eyes away from their linked hands. I felt pretty uncomfortable. I thought about my father in that Area 51 cell. It didn't matter to me that it really happened months ago, or that he'd died since then.

Lorena sat down. She smiled at me, then at my mother. You didn't need to be psychic to see that they were both nervous. It took all my self-control not to start shaking. I dragged in a couple of long breaths and held them there, releasing the air slowly through my mouth. Just the way they showed us in capoeira.

Lorena cleared her throat. "From what I can tell, Josh, the news is good."

My mother began to sob with relief. I leaned over to hug her. Montoyo watched us, his expression unreadable.

I closed my eyes so that I didn't have to look at him.

Tyler, Ixchel, and Benicio are hanging around in the lobby of the Tech. When we come down the stairs from Lorena's office, they turn anxiously.

I break into a grin. All three of them rush forward, Tyler and Ixchel hugging me at the same time.

"You're all right?" Tyler asks, breathless.

"Probably," I tell him.

"So, what did they do to you?"

I take a deep breath. "I've got all four Bakab genes now; not just the Ix gene, but the other three too."

Ixchel and Benicio are wide-eyed with amazement. "You have the abilities of all four Bakabs . . . ?"

I nod. "Yep."

Benicio frowns. "It's kind of worrying that the Sect can do that."

"The good part is that they don't know for a fact that it

worked. They didn't do any tests after I woke up. So hopefully they'll still have to test it on someone else."

Benicio shrugs. "Still . . . it's only a matter of time."

I'm actually pretty annoyed with his attitude. Sure, it's not great news all around—but at least I'm not being turned into some monstrous genetic superwarrior . . .

Ixchel gestures at my eyes. "And the eye color? Do they have some Aryan fantasy of repopulating the world with blue-eyed specimens?"

"Some *what*?"

"Like Hitler," she says.

I dart a look at Ixchel to see if she's kidding. I guess she really doesn't like my eyes like this . . . and I'm starting to wonder why.

"Lorena thinks it was the 'positive control,'" I tell them. "The Sect used their genetic technology to change my eye color—an obvious change that they could see. If that worked, if that was 'positive,' then there would be a good chance that the other genetic changes also worked."

"So you're a quadruple Bakab now," Benicio says. "Hmm, I wonder how the other Bakabs will feel about that."

I don't mention the other change that Lorena spoke about. That's something that I still have to come to terms with, something that Lorena's going to be working on.

"They put something else into you too, Josh," Lorena

told me, back in her office. "A gene that makes the Key peptide."

"The Key . . . you don't mean . . . ?"

"The substance that makes up the Crystal Key . . . yes. It can be produced by your own cells now. And isolated from your blood."

I have the Key inside me. It's just like Arcadio wrote in those postcard messages.

WHAT.KEY.HOLDS.BLOOD.

Arcadio knew. I feel sick just thinking about it. Something else he knows about my future.

"Why?"

Lorena shook her head. "I have no idea. Aside from activating the Adapter in the Revival Chamber, we don't know what the Key does."

"But you can find out, right?"

Lorena smiled then, gently, first at my mother, then at me. "Sure, Josh. Finding things out—that's my speciality."

Montoyo and my mother follow me down the stairs. Benicio and Ixchel still appear shaken by the news about the genetic changes that DiCanio and the Sect made to my DNA. In fact, they've gotten pretty quiet.

It's not the first time I've had to face up to the fact that something I did has helped the Sect.

At least I made it back to Ek Naab. More importantly, so

338

did Mom, Tyler, and Ixchel. As long as we're all together, I feel as if I can tackle any problem.

Tyler draws a breath. "The Sect has a leg up now, no doubt. But you made it back alive, didn't you? That's what really matters."

For a second or two I can't speak; then I nod a couple of times and say, "Thanks, Ty."

Montoyo passes me and taps my shoulder.

"Josh. We need to speak."

He motions me outside the lobby and past the huddle of students gathered near the front of the building. There's a consistency to the air that's unusual in Ek Naab. It feels almost powdery. I glance upward and realize that above the surface, it's raining. But this rain stops at the ceiling mesh. Only a very fine mist descends, almost imperceptible.

"It stops the rain . . ."

Montoyo nods. "Things are different here. But you'll adapt." His expression becomes sterner. "Now, let's get this done. The Bracelet of Itzamna—you're going to give it to me for safe keeping."

It's a struggle to hide my resentment. "Okay. It's at our apartment. But what about Vigores? You said we'd talk to him . . ."

"Yes, Vigores. I've been trying to get in touch with him. No luck. His assistant says he left a few days ago."

"Left? For where?"

"He had business outside the city. That's not unusual for Vigores. He traveled widely in his youth—he still has many friends in Mexico."

"He does . . . ?" For a few seconds I just stand in silence, gazing at the ground. Slowly it's dawning on me how little I know about the daily lives of any of the people who have so much influence over me.

What do Montoyo and Vigores *do*? What were their childhoods like? Did they ever have normal jobs? Girlfriends, wives? Any kids? Montoyo seems to be forever on the go: putting in appearances in the Yucatan University in Merida where he's supposed to be a lecturer, while fixing financial deals for all the technology in Ek Naab. Vigores lives in his mysterious apartment in the middle of an underground labyrinth and famously disappears for weeks at a time.

One thing is for sure—the members of the ruling Executive of Ek Naab, like Montoyo, Vigores, and Lorena, seem to have way more freedom than other citizens.

Or maybe that's just my impression. After all, Ixchel was allowed to run off to live as a maid and waitress in Veracruz—when she was only fourteen. More freedom than any fourteen-year-old I know would be given. I wonder then if it had something to do with the fact that she lost her mother so young. She never told me the details of that. But I'm willing to bet Benicio knows all about it—another advantage he has over me. I stare over Montoyo's shoulder, watching Ixchel through the glass. She and Benicio still seem tense.

I need to learn more about these people.

"Can you help me to get to know people here?" I say suddenly. Montoyo peers at me. He looks more surprised by the minute.

"Anything I can do, Josh, of course."

"People my own age," I tell him firmly. "I want to meet them first. If I'm going to stay here, I need some friends. More people like Ixchel and Benicio."

Montoyo nods, but now he looks a little wary. "Okay. Yes, I can see that. All right; why don't you have a party?"

I consider this. "Like, a housewarming party?"

"Yes, Josh. Exactly like that."

"I guess . . . it could be cool."

BLOG ENTRY: BLINDED BY NOSTALGIA

Tyler asked me, "So, you still keeping up with your blog?" And I replied, "As if . . ."

There's no point having a blog that people you know are going to read. Where's the fun in that? If your friends—or your enemies—are reading it, you can't be truthful.

Since there's not a person alive I can be truthful with, I'll have to stick with the secret blog.

Tyler and Mom help me to get the apartment ready. Mom buys paintings from the market, and vanilla-scented candles. We make the living room feel really inviting. The baker delivers hot *empanadas*—tasty little pastries filled with cheese, pork, and chicken.

I plug in my dad's iPod and select some jazz. Tyler wrinkles his nose. "You're kidding, right? It's like Summertown Starbucks in here . . ."

Well, why not? I could do with a reminder of home. It's sad to think of someone else living in our house. At least Mom is only renting it out. I'd like to think I could go back there, one day.

As we're waiting for the guests to arrive, Tyler says, "You didn't tell us everything about the Bracelet, did you?" I try to avoid his eye, but he just grins. "It's all right, man; you don't need to tell me the details. Me, I figure you used it to go back in time, further than ten minutes, and not just to rescue your-self from that hospital bed. You'd never let Montoyo have the Bracelet . . . not unless you'd already done what you wanted. Unless you'd found your *zero moment*."

I point out that Montoyo didn't exactly ask—he basically laid down the law. That I didn't know how to control the Bracelet, so it was a nonstarter.

I haven't told anyone about going back in time and meet-ing my dad. If time travel is risky, then it stands to reason that talking about it might be risky too. Maybe what happens in the past should stay there.

Tyler's comment about the zero moment stays with me, though. Was that it, I wonder—meeting Dad in the under-ground base in Area 51?

Things are different since that happened, it's true. I don't have the same drive to change the past anymore. Not when the future seems so uncertain—and so exciting.

In less than fifteen months I'll be sixteen; a member of the ruling Executive. It's a lot to prepare for . . . and I'm starting kind of late in the day.

People begin to arrive, the first bunch with Benicio. Some faces I recognize from the Tech. Benicio himself acts very laid back, introducing me to everyone as his "cousin Josh from England," not as the Bakab Ix, which is a relief. I wonder then how Benicio feels about the way Montoyo keeps ordering him around the world. Is he bothered that he isn't going back to Oxford? It doesn't look like it. In my apartment that night, Benicio doesn't seem to have a care in the world.

Then Ixchel arrives with four or five girls. They're all wearing dresses and skirts, much more formally dressed than any girls I know would be for a party. None of the girls are as pretty as Ixchel.

It feels like a dream, sitting in my new apartment, entertaining friends. Like a scene from a movie. The playlist reaches the Brazilian jazz numbers—a familiar tune by Tom Jobim, one of Dad's all-time favorites.

This again.

It's a different recording than the one I heard in the dream with Camilla, or in Dad's cell; this time the singing is in Portuguese. But I'd recognize the tune anywhere. Now that I think of it, this was playing in Brazil too, the night we sat in that restaurant on the beach.

Standing by the window, I stare at the title of the song. Then I smile. There's nothing else I can do.

Ixchel wanders over, giving me a quizzical look. "Something funny?"

If only you knew.

My mind goes back to that first night in Brazil. If I could use the Bracelet to time travel, that's when I'd go back to. Forget Arcadio and the galactic superwave; if I had to pick just one moment to revisit, I'd want another shot at that evening on the beach in Brazil.

This time I wouldn't let Ixchel go straight to Benicio. I wouldn't play it so cool; I'd let her see how excited I was to see her again.

But really—would that have changed anything? After all—what did Arcadio write to me, the quotation from that writer Borges—"Time is a river which sweeps me along, but I am the river"?

And a river flows only one way . . .

I think of the Bracelet, now locked away in Montoyo's office. I don't think I'll ever totally get rid of the urge to "swim against the stream of time." If I really am Arcadio, that sounds a lot like a warning from my future self.

Wonderful idea—but it can't be done.

Whatever purpose time travel serves, I guess Tyler and Ixchel were right. The Bracelet of Itzamna isn't a tool for solving my personal problems.

Ixchel continues to stare at me, her puzzlement turning into a grin. "So . . . what? Why are you smiling, Josh?"

"This song," I tell her, "is called 'Wave.'"

"'Wave' . . . ?" she echoes.

"Yeah. 'The wave is on its way.' Kind of like the superwave, don't you think?"

She's still slightly puzzled. "I guess that's funny . . ."

"Yeah, a bit."

"I like it," Ixchel says, thoughtfully. "It reminds me of that night we arrived in Brazil. Portuguese sounds so great there, doesn't it? I really should learn to speak it."

She's thinking about that night too.

I raise a glass of fruit punch to my lips, hiding my face. She starts to look a little nervous too; she lowers her eyes.

"I never really got to thank you . . . ," she begins.

I stare in disbelief; I get butterflies in my stomach.

Still not really looking at me, Ixchel continues, "I always knew you'd come back for your mother. But by that river, in Brazil." She looks up. "You could have gotten away. You didn't have to come back for me."

"It's okay," I mumble. "'Course I had to. That was the point—to get you all back."

Ixchel smiles. "Well . . . I'm grateful."

Then, as if she's just thought of it, she leans over and kisses my cheek. For some reason I can't make myself move.

Say something. Say anything. Now.

But all I can do is nod, smile a bit and take another sip of my drink. There's a lump in my throat the size of a plum.

After all the stuff I've been through, why is *this* so hard? The truth is, it's impossible. I don't know where to start. I might as well try to speak Japanese.

Warm air wafts in from outside. It smells of the rain-drizzled blossoms that fill the lanes and alleyways of Ek Naab. Ixchel stands inches away from me, facing the crowd of her friends from the Tech. The silence between us lengthens, becoming awkward. I pretend to glance away, but out of the corner of my eye I watch her twist her ponytail between two slender fingers. Then Ixchel turns, and I follow her gaze.

She's looking over toward Benicio. She just stands there, waiting for him to notice.

Ixchel is the one person I would love to tell everything. But I can't bring myself to do it. I can't say anything; not a word.

Acknowledgments

Eternal thanks to Team Joshua at Scholastic Children's Books UK, especially my new editor, Polly Nolan, who joins us mid-series, and to Jessica White, Alyx Price, Alex Richardson, Sarah Lansbury, Elaine McQuade, and Hilary Murray-Hill for continued energetic support. To Elv Moody for a brilliant suggestion when we first discussed the plot. To my agent, Peter Cox, for being generally wonderful. To Matt Barnard, barista and manager at Summertown's Starbucks, for providing me with such a wonderful "office," and to fellow children's author Susie Day for sharing long hours and laughs at the "office." And mostly to my husband, David, for always supporting me, letting me take the family to Brazil, and for jumping on the manuscript as soon as it's finished and not putting it down until he's read right to the end.

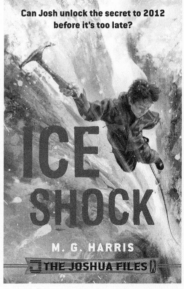

MAYAN MYSTERIES of 2012
A Young Person's Guide

Some readers of *The Joshua Files* have been asking if there is any truth in the "2012 prophecy" that features in Josh Garcia's adventures.

In fact, the Mayan calendar end date really is December 22, 2012.

But don't worry—the rest of the details of 2012 in The Joshua Files are fiction, based on some of the more entertaining theories about what might happen. There is no proof that there's really any danger at all.

Fact or fiction?

FACT:

• The ancient Mayan civilization existed in countries we now call Mexico, Guatemala, Honduras, and Belize.

• Between 500 and 900 A.D. they enjoyed a "golden age" of city-building and writing.

• Mayan astronomers made remarkably accurate observations and used their Long Count Calendar to commemorate historical and astronomical events.

• Like the Gregorian and Julian calendars, which start with

the presumed date of Jesus of Nazareth's birth, the Long Count Calendar (the Haab) has a start date.

• Unlike those calendars, however, the Haab also has an end date.

• The Haab start date is August 11, 3114 B.C.

• The end date of the Haab is thirteen baktuns later—which translates as December 22 (or 21), 2012.

If the start of a calendar commemorates the most important event a society can remember, what might the end date of a calendar commemorate?

FICTION:

• The Ix Codex and the Books of Itzamna are fictional.

• Josh Garcia's adventures happen in a fictional world where the 2012 threat is real.

What the ancient Maya wrote about 2012:

Almost nothing. Pretty surprising, don't you think? If they really did believe it was the end of the world, you'd expect many mentions of the date. But in the Mayan books and temple inscriptions that survive, there's only ONE reference to 13 Baktun—December 22, 2012. That inscription is known as Tortuguera monument 6. Mayan writing expert Professor David Stuart translated the inscription.

Here's his translation:

"The Thirteenth 'Bak'tun' will be finished
(on) Four Ajaw, the Third of Uniiw (K'ank'in).
? will occur.
(It will be) the descent(?) of the Nine Support(?) God(s) to
the ?"

As you can see, it's not clear at all what the "2012
prophecy" actually says or means. Which means we can
use our imaginations. Most of what you'll hear about
2012 is just that—pure imagination.

If you'd like to know more about the Maya or the mysteries
of 2012, please visit this website on the topic, written by
M. G. Harris:

www.mayan2012kids.com

BLOG ENTRY: JOSH NEEDS YOU!

Help Josh solve a murder!
Enter www.thejoshuafiles.com to join the
    Alternate Reality Game
Plus:
Watch exclusive trailers
Enter competitions
Win cool prizes

BLOG ENTRY: THE COUNTDOWN HAS BEGUN!

Is the world really going to end in 2012?
Where did this all come from?
Is there any truth in the stories we're hearing?
Find out more at www.mayan2012kids.com

Keep up with M. G. Harris at:

www.themgharris.com—M. G.'s website
www.mgharris.net—M. G.'s blog
www.facebook.com/joshuafiles—join the official
Joshua Files Facebook group
www.youtube.com/user/mgharrisauthor—visit
M. G.'s author channel on YouTube